The impulse was so strong it nearly took Daria's breath away. She couldn't do it, of course. It would be wrong for her to take advantage of his good nature by jumping him.

Either William was a mind reader or a very good guesser because he used his knuckle to lift Daria's chin, then slowly lowered his head. His lips were soft and warm, gentle but persistent, coaxing her to respond. She couldn't not. Hormones, pheromones, whatevermoans conspired against her rational mind and she kissed him back.

She opened her mouth and touched her tongue to his. Bold, impulsive, gratifying beyond words. He tasted new and novel and very, very good.

"Oh, dear," she gasped, pulling back. "Oh, that was so not supposed to happen." She blinked and swallowed hard, still tasting his sweetness. "In fact, it didn't happen. It was a dream. Dreams aren't real."

He placed both hands on her shoulders, more to steady her than hold her in place. "I've been working in Hollywood for half my adult life and, believe me, I know the difference between make-believe and reality....

"And that kiss was real."

Dear Reader,

One of the joys of writing a connected series is having the opportunity to delve into the lives of secondary characters. Such was the case of William Hughes, Hollywood agent, pilot and business associate of Cooper Lindstrom and Shane Reynard. William always stood out—partly because of his British accent, partly because I adored his dry sense of humor. And I was curious why someone so successful had no fairy-tale romance to call his own. The lonely little boy I found at the core of him nearly broke my heart. I knew I had to find him a very special heroine.

At first glance, Daria Fontina seems a most unlikely fit for William. A single mother with two daughters, Daria is starting from scratch after a difficult marriage and brutal divorce. She's ready to stand on her own and show the world she's capable of providing for herself and her children. That is, if she can get down from the pedestal William wants to put her on.

Thanks to Dave Ardell for his help with my questions about private airplane travel. All mistakes can be attributed to my tendency to spin his answers.

The copilot in this book is named Lucas Hopper. The *real* Lucas Hopper—my dear neighbor's grandson—was killed while on duty in Iraq shortly before Thanksgiving 2009. His full military burial in our tiny country cemetery left an image that will be with me always. I wish with all my heart that I could go back and give Lucas—a real-life hero—the story he deserves.

Check out my Web site, www.DebraSalonen.com, for details about future books.

Happy reading,

Debra Salonen

The Good Provider
Debra Salonen

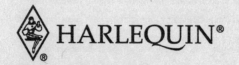

TORONTO • NEW YORK • LONDON
AMSTERDAM • PARIS • SYDNEY • HAMBURG
STOCKHOLM • ATHENS • TOKYO • MILAN • MADRID
PRAGUE • WARSAW • BUDAPEST • AUCKLAND

Recycling programs
for this product may
not exist in your area.

ISBN-13: 978-0-373-71662-3

THE GOOD PROVIDER

www.eHarlequin.com

Printed in U.S.A.

ABOUT THE AUTHOR

Debra Salonen attributes her love of reading to her late parents, Daisy and Reuben Robson, who kept Deb's childhood home stocked with more magazines than anyone could read, everything from *Popular Mechanics* to *Time* and *Newsweek* to *TV Guide.* The fabulous photos in *Life, Look* and *National Geographic* offered a glimpse into worlds far beyond the rolling plains of South Dakota. The wonderful art in *The Saturday Evening Post* and poignant stories in *Redbook* and *Reader's Digest* spoke to the budding artist in her soul. It seems fitting that Deb's first freelance sale was an article entitled "The Bulls That Fell from the Sky," which appeared in *Country* magazine.

Books by Debra Salonen

HARLEQUIN SUPERROMANCE

1196—A COWBOY SUMMER
1238—CALEB'S CHRISTMAS
        WISH
1279—HIS REAL FATHER
1386—A BABY ON THE WAY
1392—WHO NEEDS CUPID?
        "The Max Factor"
1434—LOVE, BY GEORGE
1452—BETTING ON SANTA
1492—BABY BY CONTRACT*
1516—HIS BROTHER'S SECRET*
1540—DADDY BY SURPRISE*
1564—PICTURE-PERFECT MOM*
1588—FINDING THEIR SON*
1633—UNTIL HE MET RACHEL*

**SIGNATURE
SELECT SAGA**

BETTING ON GRACE

**HARLEQUIN
AMERICAN ROMANCE**

1114—ONE DADDY
        TOO MANY
1126—BRINGING BABY
        HOME
1139—THE QUIET CHILD

*Spotlight on Sentinel Pass

To Paul, for everything.

CHAPTER ONE

"WHATCHA DOING, MOMMY? Can I help?"

Daria Fontina looked up from the two enormous plastic storage containers she'd bought that morning at the post-holiday clearance sale to see her youngest daughter standing in the doorway of the family room watching her. Daria had been meaning to organize their Christmas decorations for years, and now seemed like the perfect time. Half for her, half for him.

"Taking down the tree, sweetie. Christmas is over. It's time to move on," she told Hailey, who was tossing the shiny black ball she'd received in her stocking Christmas morning, a gift from the Santa Claus she no longer believed in—thanks to her sister.

"I'd love your help. What does the Magic 8 Ball say about putting away Christmas ornaments?"

Hailey shook the plastic orb vigorously, then peered at the little window on the bottom. "It says…'Seems likely!'"

She and Daria both laughed.

Hailey, who was five going on fifty, and her older sister Miranda were Daria's purpose for living, her one true joy, her passion and her drug. Her love for them was probably partly to blame for the Grand Canyon-size wedge that had grown between Daria and Bruce over the years. That and his election to the State House of

Representatives in Sacramento. Two worlds and three hundred miles apart.

He hadn't understood how much they'd grown apart until last August when she'd asked him for a divorce. In the five months that they'd been separated, Bruce had done everything in his power to prevent the inevitable from happening—further proof of their complete and utter disconnect, in her opinion.

Still, they'd agreed to a cease-fire over the holidays. "For the girls' sake," he'd claimed, but Daria was certain he wanted the détente to prove to his family that he was still in control. She'd expected there to be fireworks, but Bruce had been a complete gentleman. In fact, his courtly, model behavior had reminded her so much of the man she'd fallen in love with and married, she'd almost—*almost*—started to have second thoughts about the divorce.

"See the two piles? You can start wrapping the more delicate ornaments and putting them in this box for Daddy." She scooted sideways and patted a spot beside her on the plush white carpet. Bruce's pick. Only a man who wasn't part of the day-to-day business of living with two young children would insist on white carpet.

"When is Daddy moving home?" Hailey asked, joining her.

Daria nearly dropped the fragile glass ball in her hands. "I'm sorry—what? Honey…" she said, brushing aside a lock of the child's thick curls to see her eyes. "Daddy isn't moving back in with us. He was only here to see you open your presents and have Christmas Eve dinner with us before midnight Mass, like always."

Hailey frowned. "But Miranda said Daddy was coming back with some of his stuff today. She heard him talking to Grandma when we went to her house for Christmas."

Traditionally, the entire Fontina clan gathered at Bruce's parents' on Boxing Day for their holiday celebration. This year Daria had enjoyed a peaceful, catch-up day doing absolutely nothing. A first. "He told Grandma you were done being mad at him. That you kissed and made up."

Daria's cheeks flushed with heat and she quickly returned to wrapping ornaments. *Damn. Make one little mistake and look what happens.* She wished she could blame the holidays or that extra glass of wine she and Bruce had shared after they'd put the girls to bed, but she knew that wasn't why she'd done what she had. It had been watching Bruce read *The Berenstain Bears' Christmas Tree*—a book that had been Daria's favorite as a child—to Hailey that had softened her heart so much she was completely powerless to resist Bruce's tentative, wounded-little-boy kiss under the mistletoe.

Which, of course, had led to a much more fiery exchange that had wound up in the bedroom they'd shared for twelve years. She was human, after all, and all the women's magazines made a point of saying that she was at her sexual peak. She'd caved in to need and nostalgia. Once. She'd slept with her husband. Once. Then sternly insisted he go back to his mother's house instead of spending the night. "I don't want to confuse the girls," she'd told him.

Now, it turned out, she'd done just that.

"Well, my sweet girl, I wish that a kiss was all it took to fix what was wrong with Mommy and Daddy's marriage, but that isn't the case. We talked about this with the family counselor, remember? Daddy and I both love you and Miranda no matter what, but we can't live together and make each other happy."

Hailey's index finger began inching upward toward

her right nostril—a bad habit that had gotten worse the past few months. Daria handed the little girl a sheet of crumpled tissue paper to distract her. "Would you like to wrap the ornaments that your great-grandmother brought over from Italy? I'm putting all the special Fontina family ornaments in this container." *For Bruce to put on his own damn tree next year.*

"Can I?" Hailey beamed, her light brown curls framing her beautiful round face. She still had a few charming pounds of baby fat that made her look younger than her age, but she was smarter than any five-year-old Daria had ever met. Sober, quiet, thoughtful—pensive, even. Proof in Daria's mind that her daughter had seen and heard too much within the walls of this two-story McMansion that Daria hated. "I'll be extra careful. Daddy says these are very old and valuable."

To Hester, maybe. Daria's soon-to-be-ex-mother-in-law had made such a big deal of presenting Daria with the set of eight—now, seven—white-and-gold-flecked glass globes, you would have thought the gilding was fourteen-karat. In Daria's opinion, the balls were ostentatious and cheaply made, which was why they broke so easily. "They're only things, my love. Do the best you can."

Daria started filling the second box with things she'd accumulated before her marriage. Her mother had bought her a dated ornament every year she'd been alive. They were funny, silly, sentimental, and all very special to Daria, but she would never berate her daughters or make them dig into their allowance money if one broke, as Bruce had last year, ruining everyone's Christmas Eve.

"Here, sweetie," Daria said, grabbing the tree skirt she'd folded and set aside earlier. "Let's use this to add some packing between layers."

The handmade quilted skirt was adorned with gold ribbon and sequins. Daria had never seen anything like it, and while she gave Hester credit for the tremendous amount of time and effort it must have taken to make it, Daria hated the darn thing. Always had. She found it gaudy and sort of cheesy, and yet, she'd used it for twelve Christmases without argument.

Wuss, she silently chided.

Some battles weren't worth fighting, though, she'd decided a long time ago. If that made her a coward, so be it. But this was the last holiday she'd put the ugly thing around the base of her tree. She'd only used it this time as a sort of peace offering. Plus, money was tight, thanks to Bruce's legal shenanigans.

"Oh, Mommy, look. Here's your Kermit ornament," Hailey said, digging the spindly green object out of Bruce's pile. "Uh-oh. His ski is broken. I didn't do it, Mommy."

The tremor in her daughter's voice fueled the quietly stoked fire that burned in Daria's belly. Her hand was trembling as she reached out to stroke her daughter's hair. "I know that, my love. Kermit lost his ski a long time ago. When I was in college, I think."

"Did you get in trouble?"

"No. It was an accident. And, even though I like Kermit a lot, he's just a thing. And things aren't as important as people."

"That's right, Hailey," a voice said from the doorway behind them.

Daria and Hailey both jumped guiltily. Kermit fell between them as Hailey flew into her arms. Daria could feel her daughter's heart racing against her own.

"Your mother knows all about how important people are. Especially the people in your family."

"Hello, Bruce," Daria said, trying to sound calm and in control. She patted Hailey's arm and eased her to one side. "I didn't hear the bell. Did Miranda let you in?"

He stood with arms folded across his chest, leaning against the door jamb. She guessed that he'd been leisurely eavesdropping for quite a while. In the past, she'd been able to sense where he was at any given moment that he was home—behavior typical of people living in highly charged abusive environments, she'd learned in one of the counseling sessions her lawyer had encouraged her to attend.

Their months apart must have removed her edge.

"Hi, Daddy."

Was Daria the only one who noticed how tentative and thready her daughter's voice got when Bruce was around? Probably. Bruce thought of himself as a wonderful father—stern and uncompromising when necessary, fun and playful at other times. *Like never,* Daria said to herself, using Miranda's preteen tone of utter ennui.

"What are you two up to?"

"Um…putting away the ornaments. Mommy said I could help. I'm being careful. I didn't break this. Mommy did." Hailey gulped, realizing too late she'd ratted out her mother.

"In college," Daria added. She gave Hailey's thin shoulder a little squeeze. "Do me a favor, hon, and check on your sister? She's supposed to be taking down the decorations in the rest of the house."

Hailey picked up her Magic 8 Ball and dashed toward the kitchen, avoiding contact with her father. Subtle, but crystal clear to Daria.

"What are you doing here, Bruce? I figured you'd be on your way back to Sac to get ready for the big New Year's Eve party."

"Not happening this year," he said, his eyes trained on the two big bins. Worried, perhaps, that he might get shorted in the deal? Daria was being overly generous to avoid any such accusations. "The budget being what it is, nobody wants to get caught spending big bucks with lobbyists. Where'd these boxes come from?"

"The girls and I did some post-Christmas shopping this morning." She shook her head, remembering the chaos. "Good buys, but I had to outmaneuver an old lady in one of those motorized chairs to grab the last two."

She was exaggerating, of course. The store had had hundreds of bins in stock.

Bruce frowned, his thick black eyebrows uniting in what Daria couldn't help but think of as his unibrow. The first time she'd heard the term, she'd known it described Bruce's scowl exactly. "You better hope the TV cameras weren't around. The last thing I want is to hear the news media making a big stink about Representative Bruce Fontina's wife mowing down an elderly cripple. What were you thinking, Daria?"

"Well, Bruce," she said, getting to her feet. "I'm thinking you can't take a joke. There were several hundred storage boxes on the pallet when I left Lowe's. And let's not forget that I'm soon to be your *ex*-wife. I'm pretty sure nobody in the media gives a damn what I do, and frankly, that sounds pretty good after years of living in a fishbowl."

He gave her a look that made her stomach twist like a wet dishrag. "What are you talking about? We're not getting divorced."

Daria felt a chill of ice water course through her veins. "Yes, we are," she said, regret and apprehension suddenly rendering her about as articulate as Hailey.

He looked at her and shook his head, as if she were a

woefully uninformed child. "No, Daria, we're not. You proved it yourself. You're not over me. You got your tail in a wringer over my being gone so much, but, I promise you, I'll do better. You can't deny that you still love me, Dar."

Damn. Damn. Damn. They were back to square one. His refusing to accept that what they had was over. Long gone and dead.

She took a moment to get her nerves under control, bending over to finish what Hailey had started, quickly wrapping one of the two remaining glass balls in tissue and nesting it carefully in the soft material.

"Can't we just call the other night one last booty call for old time's sake and get back on the divorce track?" She wasn't trying to sound flippant, and she regretted her words instantly.

She reached for the last ball as Bruce grabbed her elbow, causing it to fall from her hand. It bounced on the carpet and rolled against the corner of the hard plastic lid. A distinct cracking sound made her throat close as adrenaline flooded her bloodstream.

"Did you just break that?" Bruce cried, yanking hard on her arm. "What the hell is wrong with you? Have you been drinking? Good lord, Daria, it's not even noon."

She tried to shake off his grasp. "I...no...of course not...I was shopping. It...slipped. You startled me." He tightened his grip and stepped closer, using the thickness of his upper body to intimidate her.

"First, you invite me into our bed, then you act like it was nothing," he said, his voice dropping to a low, angry snarl. "*Nothing* is spreading your legs like a cheap hooker. Is that what you've become? Because sleeping with a man you don't love pretty much qualifies. Is that how you're going to finance this new life you're so eager to begin?"

His fingers squeezed, cutting off circulation to her fingertips. "Huh, Daria? *Is it?*" he asked, giving her arm a shake. "Do you have some regulars already lined up? I hope they aren't too attached to their balls because I know people who will cut them off, for a price. They'll do *anything* for a price, if you get my drift."

Fear gripped her belly. At the last Fontina family gathering she'd attended before filing for divorce, she'd overheard his brothers' wives talking about a man who'd stolen from the family's import-export company. Two weeks later, his body had washed up a few miles from the warehouse Bruce's family owned in Alameda. The guy had been missing all the fingers on his right hand. Freak accident or murder? The question had made Daria slightly ill, but she was determined to stand her ground.

"The other night was a mistake, Bruce. The holidays can make people nostalgic. I'm sorry you misinterpreted what happened, but, trust me, the things that are wrong with our marriage didn't get fixed with one night of sex."

He blew out a sound of disgust. "What's wrong with our marriage all comes down to what's wrong with you. And why the hell do you get to call all the shots—that's what I want to know!" His voice rose to a shout, a sound their daughters had heard many times in the past. Daria hated putting them through another argument. One that, obviously, was all her fault.

He pulled her against him, twisting her arm in a way that added to his leverage. Her chest pressed against his, her breathing shallow and fast from fear and anger. "Let me go, Bruce."

He buried his face in her neck. "Your lips say no, but your pulse says yes. I can feel it racing," he said softly, licking his tongue across her flesh.

Racing, yes, but not because she was turned on. "Stop it, Bruce," she cried, twisting to get free. "This isn't happening. We're separated. The girls could walk in any second. I don't want to give them any hope that we might be getting back together."

His fingers squeezed tighter. "That's exactly what they want, Daria. What they deserve. A mother and father who love each other and live together in the same house. Is that so much to ask? We both had that in our lives. Why are you depriving the daughters you claim to love of the same stability? What kind of mother are you?"

"Let me go and we can talk about this."

Her bargain felt like bartering with the devil for another piece of her soul. She'd heard all of these arguments before. They'd attended counseling the year before Hailey was born. Daria had attempted to end the marriage then, but getting accidentally pregnant—or perhaps not so accidentally, if Bruce's brother was to be believed—had curtailed her plans. Her brother-in-law claimed Bruce had gotten drunk the night their youngest daughter was born and bragged about messing with Daria's birth control pills. "Keep 'em barefoot and pregnant," he'd boasted. "Isn't that what Dad always claimed was the only way to stay married?"

Back then, she'd succumbed to family pressure and postpartum depression and had given their marriage another try. That wasn't going to happen again.

He pushed his face within an inch of hers. "Don't screw with me, Daria. I mean it. If you learned nothing from our twelve years of marriage, you should know that

I can make you regret this decision every day of the rest of your life. However long—or short—that is."

She gave a mighty push and backed away until she felt the prickly needles of the now-naked tree. "You're threatening me, Bruce? How charming. And you wonder why I don't jump at the chance to stay married to you?"

His eyes narrowed; anger made his face as red as the plush Santa hat lying on the floor a few feet away. "That never seemed to be a problem when we were picking out your new, top-of-the-line SUV or redecorating the f'ing kitchen that you now want to take ownership of—even though *I* paid for it." He threw up his hands. "What's wrong with you, Daria? There are women who would kill to have this kind of life, and you're throwing it all away. Private school for your kids, a gardener, caterers when we entertain. My God, woman, are you sick? Or just stupid?"

Both, she thought, absently rubbing the ache in her side. The same sort of pain had sent her to the emergency room last summer. A barrage of tests had revealed no conclusive diagnosis, but her physician had warned that it could be the start of an ulcer. "Stress and diet. Two things you need to address so it doesn't get worse," he had advised.

She'd changed both—no more spicy pasta dishes and no more hot-tempered Italian husband. And it had worked; she'd been pain-free these past few months. Until today.

She was well aware of what she was doing, and she knew her choice would impact her daughters' lives forever. She was prepared for how much Bruce's family would hate her and anticipated them trying to turn the girls against her. The only way she could hate herself more was if she did nothing about her situation and stayed. But there wasn't enough money in the world to bribe her to do that, or enough booze in the world to mask her pain if she did.

She'd been thinking about moving for almost a year. She'd confided in no one except her grandfather, Calvin, whose support had been the one constant in her life. She was beginning to think maybe he was right—maybe she couldn't remain in Fresno. She'd wanted to stay in her house until the girls completed school, but the look in Bruce's eyes told her that wasn't going to happen. This disappointment seemed to have taken his antipathy to a new level.

"We're not good together, Bruce. Look at you. You're clenching and unclenching your hands like you want to wrap them around my throat and squeeze until I'm dead. It isn't healthy. Why do you even want to be with me?"

He drew his hands up to look at them. He made two fists then let them drop to his side. He lowered his chin and stared straight into her eyes. "It's not *you* that I want, Daria. Never was. It's the perfect wife and mother image you bring to the table. Your leaving negates every possible benefit you offer, making you virtually worthless to me. The only thing keeping me from beating the crap out of you is knowing how traumatic that would be for the girls. But believe me, once they're old enough to see what a lying, worthless bitch you are, if something happens to you, the loss won't hurt so bad."

He flipped her off for good measure, then turned and left. Daria's knees were shaking so badly she barely managed to stumble to the closest chair. *Oh, God, tell me he didn't mean what he said.*

But when she closed her eyes and recalled the venom in his tone and the glittery shards of hate in his eyes, she knew the man she'd once loved and promised to be with for life wanted her dead, and he'd find a way to make that happen when her death would be less of an inconvenience.

With violently trembling hands, she punched her grandfather's number into her cell phone. "Grandpa Cal," she cried softly the moment he picked up. "I need to come to Sentinel Pass. Now. As soon as possible. With the girls. Bruce is…oh, Grandpa, what have I done?"

"A TOAST TO THE BRIDE and groom. Where's William? He's really good at this sort of thing."

William Hughes heard Cooper Lindstrom's voice echo off the stretched canvas walls of the oversize teepee. Everyone did. The sixty or so people squeezed into the odd, distinctly Sentinel Pass venue turned to look at him.

"My pleasure," he lied, crafting a deliberate smile that he was certain would fool most people.

It wasn't that he didn't care about the newlyweds. He did. Kat was one of the sweetest people he'd ever met, and Jack seemed like a decent chap. The two were the embodiment of love. At the moment. No, the problem stemmed from William's total lack of faith in the institution of marriage.

A part of him wanted to cry, "Why bother?"

But, of course, he couldn't do that. Never mind that one of his clients had texted him earlier that day to say she'd met lucky husband number six—or was it seven? Never mind that William's parents, who had been married six months longer than William had been alive, had spent the vast majority of those years on separate continents, maintaining completely separate lives that only included him when it was convenient.

He would do his duty, support his friends and give it

the old-school try. The English way. Forget the fact he was only half Brit.

He set his empty champagne glass beside one of the many poinsettia plants anchoring the reception's holiday theme and walked to the center of the circular room. Famous faces, like Cooper and paparazzi favorite Morgana Carlyle, shared space with regular folk, the disparate group brought together by *Sentinel Passtime,* a TV show based on Cooper and his wife Libby's real-life love story.

He looked at the pair, sitting shoulder-to-shoulder, Coop's hand resting on Libby's pregnant belly. William was glad he wasn't flying them back home after the wedding. Libby's doctor had provided a written okay for her to fly in her third trimester, but only on a commercial airline. That was fine with William—his mother might be able to deliver babies under extreme conditions, but William was a pilot, not a selfless doctor-slash-saint.

"Ahem. If you please. Don't make me shout. You won't like me if I shout."

The threat drew a few chuckles, but it also accomplished what he'd intended. The crowd quieted. The only noise was that of the caterers in the adjoining shop.

"Friends and family of Kat and Jack, we've come together on a snowy night in the Black Hills of South Dakota to witness a union between two friends who have decided to make this odd journey we call life together. By lifting our glasses high—" he snagged a glass of bubbly from a passing waiter, his last, since he planned to fly in the morning "—we wish you a beautiful life filled with all the mayhem and excitement that makes for a good story in the twilight of your years. To you both."

He clinked his glass around the bridal table. "Your gift from me awaits you at the airport, fueled and ready to take you on the first leg of your honeymoon," he told the bride and groom.

The bride's sons let out a loud cheer, since they were included in the first part of the trip—a visit to Disneyland. As he understood from Cooper, the two boys would then spend a few days with Shane and Jenna, two close friends in L.A. who weren't able to make the wedding.

"A fabulous gift, William," Kat said, her sparkly tiara slightly askew. "We appreciate it so much. We'll be packed and ready to leave on time, I promise."

He nodded at Jack, intending to leave, but Kat suddenly reached out and caught his sleeve. "Wait. Um, could Jack and I speak with you in private a moment?"

"Of course. Where…?"

She looked at her sons and made a scooting motion with her hand, which he couldn't help noticing was adorned with an intricate henna tattoo. "Boys, will you please take Megan to check on the cake? We'll be right there."

William's admiration for the woman grew. She was a good mom.

"I know now probably isn't the best time and place to bring this up, but Libby got a call from Calvin— Mary's…um, husband…sorta."

William had met the man and was aware of the octogenarian's relationship to Libby's late grandmother. "Yes. And…?"

Libby shifted sideways, wincing slightly as the baby she was carrying shifted position, too. "Cal's granddaughter and her husband have been separated for about six months. According to Cal, the guy's done everything in his power to slow down the divorce process. Then, over the holidays, Daria—that's the granddaughter's name—felt sorry for the jerk and… Did I mention they have two daughters? Anyway, she let him hang out with the family some and he took that to mean she wanted him back. He showed up this morning ready to move in again. Things got ugly and now she's afraid for her safety. And the girls', too. I told Cal we'd do whatever we could to help."

Cooper leaned around his wife and added, "By *we*, she means you. As in, would you mind turning around as soon as you drop these guys off in Anaheim and fly to Fresno to pick up a battered wife and two traumatized kids?"

William's heart rate spiked slightly. Flying was his drug of choice, and he rarely passed up a chance to escape into the clouds. But messy divorces were definitely not his thing. He'd babysat more than a few clients who couldn't pick a decent mate if their life depended on it, and at least once, it had.

Libby gave Coop a hefty nudge with her shoulder. "Daria was clear about this to Cal—Bruce hasn't hit her. But he did threaten her. And his family reputedly has certain underworld connections."

"Mafia," Cooper mouthed with an over-the-top look of mock horror.

Libby ignored him. "Cal is worried sick. He wants Daria and the girls to come here, at least until the divorce is finalized."

The pleasant tingle of the excellent champagne on his tongue turned flat. "Give her my cell number. Weather permitting, I'll take her anywhere she wants to go—even here."

"Thank you," Libby said, sniffling. "You're the best."

"Hey, how 'bout a little of that hero worship for me?" Coop said, obviously trying to lighten the moment.

"William might be the hotshot pilot, but it's my plane, too."

"That's correct. We use Cooper's gas," William added. "Because he's so full of it."

His joke earned a chuckle from everyone at the table and shifted the focus to Coop, giving William a chance to slip away. He didn't want anyone thinking of him as a hero. He'd already proven he couldn't be trusted in that role. He'd give this woman a lift if she called, but chances were good she wouldn't. And as selfish as it sounded, he hoped she'd try some other avenue first. Counseling, therapy, a restraining order—anything that didn't involve him.

"Something's wrong, isn't it?"

Yes. Apparently his social radar was broken. He hadn't even heard Morgan approach the small bistro table where he was standing.

"No, Morgan," he said. Morgana to the world, Morgan to her friends and family. And agent. "Everything's divine."

"Liar. Do you know how I know something's going on with you?" She'd been his client for several years, and she knew him as well as anyone did.

"You're fidgeting. You never fidget."

He looked at his hands. Good heavens, she was right. A napkin he couldn't recall picking up was in a shredded heap at his feet.

"I had word today that my father is ill," he admitted.

"He called you?" Her surprise showed on her expressive face. Morgan was one of the few people who had some small inkling of the disconnect between William and his parents.

He wiped his hands on what was left of the napkin

and deposited it in an empty glass. "No. Uncle Notty e-mailed."

"You have an uncle named Naughty? How very British."

"Short for Naughton. We're not blood relatives. He and Father were school chums. They've shared a flat in London ever since Father won his election. I told you he's a member of Parliment, right?

"Father is a bit of a Luddite, so Notty acts as an online go-between."

Her gaze shifted to a point over his shoulder. Keeping track of her betrothed, no doubt. "What's wrong with your dad? Not the computer-hating thing—that, I get—I mean, how ill?"

William suppressed a sigh. His father had never— ever—been a dad. No tossing of a ball, no cheering on his son at a rugby match, no shooting the breeze over a pint at a local pub. Father was brilliant, high-brow, reserved. A dedicated servant of the realm. And a smoker for most of his adult life. "Lung cancer."

"Oh, William." She hugged him but quickly stepped back as if suddenly realizing who she was hugging. "Sorry, I know you're not a touchy-feely kind of person, but that's so awful. Cancer."

"The C-word," Jack's sister had called it. William's minor involvement in the planning and execution of this wedding had put him in contact with her on several occasions. She'd mentioned her father's death and her boyfriend's remission almost in the same breath. While not privy to the details of either case, William assumed that meant the disease wasn't a mandatory death sentence.

"Your mother's a doctor, right? What does she think? Is it bad? Did they catch it early? Will they operate?"

Those very same questions had been ruminating

around in his brain for hours, contributing to his current headache. "I have no idea. I only heard the news a few hours ago. I haven't spoken with Mum, but Notty did mention she was returning to England."

"Does she specialize in cancer?"

No, she specializes in sainthood. "She works in third-world countries treating AIDS patients and undernourished children. I don't know how much practical help she'll be, but her returning is a nice gesture."

"Gesture?" Morgan tilted her head in obvious confusion. She'd dyed her blond hair a rich mahogany color to play the role of Libby in *Sentinel Passtime,* and the color made her look more serious and less like a Hollywood starlet. "She's his wife. Aren't sickness and health part of the vows she signed up for?"

William must have believed that at some point in his life, but sadly, he no longer thought so—particularly where his parents were concerned. "Some marriages are less...devout than others. My parents have spent the better part of their forty-plus years of union on separate continents."

She frowned in a way that made most men suddenly want to jump up and fix whatever might be troubling her. "But they've remained married so their feelings must be there on some level," she insisted. "And she's rushing home to nurse him. What does that tell you?"

"That Mum is a doctor first, wife second?"

"You're a very cynical man, William Hughes-Smythe," she said, using his full name. He'd dropped the Smythe when he moved to America, thinking the combination seemed a bit pretentious when paired with the accent he couldn't completely shake. Maybe a part of him had hoped for some sort of reaction from his parents. Outrage. Annoyance. Even relief that his underachieving choice of job wouldn't sully the family name. There had been none.

"Merely honest. My parents live their lives. I live mine. Keeping an ocean or two between us facilitates the arrangement."

Her eyes narrowed. "Does that mean what I think it means? You're not going to see him?"

"I have a business to run. Clients' hands to hold, noses to wipe." Morgan was one of the few on his client list who didn't need coddling. "Abused women to transport," he added, grabbing the one straw that might deflect her obvious concern.

Before she could say anything, a piercing whistle filled the teepee. "The bride and groom are cutting the cake," Cooper announced. "Cameras ho."

William spotted Mac, Morgan's fiancé—and Libby's brother…Lord, the interconnectedness of this group made his head spin—motioning for her to join him and the child pulling him toward the cake cart. Morgan turned back to William. "I have to go, but I am really sorry about your dad. And while I appreciate you helping Daria—and I know *why* you're doing it—" she added meaningfully, "I think you're making a mistake by not going home to see your dad as soon as possible. Cancer's wicked tricky. You never have as much time as you think you will. I mean, look at Kat."

She pointed toward the bride and groom, dueling playfully with frosting-tipped fingers. "When Kat and Jack set this date, Kat was sure her mom would be here. Helen's cancer was in remission, and although she had some breathing issues, overall she seemed fine. Then, suddenly, something changed. Kat said her aunt called in hospice this morning."

William had heard a rumor to that effect. "I appreciate

your concern, my friend. Truly. And I'm very sorry to hear about Kat's mum. Now, hurry off. Your future groom is shooting daggers my way. Be quick." He made a shooing motion with his hands. "Mac's a miner. He could hurt me."

William watched her traipse across the room into the waiting arms of Mac McGannon. William liked Mac a great deal and didn't feel the least bit threatened, but he couldn't blame the man for feeling possessive. The couple spent a lot of time apart given Morgan's job and Mac's obligations in Sentinel Pass.

They planned to marry sometime in the future and William wished them all the luck in the world. He could speak volumes on the subject of long-distance marriages—at least from the point of view of such a marriage's child. But what was there to say, after all? So he hadn't had a storybook upbringing. What did it really matter? He'd learned a long, long time ago not to expect anything from his mother and father in the way of warm, familial exchanges. They simply weren't that sort of people, and no amount of wishing or hoping or dreaming would ever change that.

He looked around the room at the many outwardly happy people. Morgan and Mac were wrapped in an embrace now, smiling with such tenderness they could have been a poster for Hollywood's next blockbuster romance.

Unfortunately, the cynical part of him knew that appearances rarely told the whole story. His father had repeated many times the tale of how he met William's mother and was knocked "tail over toes." "Your mum was the most confident, imperturbable woman on campus," his father would say. "When Laurel made up her mind to do something—even marrying me—it would have taken an act of God to dissuade her."

And while the marriage had lasted—on paper, at least—their family was a complete and utter sham. No wonder, he supposed, that while he might wish for a wife and family of his own, he had little faith that he'd ever manage to acquire one.

He turned to leave. The thought of cake made the champagne in his gut start to curdle. He'd nearly reached the exit when Libby caught up with him. "Wait. William. I. Can't. Run."

He turned to watch her hurrying toward him with far more grace and speed than she gave herself credit for. She grabbed his arm like an exhausted swimmer clinging to a buoy.

"I heave like a huge boat listing sideways," she admitted. "Sometimes left. Sometimes right. Depends on how the baby is lying. At least, I hope it's a baby. Lately, I've had dreams of giving birth to a hippo."

He smiled. He couldn't not. Libby was a delightful person. Since she'd moved into Cooper's Malibu home, which was only a few miles up the beach from William's own house, William had noticed a distinct and positive change in his previously flighty, slightly manic friend. Libby was bedrock, even when balanced on the fault line that was Hollywood. "How much longer?"

"Till I explode?" She patted her belly. "Three weeks, they say. But what do they know? Hippos sometimes have minds of their own."

William laughed. "I don't think it would matter to Coop if you actually did give birth to a hippo. The man is obnoxiously happy about the prospect of becoming a father."

She cast a glance over her shoulder toward the sounds

of merriment in the teepee. "I know. He's still a kid at heart, so he'll be a great dad. Um…while we're on the subject, Morgan just told me about your father."

He blinked in surprise. "That was fast. Gossip at the speed of sound?"

She fished her phone out of the pocket of her simple but glamorous cashmere sweater. "Text message. Even faster." She threw her arms around him. "I'm so sorry, William. I had no idea when I asked you to fly Daria here. We'll make other arrangements. Cal will understand. Family is everything to him, and he'd never want to be the cause of you not making it back to England in time. Truly, it's—"

He stopped her. "Libby. Your compassion is as genuine as it is misplaced. I only got the news about Father's condition today. There's a great deal of doctoring to be done. I'm not privy to all the details, but I'm quite confident he will still be with us after I help Cal's granddaughter."

She didn't appear convinced, so he changed the subject. "Speaking of Cal's granddaughter, isn't Daria the name of Cooper's former secretary? The one who ran off with his first ex-wife?"

Libby rolled her eyes. "I was hoping no one would remember that. Trust me, the two women have nothing in common except their name. Cooper's assistant was a twenty-year-old opportunist looking for a shortcut to fame and riches. Cal's Daria is a stay-at-home mom by choice. She has a college degree but quit working to be with her daughters. Something I understand completely. *Now*."

William wondered how different his life might have been if his mum had chosen to live in the same country as he, let alone the same house. That kind of devotion and selflessness deserved to be honored and protected. "I'll do whatever I can to facilitate her decision."

She patted his arm in a very motherly manner. "Of course you will, William. You're the most gallant man I know."

She gave him a soft peck on the cheek then waddled toward the crowd.

Gallant? He gave a wry smile and shook his head. The word brought to mind swordplay and white chargers. He was nobody's hero. He might have aspired to the role at one time, but he'd learned the hard way that he didn't have what it took, and an innocent person had paid the price. Maybe that was the real reason he couldn't say no to helping this Daria woman and her children.

Penance.

CHAPTER TWO

JANUARY WAS William's least favorite month. He couldn't complain about the weather, as he had in England. Storms in Southern California passed through quickly, dousing the usual brownish-gray haze from the air, churning up the ocean and lowering temperatures enough for a jacket. Nothing like England.

Unfortunately, January was still the worst time for his business. Privately, he called it post-holiday distress month. None of his clients were happy, and everyone wanted something William was powerless to give them—a part in that new sure-to-break-box-office-records movie, micro changes to already eye-straining fine print on a perfectly adequate contract, permission to bring a pet snake back into the country. The latter was part of a thirty-message text conversation with JoE, a rapper who had more money than common sense.

Dude, du somting now. LAX sucks. Nazi snake patrol coming 4 him.

William sat forward to read this latest message.

With a groan, he put one hand to his face and squeezed his temples. "What, JoE?" he muttered. "What am I—your agent in *Malibu,* for God's sake—supposed to do about the illegal python you tried to sneak into the country in your amplifier?"

"Are you talking to yourself again?" a woman's voice asked.

Morgan had dropped by after her run. She and Mac were renting Cooper's neighbor's house for a couple of months.

"Yes. I've told you before, my clients are going to be the death of me—one brain cell at a time."

She took a sip from the water bottle he'd given her earlier. She wanted something from him, too, but she had too much class to come right out and demand it. "Poor William. An agent's work is never done."

"Truest statement I've heard today. And the reason for that is most clients consider an agent their surrogate parent. But even JoE's mum, who happens to be a very nice lady, would tell him what I've told him ten times so far—'You can't bring a snake into the country without going through the proper channels.'"

She tossed her ponytail from side to side. "Could be worse. Don't most rappers try to smuggle drugs into the country?"

William scrolled down until he found the number he wanted, then hit send. "John? William Hughes here. How would you like a new slant on an old story?" He quickly rattled off the details—to Morgan's obvious amusement—then hit end.

He held up one finger to indicate he wasn't done. With thumbs flying, he quickly texted.

L.A. Times on their way w/ camera guy. Headline tomorrow: JoE's Snake on a Plane.

"Clever agent saves day," Morgan said, offering a headline of her own.

William sighed. "A really clever agent never would

have gotten sucked into signing a rapper in the first place. What do I know about the music industry?"

She shrugged. "You know words. Your literary background has served you well, I think. And JoE's lyrics are some of the best poetry of our day. It's your nature to try to protect him."

"Only a fool would try to protect a man bent on self-destruction. Mostly, I despair about the loss of his natural talent if he fails to get his act together. As we both know, you can't force someone to get help."

She jumped slightly. "Help. That's why I stopped. I almost forgot. Mac talked to Calvin this morning. His granddaughter is supposed to be calling you today. Her little girl had a bad asthma attack right after the holidays so Daria had to postpone their trip. She wasn't sure you were still available to help, what with your dad's situation and all."

A slightly metallic taste developed in his mouth. He was tired of people fretting about his father's health. "Does the whole world know about my father's condition?" he grumbled. He was sick of dealing with e-mails, calls—even tweets. "What has happened to the right to privacy?"

He stood, intending to get a bit of vodka to go with his sparkling water. He'd only made it two steps when his phone rang. He picked it up without looking at the display, certain it was JoE.

"Snake or no snake, you need to clear customs so you can get your butt in the country. Are we clear on that?"

"I beg your pardon? I'm trying to reach William Hughes. This is Daria Fontina."

Daria. He scrubbed his hand across his face. "My

apologies. I was expecting someone else. How may I be of assistance?"

"No problem. Is this a good time to talk?" The voice on the other end of the line sounded slightly breathless, as if she were standing outside in the wind to hold this conversation.

"Yes, it's fine. Go on."

"My grandfather said you would be willing to fly us—my two daughters and me—to South Dakota. I know that was a week ago, so I'm wondering if your offer is still good. I'm sorry we weren't able to leave sooner, but…something came up."

He liked that she didn't go into detail about her daughter's health problems. That showed restraint and respect for the young girl's privacy—something the people around him could benefit from embracing.

"Our plane and my services are at your disposal," he said, a bit too formally, he gathered, from Morgan's eye-rolling. "Do you have a departure date in mind?"

He walked to his desk where a large daily planner was open to this week. He had a dozen meetings scheduled, at least. Three lunch dates with clients. One phone interview.

"Would tomorrow work for you?" There was a tentative quality in her voice that told him she wasn't used to asking for help. Abusers often made their victims believe that nobody would answer their call if they reached out. She was expecting him to say no. He heard that, too. He'd heard it before.

"Whatever works for you."

Morgan clapped silently and made a Rocky gesture with her arms in the air.

"I… Thank you, Mr. Hughes."

"William. Please. Let me grab a piece of paper and

take down your specifics. I'm going to need a little information. You and your daughters' full names and approximate weights for starters. And an estimate of how much baggage you'll be bringing along."

She gave a low, rueful chuckle. "A lot, figuratively speaking. But on my grandfather's advice, I haven't told my daughters this move is permanent. 'Loose lips' as Cal likes to say. So we're only doing carry-on."

He wasn't sure what he thought of that news. Had her ex-husband upped the threat level? "Should I come armed?"

She didn't answer right away. When she did, her tone was lighter somehow. "No. That won't be necessary, but thank you for asking. I'm leaving on the sly for exactly that reason—so my ex-husband and his brothers won't show up."

He gave her full marks for that. "Then, we'll be gone before anyone's the wiser. Let me get your number so I can file a flight plan, get a look at the weather and figure out the best time to meet."

He jotted down everything she told him, including her daughters' names and ages. He was thinking ahead to what he'd need to get done between now and then when she said, "My grandfather speaks very highly of you, but he never mentioned that you sound like Hugh Grant."

How many times had he heard that? A few thousand, give or take? "Not true. I sound a great deal more American than Hugh."

"Hmm," she said. "Now that you mention it, I think you're right. But I should tell you, my husband—my ex-husband—made me stop renting English films because he said I went gaga over Hugh Grant. Apparently anyone with an English accent was suspect, as well. Even Judi Dench."

William laughed. Her quip was so unexpected, and given her situation, so brave. Suddenly, he couldn't wait to meet this woman. He looked at Morgan, who was standing a foot away, mouth open and eyes wide with shock.

"I would gladly ask Dame Judi to accompany us—she could hold her own in any fight, I'm quite certain—but I believe she's in London at the moment."

"What was that, sweetheart?" Daria called to someone else. "Okay. I'll be right there." To William, she said, "Thank you for doing this for us, William. You have no idea how much it means to me and my daughters."

Simple words, hastily spoken, but William didn't doubt their sincerity. "I will see you tomorrow, then."

"Okay. Fly safe."

He hit the off button and looked at Morgan. "Tomorrow."

"That's fast. How'd she sound? Damaged? Frightened?"

"Businesslike."

She nodded. "Oh…your type."

My type? "She's a mum, doing what's best for herself and her children. How does that make her my type?"

Morgan sighed heavily. "Look at this place, William. Your last girlfriend called you Mr. OCD."

William opened the filing cabinet where he kept the plane's log book. "She spilled a martini on my BlackBerry. Didn't apologize. Or offer to replace it. If that makes me neurotically picky, so be it. What does that have to do with Daria?"

"You've lived alone too long."

My entire life, actually.

"This kind of perfection isn't natural, you know. You need rowdy, messy chaos to shake things up a little."

"That's why I have clients. You're the exception, although I remember a few months ago when your life was fodder for the tabloids. You weren't overly pleased at the time, if I recall correctly. I think I'll stick with neat and tidy, thank you."

"Boring."

He opened a drawer and withdrew the leather-bound flight log that had come with the eight-passenger Twin Commander Turbo prop plane he'd purchased with Cooper and Shane. The others called it a jet, which it wasn't, though it was jetlike in speed and range. Since he was the only licensed pilot of the bunch, he'd recorded a fair amount of hours flying to South Dakota and back. When one of the men accompanied him, William generally didn't bother with a copilot because both Coop and Shane had taken an emergency training course. This time, however, he intended to hire someone.

The additional expense would be well worth the peace of mind an extra set of hands and eyes would provide. Daria sounded capable and in control of the situation, but she'd also mentioned keeping the intent of the trip a secret from her daughters. He glanced at his notes. The eldest was twelve. He'd worked with several young actors in the past, and he guessed there wasn't a teenager on the planet that didn't know a great deal more than his or her parent thought they knew.

Best to be prepared. For everyone's sake.

"William?"

William looked up. He'd forgotten Morgan was still there. "Yes?"

She cleared the distance between them and touched his shoulder lightly. "Your father would be proud of you."

"You have absolutely no basis for that opinion. You've

never met my father." He saw her surprise at his caustic tone and was quick to add, in a less prickly voice, "But I'm sure my mother would approve. She's spent the better part of her career trying to help women and children."

"I meant that since you can't be in two places at once, at least you're doing something worthwhile. I'm sure any father would understand and appreciate that."

His father's words that morning came back to him. "You can't blame the boy for following in the footsteps his mother and I have lain down for him," Father had argued on the extension a few hours earlier when Notty had called to berate William for not catching the next flight to England. His father's support had been a great deal harder to shoulder than his uncle's scolding.

When he didn't say anything, Morgan went on. "Anyway, Libby and I have decided to make you guest of honor at the next meeting of the Wine, Women and Words book club. It won't be until after the baby is born, but I thought I'd give you plenty of time to think up excuses not to come."

"What makes you think I won't come?"

She shook her head and walked to the door. "You might put in an appearance, but you won't stick around for the nitty-gritty talk about life, love and books. Like I said, that kind of stuff is too messy for your taste, but, William—" She paused in the doorway. "You don't know what you're missing."

Then she blew him a kiss and left.

The woman did know how to make a dramatic exit, he'd give her that. And she also knew him too well. His life might be a little predictable and polished for some people, but he liked it this way.

Or, at least, that's what he told himself at three o'clock in the morning when he paced the fastidiously neat confines of his home. Did he wish for more? Yes, of course, who didn't? Did he act on those wishes? Never. Why? Because he'd learned the hard way that the messy stuff came with a high price tag when it failed. And it always failed when William was involved.

In addition to calling him Mr. OCD, his last girlfriend had also accused him of expecting too much. "You set standards no one in the universe could hope to meet," she shouted at him the night they broke up. "Who do you think you are? *God?*"

No. William knew he wasn't God. In fact, the opposite was true. He wasn't looking for perfection in a mate—simply someone much, much better than him. He wasn't a fool. He knew that growing up without viable role models left him with very little to bring to the table when it came to creating a real family. Not perfect, but something close to the kind of cinematic standard he'd craved as a child. That would require someone who had all the tools he lacked. The hard part wasn't finding a woman who possessed those skills, the hitch came when the magnitude of their inequity truly sank in.

OCD? More like OMG.

He shrugged off the thought and grabbed his phone. He had a lot to do before tomorrow, including rearranging his entire life and business schedule. Thankfully, juggling logistics, breaking appointments in a way that avoided hurt feelings, and massaging the tender ego of clients he wouldn't have time to see for a few days was something he was good at. Very good. Godlike, even.

"WE'RE GOING TO VISIT Great-Grandpa Calvin. I already told you that," Daria repeated for her eldest daughter's benefit, not turning from the window where she watched anxiously for the taxi she'd called thirty minutes earlier.

She didn't know what was taking them so long, but irrational paranoia was starting to creep into her thoughts.

Ever since their post-holiday altercation, Daria had been looking over her shoulder, waiting for Bruce to act. Nothing had happened, but she couldn't quell the feeling that he was planning a full-blown strike. Or was he laying the groundwork for something more subtle—like trying to turn their daughters against her?

Either way, she couldn't just sit back and wait. She'd made up her mind to act, and she had, starting with a call to the man with the great voice. Sexy, yes, but also calm, businesslike, reassuring. Fly a freaked-out family in crisis to the middle of the country on a moment's notice? Damn jolly well—or whatever the English say.

"Mommy?"

Daria looked down, noticing a hint of sweat on Hailey's upper lip. She quickly knelt and unzipped her jacket. Daria had added the coat's zip-in liner last night. She'd bought both girls heavy winter coats on clearance last spring, even then planning for the inevitable.

"Yes, honey girl? Do you have your backpack ready to go?"

"Uh-huh. But, Mommy, what about school? My teacher is going to miss me." Although Hailey had turned five in August and was old enough to start kindergarten, Daria had decided to keep her in preschool another year. That decision had earned her weeks of arguments and threat of a legal injunction from Bruce. Daria's lawyer had made numerous calls to Bruce's attorney until the crisis passed without legal action. Unfortunately, the extra billable hours had put a sizeable dent in Daria's savings.

"I know, sweetness, but you'll see her when we come back." *If* she and Bruce eventually made peace and Daria felt safe living near him and his family. She honestly couldn't say for sure if that day would ever come. His family had turned their collective back on her the minute the word *divorce* had come up. His mother called her once to say, "You are breaking my heart and God's rule. I don't know how you can live with yourself."

Daria had attempted to explain herself, but her mother-in-law never gave her the chance. She'd hung up on Daria and hadn't returned any of Daria's calls since. *Fine,* Daria thought. *If that's the way they want to play this, then I don't owe any of them an explanation about my intentions.*

A flash of yellow and black caught her eye. "Oh, good. The taxi's here. Let's go, girls."

The ride to the airport didn't take long. Daria had never been to the part of the airport that accommodated private planes, and they missed the turn and had to circle around to reach the drop-off area. She paid the driver then checked the backseat to be sure they hadn't left anything behind.

"This isn't the right place, Mom," Miranda said, yanking out her omnipresent earbuds long enough to register her complaint. "We went into that building over there when we flew to Italy."

"I know, love," Daria told her, urging the girls forward. "We're flying in a private plane. A friend of Great-Grandpa's is taking us. I thought I told you that."

"Great-Grandpa Cal has a friend who's a pilot?" Miranda asked, her tone skeptical. "He's really, really old, Mom. Is this safe?"

Daria checked her watch. They were a few minutes late. "He's a friend of Libby's, too. I spoke with him on the phone. He didn't sound old. Not Cal's age, anyway. Can we please go inside?"

The doors opened for them and they entered the general aviation terminal, which was nothing at all like the recently remodeled building across the way. Fresno/ Yosemite International Airport, or FYI, as it was known, had giant sequoia replicas that appeared to hold up the roof. The airport's name had amused her when she first visited Fresno to meet Bruce's family. At the time, Fresno had seemed like an agricultural wasteland compared to Santa Barbara—the town she and her parents had moved to when Daria had started high school. California had grown on her and she'd even stayed to attend college, but she'd never considered it home—and never would. The Black Hills was home. Her mother was buried there, and Daria couldn't wait to get back.

Daria quickly scanned the area. She knew what William Hughes looked like, thanks to his Web site, which came across as hip, current and connected. As an agent, he represented several famous stars, including Morgana Carlyle. From his photo, she decided he was in his late thirties or early forties. His face was a bit narrow but he had a strong jaw and full, nicely shaped lips. His thick, wavy hair—brown or black, she couldn't tell—appeared properly tamed by a very skilled stylist. His eyes were nice, and his expression was intelligent-looking, with a hint of irreverence that seemed to imply he found life a bit boring but was willing to give it his best shot. No smile to speak of, and yet, overall, he seemed approachable.

She'd planned to investigate his site more but had gotten sidetracked by housework and an exhausting exchange of text messages with Bruce.

"Ahem," a voice said from the grouping of chairs to their left. "Might you be Daria and daughters?"

She turned to look and was powerless to suppress a small gasp as the speaker rose from his seat with smooth, athletic grace, his gaze fixed on her face. Hugh who? This man was far more handsome in person than his headshot had let on.

She catalogued first impressions as he walked toward them. Well-broken-in leather flight jacket. Khaki pants and a navy blue shirt that made *simple* a fashion statement. Leather loafers that cried, "Handmade in Italy." The man could have stepped off the set of *The English Patient,* only he was even better looking than... Her mind went blank. She couldn't remember the name of the actor who starred in the film.

"How lovely to meet you." He bowed slightly as he produced three Gerber daisies as smoothly as any magician.

"Ralph Fiennes," Daria blurted out, without meaning to.

His eyes positively twinkled when he said, "No, sorry. William Hughes. It's a pleasure to make your acquaintance."

She accepted the flower because she was powerless to do otherwise. She felt silly, though, like a gawky teen in the presence of the lead singer of her favorite rock band. "Thank you. You're very kind."

"Not at all. Simply a small gesture to brighten your day. Which, luckily, appears to be an excellent one for air travel." Their gazes met and held a moment but he didn't attempt to shake her hand. She had a vague idea that the British weren't big on casual physical contact. She welcomed the change. Bruce's family tended to hug first and ask questions later. Questions like, "Why couldn't Bruce have married an Italian girl?" A query she'd heard more than once over the years.

"There's a small, built-in vase on the plane where you

can keep them until we land," he said, his gaze shifting to include her daughters.

Hailey was twirling the thick stem back and forth between her fingers. Daria doubted if the bright orange flower would last until takeoff. Miranda, on the other hand, was standing stock-still, flower forgotten as she stared at their pilot, obviously starstuck.

Daria rolled her shoulder to keep from losing the strap of her carry-on bag. The gesture caught William Hughes's attention. He sprang forward. "Let me take that for you. Are there more bags somewhere?"

"Nope. This is it. We're traveling light, aren't we, girls?"

"Well and good," he said. "The plane is this way." He made an ushering motion, allowing them to pass by him. "Does anyone care to visit the loo before we go?"

"What's a *loo?*" Hailey asked.

"The bathroom," Miranda answered, her tone snippier than usual. To William, she asked, "Can I sit up front with you?"

Daria's eyebrows went up. Talk about a quick turn-around from sulky to flirtatious. She wished she'd had even an ounce of that self-confidence when she'd been Miranda's age. Instead, she'd stayed in the shadows, afraid to be singled out, yet wishing that someone would notice her. Eventually someone had. Bruce. And, for a time, he'd made her feel beautiful and special. For a time.

"Sorry, love. That duty belongs to my copilot, Lucas, who is currently going over our preflight checklist one more time."

A copilot? Oh, no. That will mean more money. Daria hadn't been able to get a concrete answer to what this trip was going to cost. She assumed her grandfather was footing the bill, but she planned to repay him once she was working. Would another pilot double the cost?

"A copilot?"

"Better safe than sorry, as the saying goes," he replied. "And student pilots are usually so eager to log hours in the air they'll work for practically nothing," he added, as if sensing her worry.

She decided there was nothing she could do about the cost at this point so she nodded and motioned for the girls to follow.

"Once we get in the air—as long as the weather remains clear and mild—you'll all be able to move around the cabin," their pilot told them. "There's a bench seat in the far back so you can stretch out or play cards or whatever."

"We're going to see our great-grandpa because he isn't feeling good," Hailey said. "We're going to surprise him."

William opened the door leading to the tarmac and offered his hand for her to take. "That's very kind of you. I'm sure he'll feel better the minute he sees you."

Daria let Miranda go ahead of her. The older girl looked a bit put out that her sister beat her to the hand-holding punch. Daria had had many sleepless nights worrying about the role model she'd provided for her girls by staying married to Bruce. What subconscious messages was she sending them about love, a woman's potential and what constituted a successful life? That had been the first question she'd tackled in her family counseling session.

Daria's therapist had been firm. "You can't undo what's happened in the past, but you can show your daughters the value you place on your own mental health by living genuinely."

That was her goal, and her main reason for leaving. Yes, she was worried about Bruce's threats, but more than that, she was worried about the subtle campaign of hate he'd more or less promised to wage. "Our daughters are going to love me and hate you, Daria. Wait and see," he'd told her on the phone a few minutes before UPS had delivered two new bikes. "Belated Christmas presents," he'd claimed. "They were on back order."

Yeah, right.

"Is this the plane we're flying in?" Miranda cried, using her flower as a pointer. "Way cool. I feel like a movie star."

William paused at the steps that had lowered when he opened the door. "I'll tell Cooper you said so. He loves this bird. He's a little sad, though, because he and Libby are done flying for a while. Their baby is due pretty soon, so Libby told him he's grounded. Literally."

"I'm flying in Cooper Lindstrom's private plane? Oh, my gosh. That is so cool!" Miranda lit up at the insider information. Daria could picture her texting or tweeting her group of friends at the private parochial school she attended. The same school several of her cousins attended, as well. Good thing Daria had confiscated the phone until they were safely in South Dakota.

Bruce had agreed to Daria's lawyer's written request to allow the girls to accompany Daria to South Dakota *if* her grandfather's health became an issue. Was she stretching the truth at the moment? Absolutely, but she knew Cal would back up her story if need be. Until she and the girls were safely settled at Cal's, the less Bruce knew, the better.

"Come on in. Let me point out a few things you should know about the plane. Safety is a big priority, but comfort is a close second. You can stow your bags under the seats."

After pointing out the standard safety features of the plane, he turned sideways to let Daria and the girls pass. "Would you like me to store your flowers as promised?"

Daria quickly collected the daisies. Finding a stretch of stem on Hailey's flower that wasn't crimped made the exchange a bit awkward. William used both hands, his fingers covering hers a moment. She jerked back, as if pricked by a thorn.

"Maybe these weren't such a good idea, after all. Sorry," he said.

"They were a lovely gesture. I didn't mean to be rude earlier, not shaking your hand. It's one of the side effects of being a politician's wife," she explained. "I hate shaking hands anymore."

Partly because toward the end of the last campaign, she'd known, deep down, that Bruce wasn't the best candidate for the job. By election day, she'd felt like such a fraud she'd been certain the next person to shake her hand would sense this in her touch.

"I'll try to remember that when I introduce you to Lucas, our copilot."

She felt foolish and embarrassed, but oddly intrigued by William's touch. The brief contact had produced a curious, not-unpleasant tingle that seemed to resonate through her body. One she vaguely recalled from her days of dating. But being enamored with a sexy accent was one thing, feeling a physical connection to a perfect stranger was something altogether different.

"Take any seat you like, girls," he said, removing his jacket to hang in a narrow closet behind the two pilot seats. "I'm going to see what's keeping Lucas."

Daria hurried to help Hailey, who was positively bouncing with excitement. "Look, Mommy, look at my window!" She pressed her face against the small glass porthole.

Even Miranda couldn't hide her delight as she sank into the delicious, white leather seat of her choice. "This is so cool."

Daria stifled a sigh of relief as she helped them stow their backpacks. She chose the seat immediately in front of Hailey because she knew that excitement—even the good kind—sometimes brought on breathing issues. In her purse was a mini-pharmacy in addition to their passports, birth certificates, shot records and school transcript information.

William and another man returned moments later. "Everyone, this is Lucas Hopper."

Lucas was clean-cut and college age, Daria guessed. He waved his greeting without offering to shake hands then quickly took his place behind the controls. She bit down on a smile.

"One more thing. Lucas was talking to a pilot who flew in from Salt Lake a few minutes ago. He said there's a weather system over the Rockies that might give us trouble. Hopefully we can get over it without a problem, but we need to hurry. So…" William said, switching into flight attendant mode. "Let's go over the safety and emergency features and rules. Have you flown before?"

"We went to Italy last summer," Miranda boasted.

"On a big, big, big plane," Hailey added, spreading her arms wide to demonstrate.

His gray eyes widened. "Oh-ho, I'm carrying world travelers. Very well, then. No mere pretzels and sodas for you. Good thing I tucked in some Pellegrino and baguettes."

"Whatsa baguette, Mommy?"

"Skinny bread, dear heart. Very chewy and yummy with cheese."

"I like cheese."

"Good," William said. "You'll find an assortment of choices. And wine for your mum."

"You talk funny."

"Hailey," Daria scolded. "Don't make rude comments."

"Sorry."

"Apology accepted. I was raised in England. That's a few countries north of Italy. We're practically neighbors." He smiled kindly at Hailey then looked at Daria. "Make sure their seat belts are nice and snug. Hopefully, the tower will clear us quickly. At least there's no fog."

She'd watched the weather channel religiously the past week, hoping and praying for a clear day. Lucky for her, Fresno was experiencing a drought. No rain meant no thick blanket of gray fog that grounded planes.

Within twenty minutes, they were airborne. The plane was noisy but not deafening, and her seat was more comfortable than the recliner in her family room. She was starting to think they might have made a clean break when her cell phone, which she'd forgotten to turn off, beeped, indicating she had an incoming text message.

She made sure the girls were distracted before covertly checking. It was from Bruce.

Where R U? Mom stopped by. Car there. No U. H and M not in school. I ckd. DO NOT tell me U R dumb enuf to leave. I told U I changed my mind on U going. U will B sorry.

The threat made the omnipresent ache in her side intensify, but it didn't make her sorry. If anything, his immediately hostile reaction reinforced her belief that she was doing the right thing. She could have been out for a walk, for heaven's sake. The fact that he jumped to the right conclusion told her he'd been anticipating her move.

Had he hired a detective to follow her, she wondered? Why else would Hester suddenly decide to drop by for a visit? Her paranoia kicked up a notch, adding to the discomfort in her belly. *What if he has someone waiting in Rapid City?*

She closed her eyes and took several deep breaths, willing her nausea to recede. Even if she asked William to turn the plane around, which she was certain he'd do in a heartbeat if that was her wish, she knew Bruce wouldn't be placated. He might even feel provoked to do something they'd all regret for the rest of their lives.

No, she told herself, pushing her fears into a small, dark corner of her mind. *We need distance—for all our sakes.*

CHAPTER THREE

"UM...SORRY? I hate to bother you. I know you're busy... um...flying the plane and everything."

William turned his head to look over his shoulder. Daria was in her seat, motioning that she had a question.

He adjusted his mike and looked at his copilot. Lucas Hopper had come highly recommended by the flying service he'd used before he and Cooper and Shane bought the plane. "You got the controls?"

The young redhead grinned as if he'd been handed the keys to the city of Las Vegas. "You bet, sir."

"Holler if anything comes up," William said, removing his headphones and unsnapping his safety belt. He maneuvered out of his seat and stepped to the side bench across from where Daria was sitting. "Is everything okay?"

She tried to smile but it was clear by the look of anxiety in her eyes that something was wrong. Maybe she was having second thoughts.

"You look pale. Some water maybe? Libby keeps some motion sickness pills onboard if—"

She shook her head. "No, thank you. Just nerves. I need to ask you something."

He waited, certain he was going to hear, "Can you turn the plane around? I've made a terrible mistake."

She held up her phone. "I forgot to turn this off. I

didn't screw up your instruments or compromise our safety, did I?"

He let out the breath he'd been holding. "No. We're fine. Did you receive a call?"

"A text message. From my ex." She paused, probably debating how much information to share with him. "My mother-in-law stopped by the house after the girls and I left. She called Bruce, who called the school and discovered the girls were absent."

He could tell by the slight tremble in her hand that the message must have upset her.

"Why'd he call the school?"

She shrugged. "Apparently I'm so predictable that any variation from my normal routine sends up a red flag. He called me several times but I'd turned off the ringer. I was afraid my voice might give something away or he'd overhear Hailey and Miranda talking in the background and guess something was afoot."

"Unfortunate timing can happen in even the best laid plans," William told her, not liking the way she blamed herself for something beyond her control.

She looked at the phone again. "I turned this off, of course, but I was wondering if it would be safe to send him a reply now?" She quickly added, "My lawyer has a signed release saying he was okay with us visiting my grandfather who is elderly and in poor health—I might have stretched the truth a wee bit—but I wouldn't put it past him to call the police to issue an Amber Alert. He could probably make the media portray me as a deranged kidnapper."

He gave her credit for thinking things through before acting. It helped reassure him that she wasn't an impulsive diva, creating an emotional firestorm for the attention. "We won't drop out of the sky if you send a text, I promise. But whether or not you have service depends on your phone. My hunch is it won't work at our current altitude."

She pressed the on key and waited a few seconds before typing something onto the tiny keypad. "Bruce and I text more than we talk," she muttered without looking up. "When you watch CNN and see congressmen and representatives intently focused downward, it's because they're texting their wives or girlfriends."

"Does your husband have a girlfriend?"

She glanced up. "Ex-husband," she corrected. "And not that I know of. This breakup wasn't—isn't—about infidelity. His or mine."

"What is it about?" he asked, immediately wishing he hadn't. Her motives for divorcing her husband were none of his business, but he couldn't help wondering. She didn't fit the profile he had in his head of what a battered wife should look like. Her daughters seemed well-adjusted and happy, and to the casual observer, she appeared to have the kind of life he'd always fancied for himself.

She let out a sigh of frustration. "You were right. Delivery failed."

Her lips were pressed tightly together, and he could tell she was thinking hard, probably running any number of scenarios through her mind. He did the same thing when he received bad news. After a few seconds, she shrugged. "What happens happens."

"It's not too late to turn around." He wasn't surprised when she shook her head and sidestepped his suggestion.

"I'll call him from Rapid City…right after I call my lawyer," she added softly, glancing over her shoulder to check on her daughters. Both were wearing headphones attached to a portable DVD player. "You asked what went wrong in my marriage? A thousand things. Many of them my fault, but the biggest thing was Bruce changed. I wish I could blame politics, but honestly I think the job merely exacerbated tendencies that were already there. Personality flaws I managed to overlook when he was courting me, promising me the moon."

"The moon is a pretty big piece of real estate. Is that what you wanted?"

"What girl doesn't?"

He tried to picture her as greedy and avaricious, but the image simply wouldn't materialize in his mind.

"The sad fact is, Bruce gave me everything I really wanted." She nodded toward her daughters. "And more. A lot more. But nothing's ever free. And all that stuff came with a price tag I wasn't willing to spend my life paying."

She shrugged. The gesture seemed to say she might wish things were different, but this was her lot at the moment.

"I'm going to see if the girls need anything. Thanks again."

He watched her pause to have a word with each of her children. She was an attractive woman—even dressed in inexpensive jeans and sneakers. Her wardrobe cried Witness Protection, but there was no disguising her grace and dignity. Her shoulder-length hair was thick and wavy, not exactly brown, not exactly blond.

Hailey, the young one, took off her headphones and yawned. Daria immediately dropped to one knee and dug around under the child's seat for her bag. A second later, she produced a scraggly-looking stuffed animal that might once have been a bunny. Or a bear. William honestly couldn't tell.

The little girl curled sideways in her seat, hugging the treasured beast to her chest. Her right hand inched upward toward her face, thumb sticking out, but her mother gently redirected the thumb to close around the stuffed toy as she kissed Hailey's cheek.

A *blanket,* a voice in his head prompted, but before William could reach into the overhead storage compartment, Daria shrugged out of her sweatshirt and tucked it in around the child.

A small kindness, motherly. But for some reason, it irked the hell out of him.

Selflessness was well and good, but how difficult would it have been to ask for a blanket? She was a good mother, he got that, but what about *her* needs? What was she going to do if she got chilled? And why in heaven's name did he care?

It also bothered him that she was so fair-minded toward her ex. Instead of bad-mouthing the guy to a perfect stranger—as most people of William's acquaintance would do—she shouldered her share of the blame and took responsibility for her decision.

He didn't like it when people failed to behave as he expected them to. He made a small adjustment in the cabin temperature then returned to his seat.

Or maybe, the thought struck him, the problem was that he liked her. Admiration was fine as long as it didn't go any further, he decided. Doing a good deed for a friend was one thing. Getting drawn into a stranger's drama was something altogether different.

His clients were constantly trying to pull him into whatever current crisis seemed to be reshaping their worlds. For the most part, he was able to provide comfort and advice without actually giving a damn. Morgan called him a master of compartmentalization. He took that as a compliment; he'd learned the hard way what happened when you broke your own rules. A rare few got past his we-are-business-associates-not-friends filter. Like Morgan. And Bianca Del Torres.

He fumbled with his seat belt, drawing a curious look from the young man sitting next to him. Once he had his headset in place, he heard his copilot ask, "Everything okay?"

William nodded. Everything was fine and would continue to be fine so long as he didn't let himself be drawn down memory lane. Particularly *that* street, where the loss still felt fresh and there was never a shortage of regret.

"Where are we?" he asked.

Lucas gave him their current coordinates.

"Good. That tail wind is giving us a nice little bump." And the sooner he got them to their destination the better. For everyone's sake.

"YOU BITCH. YOU DIRTY, stinking, whore of a bitch," Bruce screamed. "How dare you take what doesn't belong to you?"

He had her pinned against a tree. She didn't know where they were or how they'd gotten there. He'd appeared suddenly while she was walking a dog she'd never seen before. "Run," she tried to scream, fearing for the small animal's safety. But the word got clogged in her throat, trapped by the pressure of Bruce's fingers closing around her neck.

"Don't think you'll get away with this. I will never. Ever. Let. You. Go." He growled the words, pausing to punctuate each one. "Do you hear me, Daria? You're mine. All mine."

Daria awoke with a start, sweating and shaking. Her

breath made a hollow, raspy sound as she gulped in air. A dream. She was safe. In the air, flying away. He had no power over her. But if she closed her eyes, she could feel the heat and iron force of Bruce's grip.

She stretched her jaw to loosen the tense muscles of her neck and upper torso. Her skin felt icy—as if he'd cut off circulation from the chin down. Symbolic? Or prophetic, she wondered as her breathing returned to normal.

She checked her watch, surprised to see that she'd only been asleep for thirty minutes or so. She'd hoped the respite would serve as a power nap. Between nerves and worry and a thousand what-ifs, she hadn't been able to sleep the night before. And she had a great deal to do once they landed in Rapid City: rent a car, drive to her grandfather's in Sentinel Pass, and, of course, call Bruce to explain why she hadn't responded to his text.

"I can't live in fear, Bruce," she'd say. "You've created a hostile environment that affects every aspect of our day-to-day lives. We're going to live with Cal until you and I have a custody agreement in place."

He'd be furious, of course. He'd want to choke her. But Bruce wasn't the type to get his hands dirty, and he was far too afraid of a scandal to risk hiring a hit man.

She hoped. She closed her eyes and tried to visualize arriving in Sentinel Pass and seeing her grandfather for the first time in way too long. Bruce had refused to let her go to Mary's funeral, despite Grandpa Cal's offer to pay her way.

"She was frigging ancient," Bruce had said. "Everybody knew she was going to kick the bucket eventually. What's the big deal? I need you here to work the phones."

Bruce wasn't up for re-election until next year, but

he'd insisted on dragging Daria and their daughters to help campaign for other candidates within his party. He'd never bothered to ask her whether or not she was a member of his party.

She wasn't. And she voted against him every time, on every issue, strictly on principle. She smiled at her small, secret rebellion.

"Daria?"

She looked up to see William coming toward her, a worried look on his face.

Something was wrong. Adrenaline brought her fully awake. "What's wrong?" she asked, quickly releasing her seat belt so she could turn around in her seat and look at the girls. Hailey was still asleep and Miranda barely glanced up from the movie she was watching.

Her heart rate was almost back to normal when she swung around to face William, who lowered his long, graceful self into the seat across from her. Even at a respectable distance, her awareness of him continued. She could smell his cologne—rich, subtle and sexy as hell. It was interfering with her ability to think; that is, until she heard him say, "It appears we're going to run into some weather up ahead."

As if to punctuate his point, the plane rose and dropped, making her stomach swirl uncomfortably.

"That kind of weather?" she asked, swallowing hard.

"Exactly. A storm front has dropped farther south than expected. I'm IFR—that's instrument rated—so we could go up and over, but apparently the precipitation started as sleet and changed to snow, making road conditions impassable. They haven't closed the airport in Rapid City yet, but there's a good chance they will.

Rather than risk arriving with no place to land, I think we'd be wise to set down and stay put until it passes."

She looked out the small portal to her left. The sky seemed as blue as it had when they'd boarded. The thick white blanket of soft clouds appeared innocently benign below them. "It doesn't look bad."

He stood and leaned across her to point in the distance. His proximity should have made her nervous but didn't. She found that puzzling but didn't have time to dwell on her reaction once she spotted the voluminous dark purple thunderhead he was showing her. "Ugly."

"My thought exactly." He returned to his seat. "Lucas suggested we stop in Durango. His aunt lives there, and he did his ground school and first solo there. We'll refuel and cross the Rockies tomorrow. What do you say to that?"

Her mind immediately started calculating the cost of three motel rooms, five meals, and two cabs to and from the airport. It would be a pretty hefty blow to her finances, but she didn't see any way around it. "Do you suppose the girls and I could sleep in the plane?"

He tilted his head as if not quite clear what she was asking.

"I'm on a pretty tight budget and I don't have a lot of extra cash," she explained. "I'm going to reimburse you for the cost of this flight as soon as I can, but it might not happen until after my…um…settlement," she whispered the word in case Miranda was listening. Daria had tried her best not to involve the girls in the financial details of the divorce. "In the meantime, I need to pinch pennies."

"I've always found that such an odd and outdated saying, since people rarely seem to care about one-cent coins any more," he said, a bemused look in his eyes.

"But, I need to make one thing clear. I fly the plane. Shane handles the finances. You can bring that up with him, but he probably won't take your money. He's very fond of your grandfather. Libby and Cooper were married in your grandfather's garden, and I believe Shane said the setting was magical. He's going to use it in the show next season."

"Libby and Cooper are getting married? I mean, their characters are?"

He blinked and pulled his lips to one side. "Hmm, now you know why I didn't go into foreign service. No torture necessary to get me to blurt out state secrets. I don't believe that tidbit was meant for public consumption."

His chagrin was so real, so charming, she would have melted in a pool if the plane hadn't suddenly dropped and pulled sharply to the right.

"Bloody hell," he muttered, jumping to his feet. "Damn sorry. That's what I get for flirting with the passengers."

He was flirting? With me?

"Mommy? What happened? Is the plane okay?"

A handsome man was flirting with me and I have so little self-esteem, I didn't even know it. She put the thought out of her mind and stood, gripping the back of her seat so she wouldn't fall. She needed to keep her mind on her daughters and her present situation. Period. "Everything is fine, sweetie. Let Mommy make sure your safety belt is nice and tight. We're going to land soon."

"Are we at Great-Grandpa's?"

"Not exactly, doll." She made certain Hailey's seat back was upright and then gave her belt an extra tug. "We have to make a detour because of the weather. I'll let William tell you all about it when we land. But don't worry. We're perfectly safe and we'll be back in the air tomorrow."

"Oh, jeez," Miranda said, groaning. "Dad was right. You can't do anything right. Now, we won't get to see Great-Grandpa for another day."

Her daughter's criticism stung, but Daria ignored it. She'd put off making this decision for too long and now she was going to have to pay the price. "Turn off the DVD player, Miranda," Daria said. "The pilots will need to be able to communicate with the airport control tower. All electronic devices, remember?"

She didn't know for certain that included portable movie players, but she'd flown enough to know the drill. So did her daughter, who groused but complied.

Once back in her seat, Daria let out a halting sigh. She'd done well to keep her emotions under control to this point, and she wouldn't give in to tears now—even though William's and Shane's generosity had created a lump the size of Kansas in her throat. Kindness and compassion hadn't been a part of her life for a long time, and she vowed to pay it forward as soon as she had the wherewithal to do so.

She didn't dare look too far ahead. Life was going to get tougher over the next few weeks and months, and her main goal was to protect the two sweet, fragile souls she loved more than life.

Would she ever be brave enough to risk falling in love again? Maybe. If, by then, she'd figured out what real love was supposed to be. At least now, she knew what it wasn't. Love was not abject control over another person.

And if it turned out that she was some sort of magnet for controlling men who needed to dominate her to feel good about themselves…well, forget it. She'd rather be single for the rest of her life.

As depressing as that sounded, a part of her brain couldn't quite let go of that funny flutter in her chest that happened every time she was in William Hughes's presence.

I might never marry again, she thought. *But I could take a lover. When the girls are older and off at college. Maybe one with an English accent.*

She closed her eyes and tucked the dream in a small, dark corner of her mind. Dreams were a luxury a divorced mother of two could not afford. She'd do well to remember that. Once she had her feet on the ground, they needed to stay firmly planted because, like the big bad wolf, Bruce would huff and puff and try to blow her back into the controlling net of his world, his family.

Fighting Bruce, fighting for her daughters would take all of her focus. So no more fantasizing about handsome, inscrutable Englishmen. Period.

CHAPTER FOUR

"GOOD CALL on Durango," William told his copilot. "The only thing I know about western Colorado is its ski resorts, and I don't think that's something that would interest our passengers."

"Yeah," Lucas said, his gaze never leaving the runway that was barely visible in the distance. "Durango's a college town, but it's pretty low-key. I haven't been back for a while. Like I told you earlier, my aunt lives there—I'll stay at her place tonight, if that's okay."

"Fine with me. Do you know if there's a car rental at the airport?"

They discussed the logistics of their destination for a few minutes more, then William keyed the intercom to inform Daria and her daughters to prepare for landing.

He knew she was worried about the cost of this trip, but he didn't quite know how to reassure her that the expense would be absorbed by their corporation without sounding like a pompous ass. Pride was a delicate factor that he constantly had to keep in mind when negotiating deals for his clients. If one actress discovered that someone had received orchids in his or her trailer and he or she had only gotten roses, feelings would be hurt and there would be hell to pay. Maybe he should call Libby and ask her to explain the financial end of this arrangement to Daria.

Bloody coward.

"We'll be landing in under five, Daria," he said. "Lucas is coming back to make sure everything is secure."

Lucas glanced at him in surprise.

"Seat belts. Everything neat and tidy. You know the drill."

The young man didn't hesitate, even though William had made a point of handling all the passenger interaction himself thus far. William needed to keep the goal of this mission clear in his mind. He was providing a service for a woman in need. That was all. The fact that they had several hours to kill in a strange town didn't mean he had to get too friendly.

"CAN I SIT on your lap?"

"I beg your pardon?" William asked the little girl who was tucked in tightly beside him. They were riding in the backseat of the taxi Lucas had procured for them after they'd landed and parked the plane.

"I wanna see the snow. Our snow is way up in the mountains."

"You can sit on my lap, honey," Daria said, reaching across Miranda.

"No," Hailey protested. "You're too lumpy." William glanced at Daria, who was holding all three backpacks at her feet and on her lap.

"You're supposed to wear a seat belt," Miranda said, grouchily. William still didn't have an accurate read on the girl, who was flirtatious one minute and bite-your-fingers snappy the next. She reminded him of a parrot his uncle once had.

"We're going slow and there isn't much traffic," William said, patting the tops of his knees. "Hop aboard."

"Thank you, Mr. William. I like you. Are you our

uncle?" Hailey Fontina was as precious and precocious as a young Shirley Temple.

"Of course not, dummy. We just met him for the first time this morning at the airport. Don't you think Mom or Dad would have mentioned an Uncle William who flies his own plane, if he were related to us?"

"Language," Daria cautioned softly. "We all speak. None of us is dumb."

Hailey happily scrambled across his legs to sit with her knees brushing the door panel. He leaned forward and depressed the lock button. "A girl can wish, can't she?" Hailey responded, pressing her face against the glass as she had at the window of the plane.

William's resolve to keep his distance melted like a chocolate bar in the hands of a toddler. "Your daughters could both have careers in Hollywood, if you were so inclined. Brains, beauty *and* the it factor. In spades."

Daria's eyes opened wide when both girls looked at her excitedly. "Oh, there's an idea. Your father would have a warrant out for my arrest faster than you could bribe a judge." She shook her head, grinning at Lucas who'd let out a loud hoot from the front passenger seat.

William regretted his candor. He'd momentarily forgotten who he was dealing with—not a stage mom who would sell her child's soul for a big break, but a mother who would give up everything she had for the sake of her children.

"This the place?" the taxi driver asked, slowing to turn into the lot of a two-story chain motel that had two suites available when William had called.

"That's the one," he said, leaning forward to see the meter. "Sorry, love, I need to move you so I can pay the man."

"Can I do it?" Hailey asked, her hand out.

"What a suck-up," Miranda said, her tone betraying that she was mad at herself for not taking the initiative before her sister beat her to the punch.

"Am not," Hailey returned, big crystal tears forming in her eyes.

"I will pay the fare. You are both in charge of tipping. As soon as we get out. Agreed?"

"Okay," Miranda said, sitting up tall. Hailey's chin barely left her chest, but he took the slight head bobbing as a yes.

A few minutes later, William watched with some satisfaction as the two worked together to charm a smile out of their mostly silent driver. "Thank you kindly, girls. Have a good stay," he called once Hailey and Miranda were standing safely under the tall, open portcullis.

William picked up his bag and two others, only half listening to the sisters talk.

"He was nice," Hailey said.

"Dad wouldn't have given him that much," her sister replied.

"Why not?"

"Because of his turban."

"Daddy doesn't like turbans?" Hailey asked. "I do. They remind me of Aladdin." Hailey looked up to find William watching them. "I know the words to the song from the movie by heart. Want me to sing it for you?"

He couldn't think of anything he'd rather hear, but her mother intervened. "No singing. Not right now. It's freezing. Come on, slowpokes. Let's get inside."

Since there were no other guests in the lobby, William was able to get them registered in a matter of minutes. He handed Daria the small envelope that contained her plastic key. "Room 242," he said. He pointed toward the elevator. "Second floor, turn right. You can go on up if you like. I'm going to coordinate a time to meet in the morning with Lucas."

His copilot was standing near the door, cell phone to his ear. He ended the call when he spotted William. "My aunt's pretty excited to see me. She only lives a couple of blocks from here. I offered to walk, but she said she was just leaving to pick up my uncle from work, so she'd stop here first."

William was glad the unplanned stop was working out well for someone. "Shall we meet in the morning for breakfast? I noticed a restaurant across the way."

They were still deciding on the best hour to leave when a bright red Jeep with oversize tires pulled up. "There's my aunt," Lucas said, heading for the door. "I'll call you in the morning around seven."

William made his way up in the elevator, fingering the plastic key card as he walked to his room. Right beside Daria's, he realized when Daria and Miranda suddenly stepped into the hallway. "Do you know which way the ice machine is?" Daria asked.

"Directly across from the elevator," he said. "I noticed it when I got off."

Miranda spun around and charged down the hallway without waiting for her mother's okay. Daria sighed. "Everything is a power struggle with her. Not surprising, I guess. She learned from a pro, but still…"

William pushed open his door but didn't walk inside. "Is your room adequate?"

She seemed surprised by his question. "It's perfect. There's even a microwave. The girls are going to make popcorn and watch a movie. We don't have cable at home, so they're in hog heaven."

Hog heaven. The phrase made him smile. He might have argued that putting a couch in a too-small room and adding a microwave and noisy minirefrigerator did not a suite make, but he kept his opinion to himself.

A loud, clinking sound from the far end of the hallway told them Miranda had found the machine and was accomplishing her task. Daria brushed back a lock of hair from her face and said, "By the way, I wanted to apologize for jumping all over your lovely compliment about the girls being marketable in Hollywood. I really need to stop responding to every comment by worrying about what Bruce would say. Old habits, you know."

"Nothing to apologize for. It simply struck me that both embody an innocence and grace that Hollywood would jump at the chance to exploit. You are wise to avoid going that route, regardless of the reason behind your decision."

"Mom," Miranda called, poking her head around the corner. "The juices are only a dollar. Can't we each get one, instead of sharing?"

Hailey burst out of the room, brushing past her mother's legs like a small animal breaking from the bush. "Yeah, Mommy, can we? I want grape."

"I want cran-apple," Miranda yelled.

Daria fished a crumpled bill from her front pocket. "Okay, but that's it for the day. Water with dinner. Don't ask for anything else. Got it?"

When they were alone again, William asked the question he had no business asking. "Did you get hold of their father?"

She shook her head. "Not yet. Ever since we split up, I've made every effort to keep personal calls between me and Bruce...um, personal. I won't talk divorce stuff in front of the girls. It's not always easy, but..."

His respect for her grew. "If you'd like me to watch

after your daughters while you take a walk, I'd be happy to."

She looked down. "You've already done so much. I don't want to impose any more."

"Mine's bigger than yours," Hailey said, skipping ahead of her sister.

"That's because yours has white grapes and high-fructose corn syrup in it. Mine is pure juice. So there," Miranda responded, juggling both a plastic bottle and an ice bucket filled to the brim. "Hi, William."

He was glad to see they were friends again. "Hi, Miranda. Might I ask you something?"

She paused beside her mother. The resemblance was striking, although Miranda's coloring was much darker, reflecting her Italian heritage. "What?"

"Would you and your sister be up for a walk in a few minutes? I thought we might scout around the area to pick a place to have dinner. Your mum said you were going to watch a movie, but I have no idea what you prefer to eat so…"

"Yeah, sure. I'll go. And Hailey's dying to play in the snow. Is that okay, Mom?"

Daria hesitated. He could tell she was reluctant to let the girls out of her sight, and yet they both knew Daria needed a little alone time. "The fresh air would do you good. I'll call your dad and let him know what's going on." She glanced at her watch. "But don't pick any place too expensive, okay?"

"Give me ten to check my messages," William said, turning to leave. He had his own prerequisites for a restaurant, and price wasn't on the list. But given the fact she'd agreed to entrust him with her daughters, he'd do what he'd offered and let the girls pick the place.

He had a feeling Daria wasn't going to have much of an appetite once she got off the phone with her ex.

EXCEPT FOR THE BLINDING HEADACHE, which was slowly subsiding, dinner had turned out to be a rather pleasant interlude, Daria thought to herself a few hours later.

The pizza joint was festive, noisy and anonymous. She liked that. For a few moments, she could pretend her life was normal—that the charming man across from her was something other than her conduit to safety, and that she wasn't mid-jump between the frying pan and the fire.

"I believe I saw an arcade in the enclave across the room, if anyone's interested," William said, magically producing two stacks of tokens and placing one in front of each girl.

"Cool," Miranda cried.

"Yeah, cool," Hailey echoed. "Can we, Mom?"

Daria smiled her okay, but the minute they were gone, she looked at William and asked, "Where did you get the tokens?"

"I bought them when I paid for the pizza. I was hoping to linger over this fine wine with a tiny bit less chatter." He held up a hand. "Not that your daughters aren't delightful. They're most charming and very easy company, considering their ages. But I can only handle so much talk about teen pop stars."

Daria laughed for the first time in what felt like eons. "Me, too. Thank you." She took a sip of wine. "I seem to be saying that an awful lot."

He emptied the carafe, topping off each of their glasses. She knew that this sort of wine was not his usual fare, but he'd been a good sport about the kid-friendly place. "Then, let's make a deal," he said, lifting his glass to hers. "Gratitude extended and accepted. End of story."

She lightly clinked her glass to his, knowing the challenge would be next to impossible to meet. She was thankful—more than he could ever know. Her phone conversation with Bruce had been the most vicious to date. She was beginning to think something else was going on with him—business pressures from his brothers or party pressures from National. Who knew? But he seemed very close to the breaking point.

"Tell me about your life. How long were you married?"

"Too long," she said, only half joking. "During the early years, when Bruce was in business with his brothers—they own an import-export company—and was traveling all the time, we got along great. I loved being a stay-at-home mom with Miranda. The problems started when we couldn't conceive a second child." She shook her head. "Bruce had this image of himself as the patriarch of a big Italian family, like his father. I had a miscarriage and, although he tried to be supportive, I truly felt as though he blamed me."

Now, she looked back at that as a huge red flag, but she'd minimized their difficulties at the time. In part because her mother had passed away about then, and she was dealing with grief and issues of her own.

"We separated for six weeks. Miranda and I spent some time in Santa Barbara with my dad after my mother died. I was seriously thinking about moving there, until Bruce showed up, tearful, sincere, begging for a second chance. His brother was diagnosed with an inoperable brain tumor. Doctors gave him six months. The family decided to back Bruce to fill his brother's seat in the legislature."

She could still remember his pleas. "I can't do this without you, Daria," he'd begged. "I need my family behind me. Please. Please, come back. I promise to do better."

If only Dad hadn't found someone to replace Mom so fast, Daria thought, not for the first time. Bitterness and confusion were two things that didn't facilitate clear thinking. "I succumbed to pressure from both families. And Miranda, too. She loves her father, and she missed her cousins and friends. I gave it a second try. Hailey came along a year later, and Bruce was elected, fair and square, to his own term. He didn't have to stand in his brother's shadow anymore."

"So, when the legislature is in session, he lives in Sacramento?"

"Yes. Those three hundred miles are probably the only reason I've stayed married as long as I have. Once he left for the week, I could pretend I was a single mother… more or less. Shocking, huh?"

He shook his head. "Not to me. My parents have lived separately for most of their married lives."

"Really? You're not just saying that to be nice?"

He took another drink of wine then shook his head. She really liked his hair. It seemed determined not to look as neat and fastidious as he wanted to appear. "I'm not that creative."

"How did they meet? I've read a lot of books on relationships recently, and I'm fascinated by how much fate seems to play into things."

"Well, Mother was a medical student at Harvard when my father had a visiting fellowship in economics. It was the late sixties, and the sexual revolution was in full swing. My father was handsome and lonely. My mother was feeling adventurous. They had a semester-long fling that resulted in me."

"Oh."

He tossed out his hands. "They chose convention over abortion, for which I'm thankful."

She sensed a great deal more emotion behind his cavalier attitude than he wanted her to see. "Me, too," was the only thing she could think to say.

The awkwardness of the moment was relieved by Hailey who ran up them. "Mommy, Mommy, look at all my tickets!" she said, holding out a fistful of hot pink tickets. "Come see all the cool stuff we can buy. I wanna get something for Great-Grandpa Cal, but I don't know if I have enough, and Miranda won't share hers."

Daria glanced longingly at the wine carafe. Some days the competition between sisters got very old. To her surprise, William jumped to his feet. "Prizes? I didn't know there were prizes. What say we buy some more tokens and grow that stash of tickets into something really substantial?"

Hailey clapped with glee, even though Daria was quite sure she didn't know the meaning of the word. "Mom? Will you play with us, too?"

Daria knew what kind of faux treasures awaited them—the stuff you paid a fortune to "win." But what the heck. It beat the alternative—sitting in a motel room worrying about the juggernaut she'd unleashed.

"Sure. I'm pretty good at skee ball, if I do say so myself."

She wasn't really. In fact, she was terrible, and she proved it a few minutes later, but William wasn't a darn bit better.

"They must not have this game in England, huh?"

He fished a handful of tokens from his pocket, handing

her half. "That is an excellent excuse and I'm going with it. What's yours?" he asked after tossing the first of his heavy balls toward the ridiculously challenging arrangement of holes and plastic ledges.

She selected a ball of her own. She could have resurrected any number of slights Bruce had used to describe her lack of athletic prowess in the past, but she didn't. "My balls are out of balance."

William laughed. "Definitely not an excuse I'm tempted to steal." He tried another pass, this time scoring the highest number on the machine. Hailey clapped and cheered. She'd lost interest in the game twenty or thirty dollars earlier. Daria had lost track of how many times William had returned to the counter to purchase more tokens.

Truthfully, she didn't really care. She was having fun. A woman running away from her ex-husband probably didn't deserve to have fun, but Daria refused to think about that, either. For once, she gave herself permission to do what felt right—even if she might regret it tomorrow.

"Well, Hailey, I fear we've come to the end of our token supply. Will you and Miranda collect all our tickets? Let's go see what we can buy for Cal."

Daria paused to gather their jackets and tidy up the area where they'd been playing. When she joined them at the redemption counter, she heard Miranda tell William, "He's our great-grandfather. Our mom's dad lives in Florida with a young wife Mom hates. Our dad's dad is dead. Our Grandma Hester lives close by us in Fresno. Mom doesn't like her much, either, although she says she does."

The insights and personal revelations robbed Daria of speech—momentarily. "Miranda Grace, that was entirely uncalled for. You may wait for us at the table while Hailey picks out something for Great-Grandpa Calvin. You, young lady, may use the time to rethink what is appropriate to share and what is not."

Miranda blushed and dashed away, diving for the obscurity of the booth. Hailey moved a little closer to Daria, taking her hand for comfort.

"It's okay, sweetheart. Miranda is still upset because I won't give her back her phone." To William she added, "You'd have thought I untethered her lifeline and set her adrift in the Atlantic."

William extended his hand to Hailey. "Miss Hailey and I can browse while you discuss matters with Miranda, if you like."

She looked toward the booth where they'd been sitting earlier. Miranda—her stubborn, strong, too-savvy-for-her-own-good child. "Good idea." She dropped a kiss on Hailey's cheek and cautioned, "Nothing big. Grandpa doesn't have a lot of space, remember?"

William knew that message was for him, too. And he tried to keep the child's purchases to a ticket-only minimum, but it became imminently clear that even a basketful of tickets wasn't worth squat. Anything of quality required cold, hard cash.

Hailey proved to be a serious shopper. After a great deal of deliberation, she finally settled on two very realistic-looking stuffed animals—a sober-faced black bear for Miranda and a velvety plush polar bear with a cub that Hailey and her mother would share. For Cal, she chose a whimsical two-story birdhouse, which, much to William's amusement, turned out to be from an artist whose name he recognized from Sentinel Pass.

"One thirty-seven sixty-four," the cashier mumbled after cracking a large wad of gum.

"How much?"

"One hundred thirty-seven dollars and sixty-four cents," she repeated, slowly and loud enough for everyone in the entire facility to hear.

He winced. "Thank you. I'm an American, and I'm not deaf."

"Is that a lot, William?" Hailey asked, looking worried. She coughed suddenly—a low, raspy sound that sounded like it came from a set of ninety-year-old smoker's lungs.

He handed the clerk his credit card. "No, love, that's half what it would have been if we hadn't won all those tickets. Good thing you're such a pro at that dance game you and your sister were playing."

He hastily signed his name and collected the large, reinforced shopping bag holding their treasures.

He took Hailey's hand and was halfway across the room when Miranda suddenly jumped up from the table where she and her mother were talking and rushed past them to the main entrance. William could see the girl was crying.

Daria followed, pausing to ask William in a low voice so Hailey couldn't hear, "Would you and Hailey give us a few minutes more? I told her we might not be going home right away and she's pretty upset."

"Of course. Hailey and I will catch up after—" he looked around, wondering how best to stall "—dessert. We forgot to order dessert." He used his free hand to cover his mouth in mock horror, which made Hailey burst out giggling, her concern for her sister apparently forgotten.

"Can we get ice cream?"

William shook his head. "Oh, dear me, no. Ordinary

ice cream is simply too…ordinary. We need sundaes, at the very least."

"Thank you," Daria mouthed on her way out the door.

The hotel was less than a block away and William had a clear line of sight to see Daria catch up to Miranda at the intersection. As they waited for the light to change, he saw Miranda throw herself into her mother's arms, obviously sobbing.

"So, my friend, what will it be? Chocolate, strawberry or butterscotch?" he asked when it was their turn to order. He was tempted to order tea, but he knew he'd be disappointed; authentic tea was the one thing he missed about England.

"B'nilla," Hailey said.

"Vanilla."

"No. *B*'nilla," she insisted, emphasizing the B. "It's how Mommy makes our ice cream. You put white ice cream in the blender with a banana. It's my favorite. Miranda likes Blu-nilla best."

Blueberries and vanilla ice cream, William guessed. Tasty and more nutritious. Clever mum.

"Maybe these nice people might make that for you. It can't hurt to ask."

"Can we take some to Miranda, too?"

"Yes," he said, impressed by her generosity and fealty toward her sister. "Absolutely. In fact, we'll order them both to go."

Ten minutes later, they left the restaurant with two bags in hand. The air was a good twenty degrees cooler than it had been when the sun was up. William feared his young charge might suffer another coughing fit in the cold air, but her breath formed smooth and steady little white clouds, the same as his.

"I don't wish to be nosy, but did I hear someone say you have asthma?"

She shook her head. "No, but I cough a lot. Sometimes I miss school. My teacher is Mrs. Bennett. She's nice. She has brown hair and brown eyes like our president. Some people call her black, but she's really brown."

William was still grinning when he knocked on the door adjacent to his room. Daria answered it right away. The TV was on in the background, but William didn't see Miranda. "Hi, sweetness," she said, giving Hailey a quick hug as she helped her out of her jacket. Hailey handed William the milk shake bag to hold.

"Thank you so much for dinner, William. And for your patience with Hailey. She's a very serious shopper. Aren't you, baby? She didn't buy out the store, did she?" She glanced at the two bags with that worried look William was beginning not to like.

"No, Mommy, we shopped good 'cause we had so many tickets. Huh, William?"

"Indeed, we did. And we supported a local Sentinel Pass artist, as well. Hailey has excellent taste." He set the bag containing the gifts to one side and held out the one containing their desserts. "You should probably pass these out, Hailey, before they get warm."

To Daria, he said, "Milk shakes. B'nilla and Blu-nilla."

Miranda, who must have been eavesdropping in the bathroom, opened the door across from them. "Really? You got me one, too? Thanks." Aside from a little redness around her eyes, she looked fully recovered from her emotional outburst.

"Why don't you open those in the kitchen?" Daria suggested. "I saw some spoons in the drawer if you need them."

Miranda took the bag from William, flashing him a wide smile. Hailey hurried after her but stopped suddenly, turned around and came back. "Thank you, Mr. William. I love you."

William's throat closed tight, but he managed to smile. "You're most welcome. And don't forget your presents."

Hailey gave a loud, excited squeal. "We both got new bears, M'randa," she cried.

Daria grabbed the bag before Hailey could. "After your milkshake, please." She peeked, inside then gave William a questioning look. "You bought all this with tickets? I don't think so."

William flushed under her scrutiny. "I'm a sucker for a sweet smile. She didn't ask, I offered. And like I said, the gift for your grandfather is not only something useful, the sale helps a friend of mine fund a very good cause. Okay?"

Daria took a deep breath and let it out. "Okay."

He wanted to ask if her phone call with her ex had gone *okay,* but he didn't. This was her business, he reminded himself. "I'll be next door if you need anything," he said, stepping back into the hall.

He reached in his pocket for the key card, ignoring as much as possible the odd shake of his hand as he tried to swipe it. The red light remained red.

"Here," Daria said, coming to his aid, "let me. You foreigners."

Her tone was teasing, but he said in his own defense, "I have dual citizenship, I'll have you know. I'm not a tourist, just clumsy."

The light turned green on her first try. She pushed on the handle and the door opened smoothly. "Well," she said, grinning, "that explains the skee ball, doesn't it?"

The mischievous twinkle in her eyes made him completely fumble with the key card when she tried to hand it to him. "Sleep well. See you in the morning."

Then she disappeared back into her suite.

He walked into the ugly room, shrugged off his coat and kicked the foot of the ugly sofa as he walked past. His laptop was on the desk, waiting for him to wade through the hundred or so e-mails that were undoubtedly in his in-box. Instead of pulling out the chair, he emptied his pockets. Key card. Wallet. Phone.

He checked the number of messages. Eleven. "Later," he muttered as he sat on the foot of the bed to remove his shoes. Directly across from him was a wide-screen TV. He could probably choose from several dozen channels if he was so inclined.

He wasn't.

He suddenly felt terribly alone.

Seclusion was a good thing, he told himself. Silence and routine helped him compartmentalize and concentrate. Unfortunately, at the moment, all he seemed capable of focusing on was what was happening next door, and how much he wished he were a part of it.

"DO YOU LIKE YOUR BEAR, Miranda?" Hailey's question was muffled by the towel Daria was using to dry her hair.

Both girls had showered and were dressed in pajamas. Hailey had asked to have her hair braided before bed.

"It's okay."

Daria couldn't decide if the ennui in her daughter's tone was real or fake. Sometimes, Miranda tried to distance herself from things that seemed too childish, but Daria had seen her petting and admiring the high-end stuffed animal when she didn't think anyone was looking.

"I think your bear is handsome. Like Mr. William."

"Daddy's more handsome."

"No, he isn't."

"Yes, he is."

Daria picked up the large comb she always used on Hailey's thick, curly hair. "Ahem. Ladies. Both men are very attractive. May we please leave it at that?"

She slowly, carefully teased loose a knot of snarls while Hailey cuddled her new toy. Hailey hummed a lullaby under her breath for a minute or two then brought the bear close to her lips and whispered, "And Mr. William is nicer than Daddy, too."

Daria felt a lump form in her throat. She'd tried so hard these past few months to help her daughters through this difficult transition. She'd sacrificed, backpedaled, and had given up so many concessions she'd practically lost sight of her original divorce offer. She told herself that if she remained calm, patient and flexible, Bruce would play fair. He hadn't. Not once. And even a child Hailey's age could tell the difference.

"I wanna call Dad," Miranda said, idly surfing the menu on the TV screen.

"He's at a big party with the governor tonight, remember?"

Bruce's boasting about the black-tie event had helped nudge Daria into making her move that day. She'd figured the party would make an excellent excuse to avoid that call.

"Maybe he's Twittered about it. I told you we should have brought the laptop."

They'd had this argument before. "If we were at Grandpa Cal's, like we'd planned, you'd be able to check your social networking sites, so we had no reason to cart along something that could get dropped or broken. Plus, my laptop isn't nearly as fast as your father's, and half the time it won't hook up with a Wi-Fi signal." Bruce made sure he had the fastest, most current technical gizmos, and Daria got his cast-offs. If she was lucky. His last laptop had gone to the student intern who'd worked for Bruce over the summer.

"I'm bored," Miranda said.

"Not for long. We're going to watch a little TV then go to sleep early in case William decides we need to leave first thing in the morning to beat another storm." She had no idea if that was even a possibility, but it sounded logical. Fortunately, neither of her daughters argued with her, for once.

I'm bored, Daria decided two hours later. Both girls were sound asleep in the king-size bed beyond the room divider that made the place a suite. The TV cast an eerie glow in the otherwise darkened room, although Daria had long since turned the volume to mute. She'd settled into bed with the girls to watch the animated show they'd finally compromised on, but had dozed off even before they had.

She'd awoken with a start, panic-stricken that she was home and Bruce would find her asleep when she should have been working. Unfortunately, the adrenaline rush had robbed her of the ability to go back to sleep.

Maybe a cup of cocoa, she decided, poking around the small kitchenette. She filled a cup with water from the tap and set it in the microwave. Resting one hip against the counter, she listened to the loud hum. A sharp "ping" made her jump to retrieve the cup.

She was in the process of stirring the thick, aromatic powder into the water when she heard a soft knock on the door between William's room and hers. She opened it hesitantly. "Yes?"

He smiled apologetically. "I heard your microwave ding. Mine isn't working. I wondered if you'd mind me heating a cup in yours. You can take a Brit out of England, but you can't take away his tea."

Mind? You're paying for this room. How could I mind? "Of course not. Come in."

He shook his head. "Are the girls sleeping? I don't want to disturb them." He handed her a mug identical to her own. "Give a knock when it's ready and I'll come back."

As he closed the door on his side, she caught a glimpse of an open laptop. Miranda's comment about Twitter had started Daria thinking. Maybe Bruce *had* posted something about the gala that night. Or maybe he'd made good on his threat to put out an Amber Alert.

Once the water was boiling, she carried both cups into the adjoining room, leaving the door open slightly behind her. "Here you go," she said, setting his near the basket of tea bags and premeasured coffee packets.

William, who was standing at the window staring out, looked around. "Thank you." He started toward her. "I was checking the sky. Nothing but stars as far as I can see. Hopefully that bodes well for our travel tomorrow."

"Hopefully," she repeated.

He walked past her with a tentative smile. "Are you a tea drinker, too?" he asked, nodding toward her cup.

"Not at night. Caffeine would not be a good idea right now. My mind is having a hard time shutting down as it is." She took a sip and licked her lips before adding, "This is cocoa."

"Ah." He ripped open two tea bags and plopped them

into the cup, then used a second cup to cover the steaming brew. "Not a fan of late-night television?"

She shook her head. "Not since Miranda was born. Once you have kids, you take all the sleep you can get." She stepped closer to the coffee table where his laptop sat. "Do you have Internet service?"

He nodded. "Do you need to check your e-mail or something?"

"Would you mind?"

He motioned her to join him on the sofa, then he quickly saved what he was working on and opened his home page. "Help yourself."

He returned to his tea preparations while Daria typed in Bruce's full name. He'd hired a professional communications coach last year to help him update his image and make his Web site more accessible—at least on the surface. "You want your constituents to feel as though you're there for them," Bruce had parroted, attempting to explain away the cost. "Not that I actually intend to read their e-mails, but one of my staffers can."

Indeed, she'd thought, wondering if there was a watchdog group that welcomed anonymous tips from concerned citizens about their representatives. Naturally, she never took the idea any further.

"Is that your ex?" William asked.

She hadn't heard him circle around. He was leaning against the partition that delineated the bedroom from the living area. She nodded. "He was supposed to be at a big gala reception tonight. I thought he might have Twittered about it."

She clicked on the appropriate link and, sure enough, his most recent post appeared. Twelve minutes earlier. Banal chatter including some celebrity name-dropping.

William leaned over slightly to read the entry. "Ah… Denzel is there. Good man."

She chuckled softly. "How come it doesn't sound pretentious coming from you, but Bruce sounds like a total gossip?"

He appeared to consider her observation carefully before answering. She liked that he listened—actually listened—as if what she was saying had value. "When you work with famous people on a daily basis, you see aspects of their lives that make them more…ordinary, I guess you'd say. They're human. Fallible. Temperamental. Subject to the vagaries of life that plague the rest of us."

"Do you like your job?"

A wry smile touched his lips. Hailey was right—he really was a lot more handsome than her father. "Not all of the time, but then who does? What I like best is knowing that I've contributed to the growth and development of most of my clients' careers."

"I read a biography of some older film star…his name escapes me, but he had a real love-hate relationship with his agent. He likened it to a parent-child thing."

He nodded. "I can appreciate that. There's a tricky balancing act that takes place when you're intimately involved in another person's livelihood. It's easy to get sucked into aspects of their lives where you don't belong."

"Has that happened to you?"

"Unfortunately, yes."

His honesty surprised her. She wanted to hear more, but he switched subjects. "But one lesson I learned early on in this business is to never underestimate the value of respect. A little deference can go a long way."

"Even if the person demanding respect doesn't deserve it?"

"In that case, the key is knowledge. With the right information at your fingertips, you never have to apologize."

She shivered slightly. A nice guy with an edge of steel. She scanned through a few other entries Bruce had made during the day. "Uh-oh. Here's a post about his wife being AWOL. Absent without leave. Like I'm a grunt soldier missing from duty." Her cocoa gurgled unpleasantly in her belly.

"I can't help noticing he still calls you his wife. He hasn't acknowledged that you've separated?"

She shook her head. "He keeps telling me this is a private matter and he isn't ready to make that sort of announcement. I told myself it didn't matter who he told or when, as long as I was moving forward with my plans." She swallowed. "I think I was in denial."

"Was he ever physically abusive?"

Daria closed the laptop and blew out a breath. "Bruises and broken bones are only one kind of abuse. In a way, I wish he had taken a swing at me. It would have made the process easier to document, but Bruce is too smart to leave a mark."

"Don't be too sure. It only takes one time."

His tone was so flat and stark it chilled her. "What do you mean?"

He polished off the last swig of tea in his cup and walked to the small sink beside the non-operational microwave. He rinsed it thoroughly and turned it upside down on a paper towel. Not something she'd ever seen her ex do.

Then he walked to the armchair adjacent to the coffee table and sat down, kicking out his feet. "Do you remember an actress by the name of Bianca Del Torres?"

"Sure. She was beautiful and talented. She died a few years ago. Something tragic. I don't remember the details. Overdose?"

William shook his head. "Murder-suicide at the hands of her live-in boyfriend. Ocho was part of her past. They grew up together in a little town near Jalisco. They went to Mexico City, where she got her start in Telemundo soaps. Eventually, she moved to L.A. Ocho followed." His sad, inward-looking smile nearly broke Daria's heart.

"She was one of my first clients. So young and needy and talented. In addition to championing her career, I became a sort of a big brother or a father-figure. She came so close to making it big. But, in the end, she couldn't cut loose the baggage that kept weighing her down."

Daria swallowed harshly. She heard a warning in the subtext of his message.

There was real pain in his eyes when he looked at Daria. "Every time Ocho knocked the stuffing out of her, she'd call me. 'William to the rescue,' she'd joke afterward, when things calmed down. She'd hide out at my house, walk on the beach. Vow never to give him another chance."

"But she did, didn't she?" Daria asked, remembering the headlines all too vividly. Murder-suicide. Promising young star dead.

"Every single time. He knew how to work her. He'd weep and beg for forgiveness. Swear on his dead madre's grave that he'd change. That no one would love her more than he did." Daria could read his anger, but there was something else there, too. Guilt. "The last time she caved in and took him back, I told her I was done. Finito. She assured me that this time was different. Ocho really meant it. He'd seen a priest and confessed. God was helping him."

Daria sat forward, wishing she was brave enough to reach out and comfort him. "It wasn't your fault."

His gray eyes looked tormented. "That's what everyone told me. But I'm the one who turned off my phone after her first call. By the time my guilty conscience kicked in and I called to check on her, the police answered. She was dead." His lips curled back in a snarl. "Ocho had killed her then turned the gun on himself. The newspapers reported that he'd bought the gun that morning. Like I said, it only takes once."

She realized that this poor woman's story was probably the reason he'd agreed to put his life on hold to fly her and her daughters to South Dakota. She owed him some assurance that history was not going to repeat itself where she and Bruce were concerned.

"I didn't suddenly wake up one morning and decide I wanted a divorce. I've known for a long time that my marriage was an unhealthy place for me. I fooled myself into believing that I could stick it out until my children were grown. For some reason, that seemed like the adult thing to do.

"But last summer, I had a health scare. A side ache that turned so horrible I thought I was going to die. Bruce was in Alaska on a fishing trip with his brothers, and my mother-in-law was out of town. It seemed as though the whole Fontina family was AWOL," she said, liking the tie-back to their earlier conversation.

"What did you do?"

"I called a friend. Julie and I hadn't really talked in several years. Her husband kept the girls and she stayed by my side the whole time in the emergency room. Talking with her, once the pain meds kicked in, made me realize how isolated I'd let myself become. I'd dropped her as a friend because Bruce didn't like her. I think he felt threatened by her."

William nodded. "Ocho hated me, called me a leech. He tried to convince Bianca that I was screwing her out of money that was rightfully hers. I'm fairly certain she never believed that." He shook his head as if to dislodge the memory. "So, what caused your pain, if you don't mind my asking?"

"The E.R. doctor took an X-ray. He thought he saw some spots on my liver, which really freaked me out. My family practitioner ran tests and ruled out liver cancer, thank God. They finally narrowed it down to either my gallbladder or an ulcer. Since the pain went away on its own, I decided not to do any more invasive testing. My mother used to say that the body heals itself." She shrugged. "We'll see."

She looked upward and took a deep breath. "The point of this much-too-involved story is that my trip to the E.R. was a wake-up call. I decided I didn't want to live a half life anymore. I deserve more. So do my girls. Bruce moved out in early September, and I'm ready for this to be over. My lawyer is supposed to present my final settlement offer to Bruce in the morning. Simple. Fair. Generous sharing of time with our daughters."

"Good."

"The only problem is, Bruce won't sign the divorce papers. He's somehow managed to convince himself that we're going to get back together. I fully expect him to go ballistic, which is why we're on our way to Sentinel Pass. I don't want him to make an impulsive, irrational decision that we'll all regret later."

"Do you think your life is in danger?"

She polished off the last of her cold cocoa—she found it sweet but hard to swallow, like a lot of things in her life the past few years.

"Bruce's family is Italian. I know this will probably sound cliché, like something out of *The Sopranos,* but Bruce has always claimed to have *connections*." She made air quotes. "When his brother and sister-in-law were having problems a few years ago, I remember Bruce saying she'd better clean up her act or he was going to have to call someone. I took that as code for hiring a hit man. I decided I'd rather be paranoid than a sitting duck."

He opened his mouth as if to say something, closed it, then, with obvious reluctance, asked, "Why didn't you leave sooner?"

She'd asked herself the same question a million times, if not more. "Because it wasn't always terrible. At first, I was so busy making my husband's career my life's work that I didn't realize I'd lost myself in the process. When Hailey started school, I figured I'd go back to work. But Bruce wouldn't hear of it. He said that between him and his family, they had enough clout to get me fired from any job."

William rubbed his hands on the tops of his thighs, as if itching to put them around someone's neck—probably Bruce's. "After Bianca died, I did some research about spousal abuse. What I realize now that I didn't even think about then is that anytime anyone limits your choices, they have wronged you."

"Wow. That's very profound. And true. Have you thought about writing a book or making a movie about her life? It might help someone in her situation. Or maybe even someone like me."

He smiled for the first time. "I started out as a book editor in New York. I learned early on that as much as I love books, I'm not a writer. I don't have the patience. But I did float the idea past a couple of writer friends. Do you know Shane Reynard and Jenna Murphy?"

She shook her head. She recognized the names but hadn't met any of the people associated with transforming her grandfather's rustic little town into a household name.

"Shane's coproducer of *Sentinel Passtime* and Jenna is head writer. They're considering introducing a storyline that involves spousal abuse into the show next season."

"Really? Congratulations—you made something positive come out of something really awful. I hope I'm that successful where my daughters are concerned. Whenever things get tough and there are more bills than money, I wonder if what I'm doing is worth it. But then I think of Miranda and Hailey. There's no way I want them to grow up believing that repression and bullying is normal or okay."

He started to say something but a sudden, worried, "Mommy?" sounded from the other room.

Daria jumped up. "Right here, sweetheart," she called, mouthing a silent "Bye" as she dashed back to her own room.

She closed and locked the door as if to keep all their dark, weighty confessions from dogging her heels. She needed a good night's sleep. Tomorrow was going to be intense. Tomorrow, Bruce would hear from Daria's attorney and be faced with a once-and-for-all line in the sand.

She needed this divorce to be a done deal. Now. So she could start living again.

CHAPTER FIVE

"LUCAS IS SICK," William told Daria the moment she and her girls arrived in the lobby of the motel. He'd already settled their bill and arranged for a ride back to the airport. "Laryngitis and a low-grade fever. His aunt is taking him to the doctor. I told him I'd pay his way back home as soon as he's able to travel."

"Poor guy," Daria said. "Thank goodness he's with family. Is there anything we can do to help?

He liked the way she put Lucas's welfare ahead of her own worries. "I don't believe so. His chief concern was not being able to get you to your grandfather's, but I assured him we'd take off as planned. The weather report is clear, and we'll have a good tailwind so we should make great time."

"Good," she said, glancing at her daughters. "Grandpa Cal called this morning. He was worried about us."

A slight quiver in her voice told William there was more to that comment, but he didn't press her. He had a faint headache, probably brought on by a poor night's sleep. He'd shared things with her he had no business sharing. Bianca Del Torres, for heaven's sake. He never talked about that painful time in his life. Too much heartache, not to mention a trip down guilt alley.

"If you don't mind breakfast on the run, we'll grab something on the way to the airport," he said as their taxi pulled into sight. "Here we go. Ladies first. And, ah, yes, the birdhouse," he said taking the gift bag from Daria's outstretched hand. "We can't forget that."

The lengthy line at the town's closest drive-through breakfast lane added at least five bucks to the meter, but the choice of meals seemed to please Hailey.

"Look, Mommy, a wiggle game."

William had no idea what that was, but he couldn't look because he was busy balancing the cardboard carrier holding their drinks on his lap. He did manage to lower the window a couple of inches. The aroma of fast food was not one of his favorites.

"Thank you," he heard Daria say softly.

They were a mile or so from the airport when Hailey sighed elaborately and said, "I like this place. Can we come back someday, Mommy?"

William spotted Miranda, who was sitting directly behind the driver, roll her eyes dramatically. "You say that about every place we've ever been. You don't know anything about this town. And look at all the snow. You've never lived in snow. You'd probably hate it."

"Would not."

"Would, too."

Daria shushed them. "Stop it, you two." Her voice was brittle and she sounded even more exhausted than William. "Hailey, love, we should make an effort to come here again. The mountains are really pretty. Miranda, please…"

Miranda gave Hailey a little shove and turned her face toward the door.

William faced forward again, wishing he had a free hand to rub the knot in his neck. He rolled his shoulders and stretched his neck to ease the tense muscles. He'd tossed and turned so many times during the night he woke up feeling as though he'd run a marathon. And his early morning call from Notty hadn't helped.

"Something wrong with your neck?" Daria asked.

He looked in the taxi's side mirror and could see a tiny-size image of her. "I usually bring my own pillow when I travel. The ones at that hotel were like sleeping on a puffy rock."

Miranda let out a loud guffaw. "When Hugh Grant was on *Oprah* he said he never went anywhere without his own pillow. He said that made him old."

He is old. Older than me, he almost answered. Instead, with as much dignity as possible, he told her, "Actually, offering a menu of pillow choices—firm, memory foam, hypo-allergenic, et cetera—is not uncommon at five-star hotels."

"So, our hotel was like a one-star?" she asked.

Their driver, who was probably in his midtwenties, snickered in a start and stop way, like a cat working up a hairball.

"Miranda," her mother interrupted, "that in-room coffee didn't agree with me. Could we ride in peace, please?"

That explained her paleness, William thought. He sat forward enough to actually turn and look at her. "You don't have a fever, do you? Or a sore throat?"

"Are you sick, Mommy?" Hailey cried, reaching for her mother's hand.

Daria gave William a cross look. A mind-your-own-business look. "I'm fine, honey. My tummy's a little upset, that's all."

William turned back around, distracted by the low hum of his phone. Balancing the tray of drinks on his knees, he reached in the pocket of his jacket. Libby. "Hi, Libby, what's up?"

"Where are you guys? I just got off the phone with Cal. He said you got waylaid by weather, but he couldn't remember the name of the town. Is everything okay?"

"We decided to sit out a storm that's now long gone. We're on our way to the airport as we speak."

"Good, I'm glad to hear you'll be there soon. Cal sounded pretty upset. I think he's heard from Daria's ex-husband."

In the mirror, he saw Daria sit forward, concern clearly visible on her face. "Hang on, Lib. I'm going to hand the phone to Daria. I'm just the pilot, remember?"

Libby's laughing, "In your dreams," was the last thing he heard as he held the phone over his shoulder. Daria took it from his fingers with great care. Her touch sent a tangible vibration along his arm and through his body. Interesting. Dangerous.

No, he decided, crazy.

The last thing either of them needed was him thinking he was physically attracted to Daria—even if she had been the real source of his restless night.

Daria didn't know Libby well—Bruce hadn't liked any of Daria's relatives, including her grandfather's extended family. But everyone knew Libby's story, thanks to the TV show based on Libby's modern-day fairy-tale romance with Hollywood charmer Cooper Lindstrom.

"Hi, Daria. I'm so glad you're on your way again—I think Cal had a rough night. Apparently, Bruce isn't very happy with the situation and he aimed some of his fury Cal's way."

Daria's stomach writhed and contracted, sending a flood of acid up her esophagus. She was half afraid she'd need to stop the taxi so she could throw up. Last night's spicy pizza, more than the coffee, was probably the culprit.

"Thanks for being there for Cal, Libby. I talked to him before we left the hotel. He seemed okay, but I could sense he was upset about something. He probably didn't want me to worry."

"No one's blaming you, Daria. I just didn't want you going in blind when you got to Cal's."

"Thank you," she repeated numbly as the taxi pulled up to the airport. "I'll call when we get to Sentinel Pass to let you know we're safe."

She practically threw the phone over William's shoulder and had her door open before the cab came to a complete stop. As quickly as her shaky fingers would allow, she undid her seat belt and got out, gulping in deep breaths of cold, fresh air.

William's door opened a few seconds later. "Would you mind...?" he asked, handing her the cardboard drink tray.

He leaned in to pay the driver, then shouldered her bag and his own after helping the girls with their backpacks. He wasn't a father, but he certainly acted the part well, she decided.

"Are we ready?" he asked. "Our plane awaits."

Between Libby's call and the dozen or so text messages Bruce had left on her phone that morning, Daria felt as though she might be verging on a breakdown. She ordered herself to stay strong. And focused. One step in front of the other. But her head ached and her stomach was on its own damn roller coaster. She might have curled up in a comforting little catatonic ball on the tarmac if William hadn't gently, respectfully walked her through the motions.

He hustled them aboard the plane, instructing the girls to eat while he made all the necessary checks. Daria remembered snapping her seat belt then closing her eyes—for a minute—to collect her thoughts.

When she opened her eyes, the plane was in the air. Looking out her window, she saw a thick white blanket of clouds far, far below them. Her mouth was dry and she was exceedingly thirsty. The cup of coffee she'd ordered from the fast food menu was sitting in the cup holder in the seat across from her. The thought of cold coffee made her queasy again, so she grabbed the bottle of water she'd slipped into her purse and took a sip.

Her stomach made a complaining sound audible even over the hum of the engines. Food. She needed food. A white bag with its easily identifiable logo was in arm's reach. She opened it and looked inside. By the number of choices available she could only guess that William had decided against sampling any of the items he'd purchased.

She didn't blame him. She wasn't a fan of fast food, either, but the granola bars she'd brought from home yesterday were long gone. She selected an English muffin and egg duo that looked fairly edible.

"Mom? You're awake. Are you feeling better?"

Daria leaned sideways to look at Miranda. The two girls had switched sides of the airplane, for some reason. She finished chewing and nodded. "Much. I didn't sleep very well last night. What are you watching?"

Miranda held up the case of a recently released DVD. It didn't belong to them, so Daria had to assume William had provided it. "Nice. You wanted to see that one, didn't you?"

She nodded. "It's good. Hailey's watching the new Disney movie. We're going to switch when she's done. *If* we have time before we get to Great-Grandpa's. William said we're cruising on a tailwind and making good time."

Daria heard an apology in her daughter's tone. Miranda had her father's temper, but she didn't stew and sulk for days the way Bruce did. Miranda was quick to forgive, like Daria.

"Do you need anything, sweetie?"

Miranda shook her head. "No. I'm good. Sorry for earlier." Then she put her headphones on and focused her attention back on the DVD.

Daria finished her not-terribly appetizing meal with a swig of cold coffee and then got up to check on Hailey. The little girl was curled around her new bear, sound asleep, the movie still playing. Daria hit the pause button, but left her exactly as she was.

"Where's your bear?" she asked Miranda, hoping it got packed. She'd been so frazzled this morning she hadn't made her usual final sweep through the hotel room.

"In my backpack. I'm not a baby, Mom. I can't be seen carrying a stuffed animal. Jeesch." She rolled her eyes and continued to watch her movie.

Jeesch, Mom, are you the dumbest person on the planet or what?

She worked her way to the front of the plane, intending to ask William about their remaining flight time. The plane hit a little air pocket and she stumbled slightly, falling against his seat. He looked around sharply. "Hey, sleeping beauty, how are you feeling?"

"Better. Thanks."

"Have a seat," he said, pointing to the copilot's chair.

"Really?"

He nodded. "Please."

She had to shimmy sideways and sort of drop into the cockpit, but once she was seated, she felt very comfortable. "This is nice. What a view." After fastening her seat belt, she leaned forward and looked around. Her pulse sped up, but she wasn't sure if she should blame the wide open sky or her proximity to William, who looked movie-star handsome and every bit the pilot.

"Are the girls okay?"

"Perfect. Miranda's watching a movie she's been dying to see, and Hailey is sleeping with her new bear as her pillow. Couldn't ask for more."

"Maybe you should start."

"I beg your pardon?"

He fiddled with the controls a moment then removed one side of his earphones and looked at her. "I hope I'm not out of line here, but is it safe to assume you heard from your ex this morning?"

"A flurry of texts and a voice message from last night. I think he might have been drunk. I listened to it while the girls were getting ready. He's very upset."

Last night's message had been tearful and rambling, punctuated by name-calling and spikes of temper as he listed all the ways she'd wronged him over the years, including emasculating him in bed.

"Judging by your appearance this morning, it's apparent that communicating with him on any level isn't good for your health and well-being. Maybe you should cut yourself some slack and let your lawyer handle that side of things."

"Easier said than done, I'm afraid. But that's the plan," she said, glancing at her watch, which was still set on California time. She kept her voice low, not certain if the cabin noise was enough to keep their conversation private. "My lawyer is supposed to be meeting with him about now. I'm hoping when the dust settles I'll have my life back, with a fair and equitable property settlement and sensible custody arrangement. That's not asking too much, is it?"

"Not at all," he confirmed.

"How soon will we be there?" She studied all the gauges in front of her. The plane was even more high-tech than she'd imagined. "Libby's call made me a little worried about Grandpa. There's no chance Bruce could beat us there, is there?"

"None. I figured you might be worried about that, and I checked in with Cal before we took off. I suggested he unplug his phone. He said he'd already turned off his recorder and was screening calls. Smart fellow."

Daria had warned her grandfather to expect the worst from Bruce if she and the girls came to stay with him, but Cal had pooh-poohed her worries. "I've lived through bad times. The low spots in life are there to make you appreciate the high spots, and you'll have plenty of those once you get started fresh."

A fresh start. Exactly what she wanted. And, if she read William's hint correctly, exactly what she had every right to demand for herself. Her friend Julie had said the same thing that night in the E.R. "If not now, when? Life doesn't come with any guarantees, Daria. My mom has this embroidered doily thing that says 'The best gift a father can give his children is to love their mother.' Well, in my opinion, the best gift a mother can give her daughters is to love herself."

Daria leaned sideways to look down. She tried to spot some familiar landmark or terrain, but the clouds whizzing by were too opaque. "Where are we?"

"Northeastern Colorado. We should be passing over the panhandle of Nebraska any minute. These clouds are leftover from yesterday's storm. Doesn't make for the most scenic trip. Sorry. I'm hoping to be on the ground in about an hour."

Her jaw dropped. "Seriously? I slept that long?"

"It's a pretty quick trip, without the weather interference."

He moved suddenly to make some sort of adjustment. A bell sounded and he muttered something incomprehensible into the slim mike on his headset. She suddenly understood the value of having a copilot.

When he gave her his attention again, she asked, "What would happen if something happened to you? Would I be able to land the plane or would we all be dead?"

He cleared his throat. "On that happy note…let me give you a—forgive the pun—crash course in landing a plane. First, put your hands on the stick. Like this." He reached out and adjusted her hands the way he wanted them on the second set of controls. His touch was different, but it felt good. As if they'd held hands for years.

"You've done this before. Reassured nervous nonpilots, I mean."

"Not really. Shane and Cooper have both had flying lessons. If you were going to be doing this a lot—flying back and forth to the Black Hills—I'd advise you to take a course. I'm no teacher."

She shook her head. "I disagree. I watched you with the girls last night. When you were helping Miranda with that jet fighter game, you were very patient. With Hailey, too, picking out her much-too-expensive prizes. And when we first arrived yesterday afternoon, Lucas told me you let him handle things that other instructors might not have thought he was ready for."

He looked surprised. "That's because he's a natural-born flier. I'm not, but I make up for that lack of instinctual knowledge with training and practice."

"Why do you do it? Isn't flying a terribly expensive hobby? Bruce took a few lessons but said he didn't want to spend the arm and leg it would have cost to own a plane and fly it."

"I'm sure there's a way to quantify the cost-benefit ratio of private versus commercial, but for me, I look at this—" he made a sweeping gesture, encompassing the brilliant blue sky "—as money I'm not paying a therapist." His tone was wry, but Daria sensed a deeper truth behind the statement.

"Have you always wanted to fly? Or was this something you realized as an adult?"

"Actually, I can tell you the exact moment I knew this was something I wanted to do. I was about Miranda's age, and my uncle was escorting me to Kenya. Mum was working with the World Health Organization or some such entity and it was her turn to shoulder some parenting time." Although he tried to sound cavalier, a gritty edge of bitterness poked through like rust on a glossy painted surface.

"Africa? My goodness, you're well-traveled."

He didn't dispute the claim or elaborate further. "Because of my uncle's connections—or his job, I've never been certain which—we often traveled on military transport planes. Not the most glamorous way to fly, but for a young, impressionable boy, these giant flying fortresses were pure adventure."

"So it was the excitement that attracted you. I was thinking maybe, subconsciously, you associated flying with a maternal connection."

"Doubtful. Once we hit the ground, there were usually long, dusty overland connections that involved large, diesel trucks loaded with medical supplies. I can't say for sure which of the two things—me or the penicillin—Mum was happier to see."

Interesting.

"Do you think all that back-and-forth traveling was a good thing or bad?" she asked, thinking that although his parents hadn't divorced, William had ended up volleying between them, much the way her daughters would once Daria and Bruce finalized a custody agreement.

He reached out and squeezed her hand supportively. "You can't compare my situation to yours. The two are as different as song and snoring."

She let go of the breath she'd been holding. She looked at their hands, wondering how William's touch could feel so reassuring when she barely knew him. Supportive, yes, but there was another element that spoke to the woman in her. Something timeless and basic that had no place in her consciousness at the moment. She was a mom first, a woman a very distant second.

He dropped his hand, as if sensing her decision. "I meant to tell you earlier," he said, businesslike in tone again. "I'm picking up a van at the airport. I'd be happy to give you a lift to Sentinel Pass, unless Cal is meeting you."

"Since I didn't know when we'd be arriving, I'd planned to rent a car, but Grandpa was scandalized by the idea. He told me this morning to call him once we arrived, but he isn't exactly the speediest driver on the road." And she truly wasn't looking forward to entertaining the girls in a small, regional airport for an extra hour or so. "So thanks. That would be great. You're sure it's no bother?"

"None at all. I'm staying at Libby's house tonight then picking up some outdoor heaters that were used at a

wedding recently. Cal's house is practically on the way."
He stretched his neck as he had earlier in the taxi. "I'm
hoping Libby has better pillows than the motel."

She smiled, recalling the hard time Miranda had given
him. Bruce would still be pouting, not joking about it.

"What time are you leaving tomorrow?" *Would it be
wrong to offer to fix him breakfast to thank him for all
he'd done?*

"I don't know yet. I have a conference call in the
morning—some tricky negotiations on behalf of a
brilliant-but-chemically-challenged client of mine."

She made a face. "Oh. Well, um…if you have time, I'd
be happy to offer you some homemade chocolate-chip
scones."

He looked interested, but a fleeting frown crossed his
face.

"You don't like scones? They're English, aren't
they?"

His smile returned. "Very. I love scones. I know
a little shop in London that makes the lightest, most
melt-in-your-mouth pastries. You'd swear their clotted
cream comes from a cow tied behind the building. And
their raspberry preserves are pure manna from the…"
He laughed self-consciously and smacked his lips. "I'd
forgotten about that place. I'll have to swing by when
I'm back next."

"Oh, right. Your father. Have you heard any news?"

Daria touched his arm supportively. She felt his muscles tense beneath her fingers and let go right away. "Not
really."

"I feel awful about distracting you from what's going
on with your dad. Is there anything I can do? Maybe I
could arrange to have those heaters shipped so you could

head straight to the East coast. Would you fly this plane or park it and take a commercial flight?"

He looked a little taken aback by her questions. "Neither. I'm not planning a transatlantic trip right this minute. My mother is with him. There's nothing I can do."

His blunt words and impassive attitude shocked her. She knew him to be a kind and caring person—look at how magnanimously he'd treated her and her daughters. She leaned between the two seats to check on the girls. Hailey was awake now and the two were passing their stuffed animals back and forth in some sort of made-up game. "I wonder if Hailey and Miranda will feel the same way about me and Bruce someday?" she wondered out loud.

William brushed his microphone away from his lips impatiently and looked at her. "No, Daria. I promise you, there is no parallel between my childhood and the wonderful, beautiful connection you have with your daughters. None. You're a great mom."

"By comparison to yours?" she asked, a bit more facetiously than she'd intended.

"Actually, when I was a young lad and first realized my home life was drastically different from my chums, I started to pay attention to details I thought were important—and missing—from my life. I'm not sure why. Maybe I thought I might run across a Family Fairy some day and be allowed to trade my parents in for a new pair. I wanted to make certain I chose good ones."

"A Family Fairy, huh? You had quite an imagination."

"Yes, but the little bugger never showed up. Anyway, by the time I gave up on the idea, I had compiled quite a list of motherly and fatherly attributes. And believe me, you embody most, if not all of them."

The twinge in her side suddenly kicked in, making her shift in her seat. "That's nice of you to say, but according to my ex, I'm a kidnapper whose actions are going to leave deep, permanent scars on my daughters' psyches."

She couldn't bear to see the look of sympathy she knew would be in William's eyes. She was so damn tired of being pitied and pitiful. She got up, struggling awkwardly to escape the confines of the cockpit, and returned to her seat.

"Hi, Mommy," Hailey said cheerfully. Her giggle made Daria want to pull the little girl into her arms and never let go. She loved being a mother and couldn't imagine not seeing her children for weeks, let alone months at a time. How had William's mother stood it?

She didn't know, but she did know that Bruce would never give up his children completely. At one time, he'd even threatened to manufacture evidence to prove Daria was an unfit mother so he could gain full custody. Despite Bruce's bad behavior, Daria had promised herself to do whatever it took to keep the girls from becoming caught in their parents' tug-of-war.

She wondered if that's what had happened with William. Had he been the prize his parents had fought over so intently that William, the boy, had become lost in the rhetoric? She couldn't be sure, but the entire conversation had left her with a pain in her side and the beginnings of a headache.

She dug an aspirin out of her purse and took it with the last of her water. A Family Fairy, she thought, shaking her head. What child didn't at some point in his or her life wish to trade in their parents? But what William didn't seem to take into account was the fact that regardless of his parents' failings, he'd turned out pretty damn special. He was kind, compassionate and successful. His parents couldn't have been all bad, right?

She pushed the question aside. William's issues—whatever they were—belonged to him. She had enough to worry about, and she didn't need any extra reminders that parents were fallible human beings whose actions left lasting impressions on their children.

The remainder of the trip sped by with such clickety-clack speed that Daria halfway wondered if fate was finally on her side. Within an hour of landing, William's rented van was pulling into her grandfather's driveway.

"Look, girls, isn't Great-Grandpa's garden pretty in winter?" she asked, sitting forward eagerly.

"It looks straight out of a storybook," Miranda said. "No wonder Great-Grandpa didn't want to come to California for Christmas."

Daria was pleased to hear such an upbeat observation from her daughter. Her improved attitude was probably helped in part due to Daria's promise that Miranda could go online and check her social networking page once they were settled at Cal's.

"Can we build a snowman, Mommy? And a snow dog, too?"

Daria and William both laughed. She liked the way he laughed—as if mildly surprised and a wee bit embarrassed about expressing his feelings so blatantly. She had a feeling he regretted his candid disclosures about his childhood, too. She didn't plan to discuss his father's health in front of the girls, but she did want him to know that she wasn't judging him—whatever he decided about visiting his family was William's decision alone.

"Seeing the smoke coming from Cal's chimney is like

having a load of bricks lifted from my shoulders. I truly can't thank you enough, William. For everything."

The words sounded trite and superficial, but she meant them. How did you thank a person for saving your life— or at least, for helping you to save yourself?

He shifted into park and undid his seat belt. "Last one in the snowbank is a hard-boiled egg."

Miranda and Hailey looked at each other and burst out laughing. "You're so silly, William," Hailey said.

"What?" he deadpanned, eyes twinkling with amusement.

"It's *rotten* egg," Miranda said. "And you are *so* it," she added with a little shriek as she opened the door and dashed away.

Hailey had a bit more trouble with her seat belt, but a moment later she was on the run as well. William followed, pelting them with loose, hastily packed snowballs.

Daria watched through the windshield, frozen by regret and missed opportunities. This was the sort of spontaneous fun she'd always wished for her children. How had she managed to find the exact opposite? Had she been blinded by promises of a story that, in hindsight, was too perfect to be real?

A rapping sound startled her out of her reverie. "Grandpa," she cried, opening her door to the gnomelike man in the heavy down parka and Cossack hat waiting to hug her.

"Hello, dear heart," Cal said, squeezing her with more strength than she'd expected. "I'm so happy you're here. Come in, come in."

Daria pulled back to look at him. Her stomach flip-flopped. She couldn't point to one single sign, but Grandpa Cal had aged since she'd last seen him.

Which made sense. He'd lost the dear woman he'd loved with all his heart. *And I wasn't here for the funeral. I wasn't here for him.*

For a moment, hatred twisted like a flaming dagger in her belly as she remembered the fight she'd had with Bruce. "Daria, she's not your *real* grandmother, and I need you here," he'd argued. "I've had this trip to Alaska planned forever, and I promised Devon you'd handle the phones in my place. Come on, Daria. We agreed to this, remember?"

Devon. A junior member of Congress facing a tough re-election bid. The old one-hand-washes-the-other sort of payback Bruce was famous for. She couldn't remember ever agreeing to campaign for the man she could barely stand, but Bruce had nagged and hounded her until she couldn't think. She'd given in, but two days after he'd left on his trip, she'd wound up in the hospital. And she'd contacted a lawyer the following week to set the wheels of this cumbrous process in motion.

"Hi, Cal, good to see you again," William said, sauntering up to where Daria and Cal were standing, heedless of the poorly thrown snowballs whizzing past him.

"Girls, that's enough. Come give your great-grandfather a hug and tell Mr. William goodbye."

The general chaos of kids and bags and snow made the leaving process easier than she'd expected. She felt a definite tenderness toward William stemming from the great favor he'd done them, but he wouldn't let her try to convey her gratitude. "I was happy to help," he said, getting into the van after sharing a quick, mostly impersonal hug. "I'm afraid I'll have to take a rain check on those scones, but I'll give you a ring in the morning before I leave. Take care, now."

She was a little piqued that he seemed to brush aside

the magnitude of his gift so casually, but her hurt feelings didn't last long because it soon became obvious that she had much bigger worries to consider.

Within minutes of unpacking, Miranda demanded access to Cal's computer. "You promised, Mom," she reminded Daria.

Unfortunately, Cal's computer turned out to be an ancient hand-me-down that was too slow to allow her access to any of her sites. This necessitated a trip into Sentinel Pass to use the computers the producers of *Sentinel Passtime* had donated to the citizens of the town.

Daria went in with Miranda and used another computer to contact her attorney. Using instant messaging, the two were able to converse without Miranda being privy, but what her lawyer had to say left Daria even further on edge.

Apparently, Bruce had called the woman that morning and threatened to have her disbarred. Not only had he cancelled their meeting, he'd sent their divorce papers back by courier—shredded like confetti. "Wherever you are, I hope you're safe," her attorney wrote. "This man has anger management issues. I'd testify to that in court."

Safe. Back at her grandfather's, the word lingered in the back of her mind as she ate a bowl of Cal's hearty beef stew and saw to Hailey's bath. Later, the four of them played a somewhat subdued game of Monopoly until it was time for bed.

Finally, when both girls were asleep, she was able to talk to her grandfather. "I'm so sorry about all this, Grandpa."

"Now, now, I told you before, I couldn't sleep at night knowing you were living under that man's thumb. I'm so glad you made your move. But, Daria," he said gravely, "as much as I hate to do this, I need to show you something."

She followed him to the built-in desk area in the kitchen where his phone and a small, older-model answering machine rested. "I know you're tired and probably emotionally exhausted, but you need to listen to this."

The somberness of his tone made her heart plummet. "Bruce?"

"He started calling yesterday afternoon. I stopped picking up after the first few times. He left a dozen or so messages. The last one was so bad, I unplugged the phone *and* the machine." Her grandfather's hand shook as he pressed the play button. "William's right. Nobody should have to listen to this sort of filth."

Even with the volume as low as it would go, Bruce's fury echoed off the walls of her grandfather's little home. "You tell that f-ing wife of mine that she is going to rot in hell for this. Does 'until death do us part' ring a bell? She's damn well going to find out. Sooner rather than later, if I have anything to say about it."

She hit Stop. "Oh, Grandpa. I wish you hadn't heard that."

Cal made a pooh-poohing motion. "Don't you fret about my feelings. What I want to know is how we're going to keep that man from killing you."

Taken at face value, Bruce's words were ugly and intimidating, and Daria knew she should be scared. But the thinking part of her head recognized the gift she'd been given. Leverage. In the court of public opinion, this tape was gold.

"Would you mind if I left for a few minutes, Grandpa? I'd like to take this to William for safekeeping. I've been telling everybody that Bruce is a bully, not a killer, but in case I'm wrong, I'd like to know the proof of his threats could be used against him. And maybe knowing the tape is in the hands of an agent with big-time Hollywood connections might get Bruce to back off."

Cal's eyes opened wide with surprise and he let out a low whistle. "Releasing that tape on one of those celebrity talk shows wouldn't do his political career much good, would it?"

She had no intention of doing that. Her daughters would suffer the most if Daria and Bruce took this war public, but she could make threats, too. She'd learned from a pro.

Cal patted her shoulder. "You're a pretty smart girl. Especially since you wised up and decided to leave that SOB." He grabbed a key ring from a hook near the door. "Take my car. And lock up when you get back. No sense taking chances."

She agreed wholeheartedly.

But if that were true, then what was she doing going out in the middle of the night to see William, a man who interested her in a way that was anything but safe?

CHAPTER SIX

WILLIAM STOOD at the large picture window of Libby's living room a moment longer, then sighed and resumed pacing. He was restless, antsy and on edge. He didn't know why. He'd crossed every to-do note off his list, including calling Lucas.

"Strep throat, not mono," his copilot had told him moments earlier. "I'm catching a ride home with some friends in the morning, man. Sorry I had to bail on you like that."

William had assured him he'd call the next time he needed a copilot and they'd hung up.

Good news. All was right with the world.

Or not.

He stopped beside the large oak rocking chair he'd been sitting in earlier. His phone sat on a small round table beside the chair, charger plugged into the wall. "Just get it over with and ring, damn it," he muttered under his breath.

He'd left a message on Notty's service explaining why he wasn't coming to England anytime soon. "Business," William had claimed as an excuse. "But I appreciate you keeping me in the loop, as they say. Until later, then."

William knew full well his uncle would call, with no regard to the time difference. In fact, William suspected that Notty enjoyed waking William out of a deep, sound sleep.

Not that such a sleep was likely tonight.

William felt guilty. The way he had as a young boy when he'd broken a window in the carriage house at Byron Manor, his family's country estate. With neither of his parents present, he figured he'd get away with the small transgression. Who would know or hold him accountable?

He hadn't counted on his conscience betraying him. After a sleepless night that followed a wildly unlikely dream where an innocent child was convicted of the crime and died at the hands of a cruel jailor, William had marched into the kitchen to confess all to Bea, their live-in housekeeper, who was busy making breakfast.

She'd opened her pudgy arms to comfort him. But, wisely, she hadn't swept the matter aside, as his parents might have. She made him work with the handyman she hired to clean up the mess *and* pay for the new glass with money from his piggy bank.

"Practical absolution," Bea had called her philosophy.

A simple woman who never traveled beyond the shores of her beloved homeland, Bea had lost her one true love in the Great War and never married. In a way, she'd provided William with his most tangible sense of family. Sadly, she'd passed away from a bout of influenza the following year. From that point on, his world had consisted of boarding school schedules punctuated by visits to his parents, either in London or wherever his mother was volunteering at the time.

He found it ironic that while his parents had provided him a broad, enviable worldview, they'd been unable to give him the one thing he'd craved most—a real home. The lands around Byron Manor, so-named for a supposed visit the famous poet made to the place, had been sold off to finance political campaigns and missions to various war-torn countries.

The house itself still belonged to the family, but until a few days ago it was rarely occupied for longer than a weekend or two. Now, apparently, both of William's parents were in residence. He wasn't quite sure what to make of that, but figured he'd find out soon enough when Notty called.

To kill time and keep his mind off Daria and her family—*Was she okay? Had she heard from her thick-skulled ex-husband? Were the girls happily settled at Cal's?*—he walked to the liquor cabinet where he knew Cooper stocked a fine Irish whiskey and poured himself a glass. The first sip burned all the way down, the second not so much. He was about to take a third when his phone rang.

"Hullo, Notty."

"William. You've read my e-mail, I assume."

"I did. Father in the country? That came as a bit of a surprise. Is this the only way to keep him from his work?"

"Quite the contrary. He resigned last week. Didn't you hear? Made quite a splash in the press over here. Someone leaked news of his cancer and…well, it seemed the most political way to handle things. Forgive the pun."

William was momentarily speechless. His father's work had been the most important thing in his life—including his son.

"Your mother thought the clean air would be good for his breathing," Notty said. "They're getting on jolly well, William. You could see for yourself if you weren't a complete and utter toad, too wrapped up in your own affairs to take the proffered olive branch and come home."

A toad? What am I? Eight? "I haven't said I won't

return, Notty. I simply can't give you a date. I'm in the Black Hills at the moment, which is set in the middle of the continent and not a particularly convenient hopping off point to cross the pond."

Notty made a skeptical sound. "Are you or are you not a pilot with his own jet?"

William's face heated the way it always did when he was caught in a lie. "I am one-third owner of a plane," he said stiffly. "My partners are expecting me back in L.A. tomorrow."

Shane and Cooper would understand if William parked the plane and booked a commercial flight to London, but he wasn't ready to do that. He wasn't sure why. Stubbornness? Maybe. He'd been told many times—usually by his father—that he'd inherited his mother's rigid sense of right and wrong.

"There's never any gray area where your mother is concerned," Father liked to say. "She would have made an excellent Knight of the Round Table."

"How bad is it, Notty? Honestly. Is Father going to die in the next few days?"

"No, I don't believe so," Notty answered, his voice raspier than usual. "But the doctors aren't optimistic about his chances of beating this. And I honestly don't know how long he'll keep trying. It's very difficult to stay positive when you're puking your guts up."

That same sense of guilt from his childhood swept over him. But a thought suddenly struck him—the only reason he'd broken that window in the first place was because he'd been angry at his father. Father had promised to help William with a science project that weekend, but instead, had canceled his trip home—as he did more often than not—choosing to devote his attention to some legislation he felt deserved his time more than his son.

"Do you know if he got the flowers I sent? And that book I ordered for him about coping with cancer?"

Notty sighed heavily. "Yes. James got them both and was pathetically delighted because he had tangible proof of what a caring son he had," he said, his tone dripping with sarcasm.

"I will come, Notty."

"So you keep saying, but the proof is in the pudding as my old mum used to say. Not that she knew the first thing about cooking, mind you, but she did like a good custard."

William smiled. He was about to ask whether or not his own mother had had any luck finding a clinical trial for his father to join, but the lights of a car pulling into the driveway distracted him. "Someone's here, Notty. I have to go. Tell Father I'll call tomorrow. Bye for now."

He ended the call and plugged his phone back in seconds before the doorbell rang. He hurried to answer it, his mind racing through a very short list of possible visitors—beginning and ending with Daria Fontina.

And there she was, shivering in the cold on the front porch. "Daria. Is everything okay?"

"Hi," she said, shifting her feet nervously on the freshly shoveled stoop. William had shoveled until he was dripping with sweat. Not his favorite thing to do, but the exercise had helped keep his mind off Daria. "I…is this a bad… Why didn't I call?"

She smacked her head with the heel of her gloved hand. "I guess I just reacted. Are you busy? Can we talk?"

"Yes. No. Um…what was the question?"

Her nose wrinkled in the cutest way. "Have you been drinking? Is there any left?"

"Whiskey. Would you like one?"

"Yes, definitely. Probably better for me than a sleeping pill, and at this point I'll never get to sleep tonight without some help."

He stepped aside to let her enter. "Something has happened with your ex-husband."

She kicked off her boots and removed her coat and gloves before fishing a small black plastic box out of the pocket of her hooded sweatshirt. "Bruce has snapped. He's always had a temper, but he's enough of a politician to make sure nothing damaging ever gets on tape. Until now."

He took the compact answering machine from her icy cold fingers and ushered her into the living room while she told him about Bruce's vitriolic diatribes aimed first at Cal, then at her. "He said things no politician in their right mind would say on the record and...hello, these messages are time stamped and dated."

William used the same electrical outlet as his charger and set the machine beside his phone, but he didn't turn it on. Instead, he poured her a stiff drink, diluting it slightly with a bit of soda water. He carried it to the sofa where she'd chosen to sit.

"Thank you." Her hand trembled slightly as she took the glass. "I hate to ask another favor of you, but, I promise, this one is strictly for bluffing purposes."

He returned to the rocker. "I beg your pardon?"

"As I told Grandpa, I'd like to leave this with you for safekeeping tonight, but in the morning, I plan to make a couple of copies. One to send home with you, and one for my lawyer."

He nodded his approval.

"In your case, I'll tell Bruce that if anything happens to me, you will release the tape to *Entertainment Tonight* or some other TV news outlet. The bad publicity would ruin him, even if a court decided he had nothing to do with my death."

She stumbled over the word, proving to William she wasn't handling this threat with as much aplomb she wanted him to believe. He lifted his glass. "Drink up. It's not every day someone gets a death threat. I remember Cooper telling me about his mother's bookie threatening to take out a contract on him. Very unnerving, to say the least."

She took a large gulp, then made a face as it traveled down her gullet. "Good," she said breathlessly.

"Miranda and Hailey didn't hear any of this, did they?"

"No. Heavens, no. The language is…well, R-rated to say the least. That I could handle, but when he started talking about wanting to see me dead…"

Her attempted smile didn't erase the worry lines across her brow, but it did make him want to try to fix the cause. But that would mean getting more involved than he already was, and hadn't he decided that was a bad idea?

"I would be happy to provide some threat of leverage if you think it will help, but let's not overlook the facts here—this man threatened your life. Your lawyer needs to get a restraining order in place as soon as possible, not to mention notifying the police."

She settled against the puffy cushions of the sofa with a weighty sigh, drawing her knees to her chest. "That's what Cal said, too."

Unfortunately, William knew all too well that a restraining order only worked if the person gave a damn. Bianca had had several in place against Ocho. He'd still killed her. "Do you think you'll be safe at Cal's tonight?

You could bring the girls here, or I could drive you to a hotel in Deadwood. As long as you don't put the charge on your credit card or use your cell phone to call him, he won't be able to find you."

Daria closed her eyes and rested her chin on her knees. She didn't know what it was about William's voice that calmed her badly shaken nerves so completely. Maybe his thoughtful, dispassionate delivery, or that unflappable British composure that seemed to say "Fear not, dear lady, all shall be well."

"Moving the girls won't be necessary. They're sound asleep and I'm fairly certain I'm going to be able to sleep, too. Thanks to you," she added softly.

"Me? But I haven't done anything."

"You listened. You didn't try to downplay how serious this is. And most of all, you believed me. Without even listening to the tape, you trusted that I wasn't overreacting. You have no idea how much that means to a person who has had someone second-guess her every single decision for most of her married life."

She reached for her drink and took a small sip. "I couldn't buy a set of drinking glasses without worrying about what Bruce would say." *Will he hate these? Will he make me take them back four or five times until he finally goes out and buys something else?* She hated the subtle way he'd robbed her of her self-confidence.

"That's a sad fact to admit to a relative stranger, isn't it?" Daria asked. "Are you wondering how I manage to walk upright without a backbone?"

He shook his head. "No. Of course not. It's infinitely clear that your ex-husband has control issues. I once worked under a senior editor at a large publishing house in New York. This guy so frequently reversed his subordinates' decisions we were left wondering if that was the only reason we'd been hired—to provide an array of people for this egomaniac to humiliate and torture on a daily basis."

Daria recalled reading a popular chick-lit book on the subject. "I bet you didn't stick around twelve years, did you? You quit after a few weeks and found some place else to work."

"Eleven months later I left to become my own boss. But I didn't have any children with this man, so it was a bit easier."

She bit on her lip to keep from laughing. She liked his droll sense of humor. She was comfortable with him in a way she couldn't remember being around any man for a long time. So long, in fact, it was depressing to think about.

"I should go. I don't know if it's the alcohol or you, but I feel a lot less panicky than I did when I first got here. Grandpa looked so upset and worried when he played that tape for me, I almost asked you to fly us somewhere else. Anywhere. The last thing I want is for Bruce's poison to spill over on Cal."

"From my observations, limited though they are, your grandfather is pretty resilient. I flew Morgan here not long after Libby's grandmother's funeral, and I had a very nice chat with Cal in his garden. He seemed at peace with Mary's passing." He paused, thinking. "Actually, I think he may have mentioned you. Not by name, of course, but he said he had a granddaughter who was going through a rough time and how much he admired her for standing up for herself and her children."

Daria was touched. It was hard not to feel like a failure when you were digging yourself out of a deep hole of your own making.

"So," she said, sitting upright. "Enough of my personal soap opera. You're returning to L.A. tomorrow, as planned?"

William got up and walked to the cabinet where he'd poured her drink. His lean, refined physique was something she doubted she'd ever get tired of looking at. "Yes. I heard from Lucas earlier. He's much improved. He asked me to relay his regards to you and your daughters."

She looked at her watch. She should go and try to sleep, but even after the whiskey she felt too wired to doze off. "That's nice."

"Can I fix you another?" His lips compressed in a line. "Probably not, since you're driving. Sorry."

"How 'bout something hot? I'd forgotten how cold it is around here in winter. Does Libby have herbal tea?"

His laugh was genuine and inclusive. "Based on the number of boxes in her cupboard, I'd speculate she owns stock in several companies. Come, name your poison." He grabbed her hand and led her into the adjoining room.

She looked at her hand in his, surprised that she hadn't jerked back automatically. A learned reaction from being pulled places she didn't want to go by someone who would squeeze her hand until she gave in.

William let go to fling open a pair of cupboard doors, then he bowed. "Your pick, m'lady."

She lifted her gaze to the proffered selections and burst out laughing. "Morning sickness."

"I beg your pardon?"

His expression was so baffled, sweet and funny she wanted to kiss him. Instead, she coughed into her fist, ordering herself to sober up. "I tried a bunch of these same brands when I was pregnant with Hailey. I swear I had morning sickness from the moment of conception 'til the day of her birth."

She reached out and selected a variety she'd never tried. "Hmm. Sit back and relax," she said, reading the label. "Definitely what I need to do at the moment."

He removed an individual bag from the box then returned it to her. "Please, take it. With my compliments. I'll replace it for Libby before she returns home."

"Are you always this generous?"

"Yes. Especially with other people's things."

What she liked best about his sense of humor was that it wasn't loud, flamboyant or demanding of a response. She found the natural give and take between them so easy and refreshing she almost commented on it. Instead, she asked, "Does Libby know if she's having a boy or a girl?"

"The last thing she told me was that the young hippopotamus she was carrying was definitely one of the two."

She snickered softly as she took a seat at the table and watched his methodical preparations. Even in an unfamiliar kitchen he moved with an elegant sort of confidence. "How's your dad?"

The sugar bowl in his hand slipped from his fingers and fell onto its side on the table. They both reached out to keep it from spilling. "Slippery devil," he muttered before pivoting quickly to return to the stove. "I was on the phone with my uncle right before you arrived."

"I hope things work out, but either way, it's your call. I hope it didn't sound like I was judging or criticizing your choice on the plane today. That was just my guilt speaking."

He turned to face her. "Your guilt? What do you have to feel guilty about?"

"I was a coward. I chose to keep the peace and avoid a fight rather than do what my heart told me to do."

"How specifically?"

"I didn't make it to my mother's side before she died. But my mistakes have no bearing whatsoever on your decision whether or not to see your father. I'm sorry I said anything."

He carried two mugs to the table and sat across from her. "When the mortal end is in sight, there's never a shortage of guilt and remorse to go around. Would anything have changed if you'd gotten to her bedside beforehand?"

"Not for Mom, probably. But it might have helped rebuild my relationship with my father. He felt lost and abandoned, which made him vulnerable to the first opportunistic woman who came along to fill the void my mother's passing left."

He seemed to think seriously about what she said. "I think most people tend to romanticize their parents' relationship, and have difficulty picturing them as men and women with lives that don't intersect with ours. Maybe my parents did me a favor by shattering that illusion early on."

He stirred his cup. "Did you ever see *Dr. Zhivago?*"

"Of course. It was one of my mother's favorites."

"I was pretty young the first time I saw it. Our housekeeper-slash-nanny took me. I was absolutely convinced that my parents were those tragic, forever lovers kept apart by distance and circumstance, not choice."

She sighed wistfully. "The heartbreak. Matched only by the ice."

He nodded. "But a few months later, I found my mother kissing some stranger behind a Red Cross field tent in the middle of the desert. He was a doctor, but he wasn't Omar Sharif."

"Oh," she groaned. "That must have been terrible.

Did you talk to her about what you saw? Maybe it wasn't what you thought."

His sardonic sneer told her no. She also guessed the subject was closed, and he was sorry he'd even mentioned it.

She polished off the last of her tea and stood. "Speaking of ice and cold, I should probably get back to Grandpa's. I don't want him to worry."

"Would you like me to ride along and walk back? The exercise would do me good," he said, following her to the door.

"No, no, that's okay. The car has snow tires. I'll be fine."

He reached down to open the door for her but stopped with his hand on the knob. Their faces were only a few inches apart. She should have stepped backward. She could have. But she didn't.

"I'm glad you came here tonight, Daria. I like you. I enjoy talking with you. You're the most honest, self-attuned, real person I've met in a long time."

"What about Libby?"

"She's spoken for."

And I'm not, she thought with a bright, glittery burst of joy. *I'm free. Available. Sorta.*

She looked at his lips. His perfect, masculine, desirable lips. "You know the baggage we brought with us on your plane is only part of the package, right?"

William put his arms around her and carefully eased her closer, as if expecting her to bolt. Which she should have. Would have, if she'd been listening to the sensible advice she'd read in a dozen or so women's magazines over the past few months. But those writers' voices were drowned out by the girlish thrill of sharing a first kiss with the handsomest man she'd ever known.

And why the heck shouldn't I? He's flying away in the morning. I'll probably never see him again. If not now, when?

Her last justification—a popular slogan adopted by several politicians she knew—made her smile. William seemed to take that as a yes. With one hand he lifted her chin as he slowly lowered his head.

His lips were soft and warm, gentle but persistent, coaxing her to respond. She couldn't not. Hormones, pheromones, whatevermones flooded her desert-dry senses. She not only kissed him back, she leaned into him, pressing close enough to feel every button on his shirt, the well-formed shape of his chest, and the ribs, sinew and muscle under his skin.

She opened her mouth and touched her tongue to his. It felt bold, impulsive and gratifying beyond words. He tasted like the honey he'd added to his tea. He tasted new and novel and very, very good.

His tongue made tentative inquiries at first, but quickly left politeness behind and explored her mouth as only a stranger would. A stranger. That's what he was.

She jerked back with a gasp. "Oh! That was *so* not supposed to happen." She swallowed hard, still tasting his sweetness. "In fact, it didn't happen. It was a dream. Dreams aren't real."

He placed both hands on her shoulders, more to steady her than hold her in place. "I've been working in Hollywood for half my adult life, and believe me, I know the difference between make-believe and reality. That kiss was real."

She turned sideways to dislodge his hands. "I've never even been to Hollywood."

He seemed amused by her non sequitur. "I also have a fair knowledge of timing, and this was not well-scripted.

For that I apologize. Not for the kiss, mind you. That was quite lovely, and I shall treasure it always."

She couldn't decide if he was being gallant or joking around. That was the problem with kissing a stranger, she decided, as he escorted her to her grandfather's old sedan—you have no barometer to go by.

"Sleep well, Daria," he said, dropping a friendly peck near the corner of her lips. "I'll run the tape back to you in the morning unless you need me before then. You have my number."

He remained standing in the driveway the entire time she backed up and slowly maneuvered her way between the snowbanks. He was still there when she turned onto the street and stepped on the gas. The guy didn't have a jacket on. That made him either crazy or inured to the cold weather.

Her bet was on the former. After all, he'd kissed her, hadn't he? A not-quite-divorced divorcée with two kids, no alimony, no job, no nothing.

The man was interesting. Intriguing. Sexy as hell, and a great kisser. But he was right about their timing. It sucked big time, as Miranda would have said. And that's all there was to it.

WILLIAM WAITED until the red orbs of her car's taillights were completely out of sight before he returned to the house. He wasn't a skier or winter sports fanatic, but ever since his snowball fight with Daria's daughters today, he'd decided he liked winter. His internal thermostat seemed set at who-gives-a-damn high.

"Maybe I'll walk into town and have a pint at the local pub," he said to himself. He remembered accompanying Shane to a joint on Main Street, although that had been in summer. He had no idea if the place remained open during the winter months or not. He vaguely remembered Jenna telling him a lot of businesses closed in the off-season.

He dashed into the house to grab his coat and phone.

"Coop," he said a moment later. "Do me a favor and ask your wife if the local pub stays open year-round."

"Sure. No problem. But I left you better booze than you'll find there," Cooper told him. "Oh, wait. Are you taking Daria out for a drink? Way to go, old man. Libby says she's pretty and—" A sudden grunt ended his comment.

Libby's elbow to her husband's solar plexus, William guessed with a grin.

"Hi, William. It's Libby. I talked to Cal an hour or so ago. He was going to bed. How's Daria?"

"Fine. She stopped by a few minutes ago. She has some valid concerns about her safety and wanted to discuss her options."

"William, I want to apologize. I had no idea Bruce was such a jerk. I shouldn't have asked you to get involved, especially after what you went through with Bianca."

A shiver of cold penetrated his euphoria. "That was a long time ago, Libby. Daria's been separated almost six months. She's made a clean break. And she was smart enough to put half a continent between her and that miserable excuse for a man before drawing her final line in the sand, so to speak."

Libby didn't reply right away. "William, I don't think I've ever heard you speak quite so passionately about anything. Is there a chance you're falling for her?"

The heel of his shoe slipped on a patch of ice and he nearly went down. Cursing softly, he apologized. "Sorry. Black ice. I'd better hang up and pay attention to what I'm doing before I slip and break something."

"You didn't answer my question, but fine, it's none of my business. But, William, promise me you'll be careful. And I don't just mean on your walk into town."

He assured her he would, then pocketed his phone. He'd avoided her question because, in all honesty, he wasn't ready to talk about how he felt. This jumble of sensations was too new, too novel. Energized. Hypersensitive to a relative stranger's slightest change of expression. Mesmerized by every little thing about her when she was close by. Dazzled and delighted by her daughters. Fearful for her. Sympathetic one moment, furious on her behalf the next.

And let's not forget passionate, he acknowledged. That kiss was definitely the most intriguing, compelling, stay-in-his-mind-forever sort of kiss he could recall experiencing. It was in a class all its own. And it made him think of all the other sorts of things he'd like to do with her.

Too much, too soon, the mature, responsible part of him scolded. *You only just met her.* And let's not forget her reaction to the Family Fairy list he'd told her about earlier.

Despite her apology, Daria clearly had strong feelings about what constituted family and what those familial obligations involved. She might not sit in judgment of him, but he doubted she'd understand the disconnect he felt toward his parents. He didn't hate them; in fact, he appreciated everything they'd done for him. It was the love and honor part of their mutual relationship that got dicey.

How could he expect a wonderful, loving mother like Daria to understand what it was like to travel thousands of miles to see your mother only to spend no more than a few hours in her company, with barely a few minutes of that time with her attention focused completely on you?

At least Daria waited until she was single before kissing someone who wasn't her husband.

He shook his head to dislodge the thought and quickened his pace. But he stopped a few steps later. *What am I doing?* he asked himself. *I don't overindulge the night before I'm scheduled to fly.*

He made an immediate about-face. The chill was starting to get to him. The fire he'd felt earlier was receding. Daria was quite possibly the *sort* of woman he'd been searching for his entire life. He'd even conceded that she embodied nearly all of the items on his Family Fairy list. But that didn't mean she was the one.

No. He wasn't ready to go there. And he was certain she would be the first to thank him for that.

CHAPTER SEVEN

"GOOD MORNING, morning glory."

Daria smiled without opening her eyes. Her grandfather's greeting took her back to her childhood visits to her grandparents in South Dakota. Warm summer mornings when she could sleep as late as she liked.

Stretching, she rolled to her back and opened her eyes. A second later she sat up, crying, "Oh, good heavens, what time is it?"

Cal set a flowery ceramic mug on the bedside table in what had once been Mary McGannon's screened porch. Cal had hired someone to install operational windows and insulate the walls to provide a third bedroom. Her daughters were sharing the room next to Cal's.

"Almost nine-thirty. The girls helped me make scones. I would have brought you one, but Miranda said you like coffee first. Cream, no sugar."

"Nine-thirty? I haven't slept that late in years." She swung her feet out from beneath the heavy down comforter and patchwork quilt. The air temperature was cool, making her glad for the new flannel pajamas she'd picked up at an after-Christmas sale.

"You already made the scones?"

"Yes. I figured you needed sleep more than food. Is something wrong?"

"No, not at all. But I did invite William to join us before he headed back to California. A small thank you for all that he's done," she explained, grateful her voice didn't betray her.

In truth, he'd slept with her all night—in her dreams. Warm and snuggly, hot and steamy, friendly and fun. She was looking forward to seeing him this morning to prove to her subconscious the man was not as wonderful as she wanted to believe.

"He dropped off the answering machine about an hour ago. I told him you were still asleep."

Daria let out a groan that was pure Miranda. "Bummer."

Her grandfather chuckled. "He said to tell you he was loading up the heaters and would stop by on his way to the airport. He won't be here for at least five... ten minutes."

"Grandpa!" she shrieked, nearly spilling her coffee—until she caught the teasing twinkle in his eyes. "Oh, you." She gave him a one-armed hug. "You know me too well."

Turning to lower her feet to the thick woolly rug beside her bed, she felt the caffeine chase the last of the cobwebs from her mind. "Do you know if Hailey took her medicine? And remembered to rinse her mouth afterward?"

"Miranda reminded her. And I brewed a special tea that might help open those bronchial membranes, too." He held up his hand as if expecting a motherly protest. "Don't worry. Not voodoo witch doctor stuff, merely homeopathic herbs. I checked with my doctor the last time I saw him to make sure it wouldn't interact poorly with what Hailey's taking. That's why I had you fax me a copy of her medicines, remember?"

Daria was impressed. "For a retired pharmacist,

Grandpa, you sound as though you might have been wooed over to the dark side."

He made a face. "Pharmaceuticals have their place in your medicine cabinet, but sometimes common sense is the best cure." He turned to go. "We saved you a couple of scones, but the mice seem to be particularly hungry this morning."

Mice named Miranda and Hailey, she'd bet. "I'll be right there as soon as I'm dressed."

"And don't forget you have company coming at ten."

Her heart rate spiked. *William?*

"Those book club gals. Libby's friends. Lib called twice this morning to make sure it was all right that they stopped by."

Right. She'd heard about the group for years from Mary and Libby, and making new women friends was one of the things on her to-do list. "Great. I'll hop in the shower, then be right there. Thanks, Grandpa."

But mention of a "list" brought to mind William and his Family Fairy theory, and thinking about William while hot soapy water sluiced over her body derailed her usual quickie sponge bath. Twenty minutes later—hair still damp and no makeup to speak of—she opened the door of her grandfather's house to three women, each as different from the other as humanly possible.

"Hi. You must be Daria. I'm Kat," said the petite blonde carrying a huge wicker basket. "I brought some things for your daughters. I hope they like them."

Daria spotted movies, books, candy and a couple of craft projects in the basket. All very pink and girly. "How nice of you! They'll be over the moon."

The second arrival handed Daria a trade paperback.

"Our current read," she said, shaking her mop of tri-color hair. "I'm Char."

The straggler was murmuring into her cell phone as she approached, pausing on the stoop to whisper, "Love you, too. Bye." When she looked up from stowing the phone in her oversize purse, she found three sets of eyes on her. She laughed and held out her hand in greeting. "Sorry. I'm Rachel. Newest book club member. Well, prior to you, of course. It's lovely to meet you."

Daria called her daughters into the kitchen to be introduced.

"Wow," Hailey exclaimed. "All this stuff is for us? Cool."

Miranda, who had a habit of turning shy when Daria least expected it, picked up the DVD she'd been watching yesterday on the plane. "This is a good movie. I can't wait to watch it again."

Daria smiled her pleasure at her daughter's good manners.

"My boys loved it. Usually, if something doesn't blow up in the first ten minutes of the movie, they're bored, but they actually liked this story," Kat said.

"How old are they?" Miranda asked.

"Tag is nine and Jordie is Hailey's age. I should warn you, though, Tag adores older women," she said with a wink.

"Do you have any pictures?" Miranda asked.

"About a million," Char answered for her. "Stick around long enough and you'll see them all."

Daria chuckled at the friendly ribbing. "Come in, everyone. Where are my manners?"

Once they were seated in her grandfather's living room, a small but homey place with a huge stone fireplace and energy-efficient wood stove, Kat brought out a glossy, scrapbook-style photo book.

"Wow. This is gorgeous. Where'd you get it?" Daria asked. She'd tried scrapbooking and had loved it, but like a lot of her creative endeavors, had given it up rather than argue with Bruce about the cost.

Rachel answered for Kat. "I made it. I have a Web design business and dabble in photography. My fiancé is an artist. We're in the process of starting up an artists' collective. If you have any hidden talents—painting, photography, writing, you name it—we'd love to have you."

"Do you have a card?"

Rachel pawed through her oversize purse a solid minute, finally retrieving one badly battered business card. "Nuts. Mine must be in my car. But here's Rufus's. You can reach me through his Web site."

Hailey, who was still sitting shyly on Daria's lap, let out a loud shriek. "Mommy, look—that's the birdhouse William and I bought Great-Grandpa Cal." She hopped off Daria's lap and raced to point to the object hanging outside the window above the kitchen sink. "Look!"

"William bought it?" Rachel asked. "Where was that?"

Daria told them about their weather-delay adventure.

"He's such a great guy," Rachel said. "Kind, sensitive, generous…"

"Freakin' gorgeous," Kat added, then blushed profusely. "Oops. Mind bubble. Not meant to share publicly. Sorry."

Everyone laughed as she covered her face with her hands.

Daria liked these women. She felt welcomed and

accepted. For the first time, she could actually picture herself and her daughters living here, not just escaping to her grandfather's until the dust cleared.

"How are the schools here?" she asked.

Miranda looked up from the magazine she was thumbing through.

"Excellent," Kat said. "My boys are doing great. Love their teachers. Hate their homework, but that's to be expected, right? I'm subbing in Hill City at the moment and can tell you who to contact if you're considering enrolling the girls."

"Enrolling us? Like in school?" Miranda asked, jumping to her feet. "You didn't say we'd have to go to school here, Mom. I like my school. All my friends are there."

Daria heard the quiver of tears behind the last statement. "It never hurts to explore other options, Miranda."

"Daddy was right. You only think about yourself. You're dumb and selfish and horrible. I hate you."

Daria's stomach turned over. "Miranda Grace, you do *not* speak to your mother like that. Go to your room. Now."

Hailey, who had run back to Daria at the first hint of conflict, was sobbing against her legs. Every other sob was punctuated by that dark, dry hacking sound Daria had come to fear. She picked up the little girl and rocked her back and forth. "Breathe, darling. Slow and steady. You know how. Do we need to find your rescue inhaler?"

Cal suddenly appeared and held out his hand. "How 'bout we go walk in the garden, Miss Hailey? A little fresh air might help."

Daria doubted that, but Hailey seemed eager to go,

so she set her down. The two disappeared down the hall and emerged in view of the front window a few minutes later in jackets, hats and boots.

"Oh, Daria, I'm so sorry," Kat said. "I've been through two divorces. I know how difficult this can be for children. You want life to be smooth and easy, but it never is."

Daria was slightly comforted looking at this smiling, happy woman. If Kat could survive two divorces, surely Daria could handle one.

Char piped up. "My fiancé recently went through a difficult divorce—well, heck, is there any other kind? All I mean to say is we're here for you, if you need to talk to someone."

"Me, too," Rachel added. "Divorced, but happier than ever."

Daria doubted any of them had experienced the kind of guilt and self-hate she'd known for so long, but their support, as women and as mothers, made her feel welcome to a community she'd been apart from for too long.

The three women left a few minutes later. The moment she closed the door behind them, Daria hurried to the spare bedroom, knocking briefly before entering.

Miranda was sitting on her bed, knees drawn to her chest, Daria's phone to her ear. She looked up guiltily. "I know, Grandma," she said. "I know you love me. So does Daddy. I don't know why Mommy took us away." *A lie.* "Do you want to talk to Mommy? She just walked in. Her new friends must have left."

Daria snatched the phone out of her daughter's hand, retaining eye contact. "Hello, Hester. I'd intended to call once Bruce and I had a chance to talk. So far, that hasn't been possible because he can't stop swearing and calling me names long enough to listen to anything I have to say. When he can speak civilly, he knows where to find me. In the meantime, the girls and I will be staying with my grandfather. For everyone's sake. Bruce's, too."

She was quite sure her mother-in-law knew what Daria meant. Bruce's temper had gotten him in hot water before. One particularly nasty confrontation had involved a highway patrol officer who'd dared give Bruce a ticket for speeding. It had cost Bruce's brothers a pretty penny to pull the necessary strings to save the family any embarrassment.

"You're being ridiculous, Daria. Being selfish. Bruce is in the middle of very important legislation at the moment. You couldn't have picked a worse time to do this."

Daria almost laughed. "So what you're saying is your son's career is more important than his wife and children? Why did I ever think otherwise? He's a Fontina."

Hester made a sound of pure outrage. "And being a Fontina was good enough for you for quite some time. Our name put a beautiful roof over your head, a fancy car in your driveway and nice clothes on your back. It sent your children to private schools and got Hailey the best doctors around. You're willing to give that up? For what? Or should I say for whom? There's someone else, isn't there?"

Daria spun around and walked out of the room. "No, Hester, there isn't." *Despite one kiss that made me wish there was.* "This isn't about love, it's about the lack of love. It's about feeling so damn empty inside I can't see myself in the mirror. Your son has drained me dry, and I won't let him do the same thing to our daughters."

She jabbed the off button as hard as she could, exhilarated and at the same time sick to her stomach. She had no idea what her mother-in-law might do in retaliation—call in all the family forces to exert as much pressure on Daria as possible, she guessed. And Daria certainly wouldn't put it past any one of the Fontina siblings or extended family to try to use her daughters against her. But none of that mattered.

Her children were the only thing that mattered, and Daria needed to find out what was up with Miranda.

"I'm sorry, Mommy," her daughter told her the moment Daria walked in. Her eyes were red from crying. "I saw you with those ladies and I remembered Daddy saying you couldn't be a good mother if you had a bunch of yappy women friends around who drank cocktails and made up lies about their husbands. I shouldn't have said those things. I didn't mean them."

Daria sat beside her and opened her arms. "I know, baby. After a while you don't know who to believe. But you can believe this. I'm not trying to hurt your father. I'm trying to start a new life for all of us, including Daddy. If two people aren't good for each other…if one of them—or both of them, for that matter—feels boxed in and unhappy, then the whole family suffers."

Miranda nodded, still sniffling. "But what if he won't take us back? Me and Hailey. Because we went with you?"

Daria hated the fear she saw in Miranda's eyes. "He's your father. He will always love you and want you in his life. *I* will never live with him again, Miranda. I can't. But I promise you I'll do everything in my power to make sure you and Hailey remain connected to your dad, and your grandma, and the whole family as much as possible."

"Mommy?"

Daria looked over her shoulder to see a rosy-cheeked

five-year-old standing a foot or so away. "What's wrong, Miranda?" Hailey asked. "Why did you yell at Mommy?"

"I don't want to talk about it," Miranda snarled. She leaped off the bed, giving her sister a small shove for good measure. A few seconds later, Daria heard the bathroom door slam shut.

"Why'd she push me, Mommy?"

Daria hugged Hailey close, smelling the fresh scent of snow on her hair. "Sorry, sweetness. Your sister is mad at me. Sometimes when people are mad, they take their anger out on other people. I'm sure she'll tell you she's sorry once she's calmed down."

"Like Daddy?" Hailey asked. "'Member when he yelled at you for not making us put away our bikes and then later he said he was sorry and you were a good mommy after all."

Bruce might have told Hailey that, but he never apologized to Daria. Never. In fact, he once bragged that being married to Daria meant never having to say you're sorry. He didn't mean that in a cheesy *Love Story* way, either. She clearly wasn't worthy of an apology—sincere or not.

Another reason the divorce was final—in her mind, at least.

WILLIAM CHECKED the list Shane had e-mailed him that morning against the collection of personal property and set props stowed in the back of the van. He was finally ready to leave Sentinel Pass and head for home. L.A., that is. Not England. Despite two other e-mails he'd received. One from Notty, the other from his mother.

The latter had been short and to the point: Come soon. Mom.

"Mom," he muttered under his breath as he walked around the van to climb into the driver's seat. The colloquialism simply didn't fit. Daria was a mom; Dr. Laurel Hughes-Smythe was dedicated physician first, parent, a very distant second.

No, even that wasn't true, he realized. Dr. Lady, as she was called by staff and those she served, was also a selfless humanitarian, a crusader against greed and corruption. A noble heroine. Parent was way, way down on the list.

At least she hadn't tried to guilt him into returning. That was more his uncle's style. Notty had devoted several paragraphs to supporting his postulation that William was an ingrate.

As if thinking about the man could conjure him, William's phone rang. He could ignore the call and carry on with his schedule, but postponing the inevitable rarely worked with Notty.

He opened the door of the van and got in. "Hello again, Uncle Naughton. What a surprise."

"Don't start, William. I'm not in the mood."

"What are you in the mood for?" William asked, putting the key in the ignition. He didn't turn on the engine. Although the temperature read a meager twenty-nine degrees, the sun had warmed the cab to a very comfortable setting.

"I forgot a couple of points in my e-mail and I didn't feel like typing. Are you ready?"

"As ready as I'll ever be, but can I ask you something first? Did you have my parents vet these complaints as well? Do they agree that I'm a worthless ingrate who mooched off them my entire childhood and never made any attempt to pay them back?"

Notty was silent for several seconds. William had

surprised him with the question. *Good.* "No. Of course not. They would never expect anything from you. They love you. You are perfect—or fairly close to perfect—in their eyes."

William slouched forward. *Bollocks.* He could take Notty's contentiousness much easier than he could handle the man's raw honesty. "Why do I have to come right this minute, Not? Why now? You said yourself Father is holding his own. He's not getting worse. His mind is still sharp. Mother is there. Why is it so damn important that I drop everything to come now?"

Another long pause followed. Finally, Notty heaved a sigh and said, "I don't know why, William. I can't put my finger on it. Maybe what bothers me is that I even have to pick up the phone to plead with you to do what most people would do spontaneously. 'My father is ill. Oh, no, I'd better go home and visit him in his time of need,'" he said in a staged voice.

"So I'm a cad," William muttered. "What can I say? I was never a priority in either of their lives, Notty, and damn it, I'm not going to drop everything to fly to England. I will come on my own terms. May we leave it at that?"

"William, do you remember when you were a lad and you told everyone you were going to be a doctor when you grew up?"

William shook his head. "I did not. I've never been interested in medicine."

"You were. For a number of years. It's all you'd talk about. When you were in the hospital camps with your mother, you'd even wear an old stethoscope and pretend to help."

William closed his eyes but no such image came to mind. "I hate being around sick people. It's one of the reasons I'm not rushing back to see Father. When I visited Mum in those camps, I'd volunteer in the supply shack or the office."

"Yes, later on. When you were older. But as a very young child, you wanted to be a doctor."

William scowled. "I don't recall, but apparently I grew out of the notion. What is your point?"

"My point is, you stopped wanting to be a doctor for a reason, William. On the flight back from wherever we were—I'm not sure which trip this was, actually—you broke down and cried. You told me you'd accidentally seen your mummy kissing a man. Some visiting surgeon from Germany. I tried to explain that your mother was not infallible. She was a woman, and human."

William felt an unpleasant tension pass through his body. "I have no memory of any of that," he lied.

"I'm not surprised. Everything in your world, William, is black or white, including your memories. There's no gray area. No room for mistakes.

"From that point on, you decided medicine wasn't for you. Although I encouraged you to bring up the subject with your mother, you refused. Obviously, Laurel wasn't madly in love with the man. She didn't divorce your father to marry him. She might not have even kissed him passionately. You were a child. What did you know of passion? But you based a pivotal, life-altering choice on your assumption." He paused to sigh. "That's all I wanted to tell you."

The line went dead.

William looked at his phone, stunned. That conversation had to be the strangest he'd ever had with his uncle. He closed his eyes and brought to mind the image that—his uncle was right—had left an impression on him. Not black and white at all. Blurry and completely out of focus. Was the man her lover? Or a friend?

He and Daria had kissed, too. With spectacular passion and possibility. But Daria was divorced. Even a child knew the difference—one was right, one wrong. So, he'd judged his mother's actions and the experience changed him. How did that make everything his fault?

He cursed softly and turned the key in the ignition. The only person he planned to offer an apology was Daria. He'd been completely out of line kissing her last night. They were the proverbial two ships passing in the night, brushing a shade too close for a split second. His hull, he feared, would always carry the imprint of that kiss, but he didn't intend to tell her that. She had enough to worry about without adding any more guilt.

"A quick, polite goodbye," he said aloud, pulling into Cal's driveway. The tires made a loud crunching sound against the hard-packed snow. His nervous buzz of anticipation began to ebb when he realized Cal's car wasn't there. Damn. Was the family gone? He thought about leaving a note but didn't have the first clue about where to find a pen and paper.

He glanced toward the garden, recalling the fun he'd had playing with Daria's children the day before, and spotted an odd bit of color. Someone was sitting on a bench in the garden. Daria. Even from a distance, he could tell she was upset about something.

He turned off the engine and got out. "Daria? Are you all right?" he asked, giving her plenty of warning of his presence. The sky was clear but the air had a decided nip in it made more biting by the gusty wind.

"I heard once that freezing to death is a fairly painless way to go," she said, her tone flat, resigned.

"Compared to say, stepping on a land mine, you mean?"

The quip earned him a half smile. When she looked up, he saw her eyes were red and puffy. Guilt stabbed him mid-gut. "Please tell me you're not tossing in the towel because of what happened between us last night. That was my fault. I'm an utter cad, who apparently has so little self-control, he takes advantage of a woman who is emotionally fragile and—"

She held up a hand. A bare hand. "No. That's not why I'm upset. I wish you were my only unplanned problem. This is much, much worse."

The word *unplanned* set off his radar.

"I threw up this morning. My stomach has been a little off for a few days. I blamed it on the travel, strange water, nerves… Remember what I told you about trying every sort of tea on the market? And why?"

He remembered. *Morning sickness.* "What about the flu? This is winter. Lots of germs around."

"I don't have a fever. In fact, my stomach is a lot better now. That's how it was when I was pregnant with the girls. Nausea every morning but once I tossed my cookies, I'd be okay."

"You think there's a chance you might be pregnant," he said, to be absolutely clear. "How?"

She gave him a "Well, duh" look.

"Wh-who?"

She wouldn't meet his gaze. "It was just the once. Over Christmas. He wanted to spend time with the girls. Brought them home from Midnight mass. We had a couple of glasses of wine." She shook her head. "I knew it was a mistake when it happened."

"Because you had unprotected sex?"

She shook her head. "No. God, no. We used a condom.

He complained about it, but I said he was either safe or sorry."

The image in William's head was not flattering. Picturing this guy in bed, making love with the woman William had come to care for—oh, hell, admit it, had a major crush on—was disquieting, to say the least. "Then, how could you be pregnant?"

"Bad luck? Operator error? The worst timing in the world? I don't know. I can't explain it. But I'm pretty sure I hate myself more than I thought possible."

He dropped to a squat and removed his gloves. Her fingers were nearly blue they were so cold. He chafed them gently between his hands. "Where are Hailey and Miranda?"

"Cal took them to Rapid City for some kind of big celebration. I was thinking about walking into town to buy an over-the-counter test."

He did a quick calculation in his head. "It's probably too soon to know for sure, isn't it?" he said, still a bit baffled that something like this could have happened. If her ex was such a jerk—the man had threatened to kill her, right?—how could she sleep with him?

"Sex was the one part of our marriage that worked pretty effortlessly," she said, apparently hearing his unasked question. "But I was determined not to have any more children with Bruce. I've been on the pill since Hailey was a month old. Until my E.R. visit last summer. My primary care doctor suggested I go off it to rule out problems with my ovaries."

With her husband out of the picture, she'd be safe. He got that. But she had condoms. She must have been planning to become sexually active at some point. He got that, too. But why with the bastard she was divorcing? That, he didn't understand.

Daria took a deep breath, grateful beyond measure that the queasiness she'd experienced earlier was gone. She felt almost normal. Freezing cold, but... She suddenly gripped William's hands fiercely. "I wonder if I'm losing my mind. When I was throwing up, the one clear thought going through my head was 'Bruce won. I'll have to go back to him now.'"

"No, Daria. Don't say that. You can't."

"I lost a lot of blood when Hailey was born. Even with a transfusion, I was so exhausted I could barely sit up to nurse her. How could I handle two kids *and* an infant on my own?"

"You ask for help. But not from the person who wants to control you." He spoke with such fierceness and conviction she had to look at him. "A baby only ups the stakes."

She suddenly understood that he wasn't talking about Bruce. "What do you mean?"

"The police never let this out, but Bianca was six months pregnant when she died. She kept it a secret from everyone, even me. I think she knew how vulnerable it would make her. In Ocho's eyes, she became his possession times two."

He looked her straight in the eyes. "You can't go back to him. He threatened your life."

She knew that. In fact, she'd been copying the voice message tape to give a copy to William when she'd become ill. Maybe her volatile stomach *was* the product of nerves, not pregnancy.

Before she could reassure him, he pushed to his feet and started pacing. "Your ex knows you're a good mother. He wouldn't hesitate to use your maternal devotion against you as leverage. Say you went back to him and managed to stick it out another five years until this new baby—if you're even pregnant—" he added pointedly, "is Hailey's age. What would you accomplish other than indoctrinating another kid to the sort of spousal abuse that might perpetuate into another generation?"

His words were tough, his tone bleak. She wondered if this was the sort of speech he regretted not giving Bianca. Such a good, good man. She jumped up and hugged him with all her strength, burying her face against his shoulder to breathe in the smell of him.

He wrapped his arms around her, too, and they stood there in the icy garden, like a modern-day Julie Christie and Omar Sharif. Until the sound of a car turning into Cal's drive made them step apart.

Daria turned. She didn't recognize the late model sedan creeping slowly ahead, but even in silhouette against the bright sunlight she could identify the driver. Bruce.

Her stomach clenched again as acid flooded the empty space. "Brace yourself," she whispered, clutching the sleeve of William's coat to keep her knees from buckling. "That devil you were alluding to has arrived."

William glanced over his shoulder as Bruce got out of the car. He stepped around her so he would be the first person Bruce encountered.

Bruce advanced like a boxer prepping for a match, his bare hands tensing and releasing as if deciding whether or not to swing first and ask questions later. His suit and wool topcoat suggested he'd taken a plane straight from the capitol.

"So, there *is* a man," he said, his hand flipping outward in a gesture of disdain. "I figured there had to be. You don't have the balls to do this on your own, do you, Daria?"

CHAPTER EIGHT

"WHAT ARE YOU DOING here, Bruce?"

"I came to take our daughters home, you psycho kidnapper. Where are they?"

Daria looked skyward for help. "You agreed that Miranda and Hailey could accompany me to my grandfather's if Cal needed me. My lawyer has it in writing. What is the problem, Bruce?"

"The problem, Daria, is your witch of a lawyer dropping the divorce bomb in my lap the minute you leave. Plus, there's the whole manner of how you left. On the sly. Without telling anyone your grandfather was sick or even that you were leaving. Which leads me to believe that Cal is healthy as a horse and you're not planning on coming back. So, I'm here to make sure that you do. Where are the girls?"

Daria's mind was racing. She knew without a doubt William was right about keeping her pregnancy fears a secret for the time being. The last thing she wanted to do was add fuel to this contentious fire.

"They're with Cal. He's feeling a bit better."

Bruce's scowl made it clear that their absence had ruined his plan for a big, emotional reunion. "And just who the hell are you?" he asked, giving William the once-over.

Daria tried to step in front of William to shield him, but he wouldn't let her.

"William Hughes," he answered, smoothly slipping one arm through Daria's so they presented a united front.

Bruce did a double take. "Oh, my, an accent. How bloody civilized," he said snidely. He took a step closer— well within swinging distance. "Listen, *William,* that's my wife you're acting so chummy with. Here in America we take it kinda personal when someone tries to steal something that doesn't belong to him. We usually call the cops, and when there's a foreigner involved that means the INS starts asking for green cards. You got one?"

Daria's nausea returned. William, deported? His business, his friends, his home was here. Could that happen? Did Bruce possess the clout? If not, he probably knew the right people who could pull the right strings. "Bruce. Leave him alone. This is about us, not William. He's a friend. There's nothing going on between us."

Bruce glanced at William's rental van. "That your ride? You're what? A delivery boy? Fine, then beat it. My wife and I have things to discuss."

Daria stomped her foot, realizing suddenly that her toes were nearly frozen. A violent shiver passed through her body. "You and I are separated, Bruce, soon to be divorced. I am not your wife."

"You're shivering," William said, touching her cheek. "Hypothermia is a dangerous thing. You need to go inside. Now."

"F— Yes," Bruce said, shuffling a bit. "Why the hell would anybody want to live in this climate? I hate snow."

"Then go home," Daria pleaded. Her toes were starting to sting. The thought of warming her hands in front of her grandfather's fire took over her brain, making it difficult to focus on what the two men were saying.

Bruce was posturing like one of those showy male birds on the science network the girls liked to watch. "Who do you think you're dealing with, Daria? Some pussy-whipped slob who's gonna sit on his thumbs while you do exactly what you want with our daughters? Hell, no. Get in the house and pack. There's a return flight out of this crappy ass hellhole in five hours, and we're going to be on it. All of us."

"Forcing a person to go somewhere they don't want to go is called kidnapping," William said, pulling his phone from his pocket. "Do I need to call the police?"

"Does this Podunk town even *have* police?" Bruce replied sarcastically.

"Stop it, you two. I'm freezing. I need to go inside. I'd like you both to leave."

Bruce laughed outright, and William looked concerned—and a little hurt. She was suddenly completely fed up with the drama, with her choices, her mistakes and her options. She marched past William to Bruce. "I never thought I'd need a restraining order, but maybe I was wrong."

His face crumpled, his bluster vanished. "I didn't come here to hurt you, Daria. Yes, okay, maybe I wanted to do that—at first. I got drunk and said some things I shouldn't have, but I was just blowing off steam. You know that, don't you? We don't need outsiders to figure this out. We need to do what's right for our girls. Together." He nodded toward William. "Alone."

William took a step closer. "With bullies, plan A is always divide and conquer. Don't listen to him, Daria."

Her head was throbbing, her feet hurt and her teeth were chattering. "There's a coffee shop called The Tidbiscuit on Main Street. I'll meet you there in ten minutes,

Bruce. That's the best offer you're going to get today. I strongly suggest you take it."

"Will he be there?"

She shook her head. "No. William has a plane to catch."

Bruce checked his watch. "Ten minutes. Doesn't leave you much time for a quickie, English Boy." He gave William a blistering look then started toward his rental car. "Don't be late, Daria. You know how much I hate waiting."

Once he was gone, Daria grabbed William's hand and headed toward the house. "I'm so sorry you had to witness that. God, what you must think of me. Drama queen. Hopeless basket case."

He opened the door and pulled her inside, then wrapped his arms around her and hugged her tight. He kissed her, too—not as passionately as the night before, but fast and hard, befitting their frozen skin. "We're like a pair of ice pops."

She wanted to collapse, cry and throw up, but she refused to do any of those things. She was a big girl and she was finally taking charge of her life. That meant making tough choices and doing difficult things on her own.

She stepped out of his arms, shed her coat and walked to the wood-burning stove at the opposite side of the room. As she warmed her icy hands, she told him, "Thank you for your support today. I mean it. I don't want to think what might have happened if Bruce had shown up first." She shook her head. "I definitely over-reacted this morning."

He remained near the door but never took his gaze off her. "Does that mean you're not going back to him?"

"Definitely not. Baby or no baby, there's no way the

girls and I will be on that plane this afternoon. I plan to call my lawyer from the café and ask her to talk some sense into him. I didn't break any law by coming here and neither did you."

"I wasn't worried about me, but from what you've told me, he's a master manipulator. He might convince you to change your mind."

She turned to face him. "You're disappointed in me, aren't you?"

He blinked in surprise. "Why do you say that? You stood up to him magnificently. You even tried to protect me. I was touched. But, for your information, that INS threat was completely empty. I have dual citizenship."

Oh. "I meant because I slept with him."

He looked at his watch. "You were right about me needing to leave. My plane is ready and I'm not even loaded." He scratched the side of his nose and shifted his feet. She'd never seen him appear so awkward and uncomfortable. Finally, he said, "Relationships are complicated, I know that. I'm in no position to judge you. I only hope whatever hold he has over you is gone now. For your sake."

Daria sensed a chill between them that had nothing to do with the ambient temperature of the room. Despite his supportive words, she knew she'd let him down. He didn't understand how she could have slept with Bruce. Neither did she, but it had happened. Once. And she vowed it would never happen again.

"You'll be safe in a public place," he told her, reaching for the doorknob. "You have your cell phone—call 911 if he loses it. The girls are with Cal."

She nodded. "You're free to go."

In fact, she wanted him to leave. She needed to prove to herself she could stand up to Bruce without a safety net. "Oh, wait. Here's that copy of the message tape we talked about," she said, walking to the desk where she'd left it right before she'd gotten sick.

She quickly dropped it in a manila envelope and scribbled her name across the front. "I'm reasonably confident you'll never have to use this, but you know what to do if..." She couldn't complete the thought.

He took it from her without letting their fingers touch. "Ruin him. I can do that."

There was a fierceness in his tone that made Bruce's bluster sound hollow and pompous. It reminded her that she actually knew very little about this handsome, compassionate stranger...and she needed to keep things that way. At least until the ink was dry on her divorce papers.

She looked at the wall clock and let out a small peep. "Ten minutes. Bruce will be starting to fume. Could I beg one more small favor? Give me a lift to the café?"

WILLIAM DROPPED Daria at the corner establishment where he'd dined several times. The place looked busy. She'd be safe. As long as she didn't let the jerk play on her emotions.

"She slept with him," he murmured under his breath as he headed toward the highway.

The idea turned his stomach. Even seeing the guy in person didn't help him understand why she'd do such a thing. Granted, Bruce was no ogre—full head of black, wavy hair, Brooks Brothers suit, three-hundred dollar tie. The start of a midbelly paunch, but nothing outwardly repulsive.

Maybe she is a drama queen. Maybe her assertion about abuse is bogus. He glanced at the business-type envelope sitting on the passenger seat.

Spotting a familiar landmark—a giant teepee—he pulled into Native Art's parking lot and popped the tape into the van's player. Daria's voice filled the cab.

"Ahem. To whom it may concern, this is Daria Fontina." She gave the date and explained the circumstances behind the recording she was about to share. William leaned forward, rested his arms on the steering wheel and cocked his head to listen.

His blood pressure began to climb the moment Bruce's voice came across the tape. The messages he directed toward Cal started off fairly sanitized. Bruce confirmed Daria's allegation that he'd known about and approved her travel plans, but when she didn't call him back right away, his tone changed. By the time he thought Daria should have been at Cal's he didn't mince words—mostly swear words—as he told her exactly what he thought of her and what he planned to do her the next time he saw her.

William hit eject and dropped the tape back into the envelope. The man might not be a psychopath, but he was a major control freak. Living with someone like that would surely be a special kind of hell.

His first impulse was to swing the van around and go back. She couldn't face this ass alone. She'd cave. She'd do something stupid—like sleep with the cretin. But as he watched the traffic pass, the thinking part of his brain kicked in. She'd asked him to leave for a reason. His presence would only antagonize her ex, who obviously had jealousy issues.

Was Bruce astute enough to guess that William was extremely attracted to Daria? William didn't think so, but why take the chance?

Attracted? How about infatuated? At least, he had

been until she told him she might be pregnant with her ex-husband's baby.

He took a deep breath, recalling what his uncle had said about William's tendency to categorize things as either black or white.

The simple facts were pretty straightforward. William wasn't Daria's boyfriend. He wasn't even her friend, really. He felt a strong connection to her and wanted to explore where that might take them, but there was a good chance that all stemmed from his guilt over not having done more to help Bianca.

He put the car in gear and pulled onto the highway. As he drove, he noticed that a glum-looking cloud cover had pushed in over the Black Hills to obscure the sun. Notty was wrong. William had no fear of gray areas—he would be flying into one as soon as humanly possible, and he honestly couldn't wait.

"LOOK," BRUCE SAID, using the plain white mug in his hand to make a sweeping gesture. "Look at what I saved you from, Daria. All *this* could have been yours if you'd moved back here instead of marrying me."

His sarcastic tone made it clear what he thought of The Tidbiscuit, Sentinel Pass and, probably, the Black Hills. Daria flushed with embarrassment, hoping none of the diners in the neighboring booths were listening.

"I was expecting more since that TV show was filmed here. Nothing." He took a gulp of coffee. "Not even a Starbucks."

"Why did you come here, Bruce? And don't tell me because my lawyer gave you my final settlement offer. You had to know that was coming. Did I time it to my not being in town? Yes. Because I knew you'd react poorly."

His face contorted with rage, and his fists shook with the effort it took to control his temper. Daria was glad to see him try. Maybe, she told herself, he would change once they were apart. Maybe.

"After what happened between us at Christmas I thought things had changed. Yeah, yeah, we had that discussion, but you can't tell me you don't have feelings for me, Daria."

The thought of her nausea that morning crossed her mind but she pushed it away. "I care about you, Bruce. You're my daughters' father and that will never change. But I can't live with you ever again," she said simply and firmly. "If you love me—if you ever loved me—you'll make this divorce as painless as possible."

He slammed the cup on the table. "When exactly did you grow a backbone? Does this have something to do with your Euro trash boyfriend? Did you play the simpering, abused wife card on him?"

She pushed her cup aside, untouched. "I mailed a copy of the voice messages you left on my grandfather's machine to my lawyer. Between that and the phone conversation you had with her, she's convinced I shouldn't have any trouble whatsoever getting sole custody of the girls."

His normally tanned skin paled.

"And if that's the case," she continued, "there's no reason for me to remain in Fresno. I've already talked to Cal about moving here permanently. I plan to research what I need to do to get my teaching credential before we return home."

She watched as he struggled with his rage, knowing he couldn't say what he wanted to say to her in public. After a few seconds, he leaned across the table and whispered in a raspy hiss, "You will fry in hell for this. I'm a good father, and *nobody's* taking my girls away from me. Nobody."

Then he got up, tossed a ten on the table and left.

She sat for several minutes, waiting for the chaos in her mind to settle. She replayed everything that had happened that day. Her only true regret was telling William that she'd slept with Bruce. The look on his face when she'd admitted her mistake had reminded her of Hailey when Miranda had told her Santa wasn't real. Miranda had apologized later and said she was kidding, but Daria knew Hailey's glossy, pristine picture of old St. Nick would never be the same.

When the waitress came to refill her cup, Daria handed her the ten and said, "Keep it." Then she stood up and pulled on her coat, noting that the sun, which had moved the thermometer up a few degrees, was now tucked behind a thick layer of clouds.

She walked fast to stay warm, but her pace slowed when she spotted two cars in her grandfather's drive. Cal and her daughters were back early. And Bruce was there, too.

"Damn," she muttered.

She picked up her pace, as too many emotions—anger, fear, regret and worry—vied for top place in her head. As she approached the house, a sharp piercing pain exploded in her side, making her bend over. *Not again,* she thought, her fingers pressing against the burning spot under her ribs. This felt very similar to what she'd experienced the previous summer.

That episode, too, had triggered nausea, she thought, suddenly seeing a connection she'd missed. Maybe she wasn't pregnant. That was the good news—the bad was that she couldn't show any kind of weakness in front of Bruce. He'd railroad her into going to the hospital, then ride roughshod over Cal and the girls until he ruined everything.

She paused a moment, trying to formulate a plan. If the side door was unlocked, she could slip into her grandfather's room. As an ex-pharmacist, Cal kept a well-stocked medicine cabinet, with an excellent array of painkillers.

Once she had her side ache under control, she'd join the family and try to mitigate whatever damage Bruce had done.

The door opened for her, and she hurried inside. She could hear voices coming from the kitchen and living room, but she didn't want to see anybody while she was doubled over. She scanned the various bottles in his medicine cabinet as quickly as possible, swallowing two pills from a bottle labeled: For Pain. Then she quickly tiptoed to her room to wait for the pain reliever to take effect.

She curled onto her side and closed her eyes, focusing on her deep breathing the way she'd learned in her birthing classes.

She was now positive she wasn't pregnant. She'd over-reacted. Probably partly out of guilt. Talking about her mistake had been cathartic. Unfortunately, she'd chosen the wrong person to tell.

Poor William, she thought.

She didn't know why, exactly, but she had a feeling he was used to people disappointing him.

That was her last clear thought before sleep over-came her.

CHAPTER NINE

Hell would be an improvement over this, Daria decided somewhere over Utah. Middle seat. Last row, so there was no way to recline. An overly fragrant octogenarian on one side of her, on the other side, an unwashed teen twitching to the beat of the overly loud music escaping past his ear buds, which were barely visible past an assortment of rings, studs and greasy black hair.

The kid was going to need hearing aids by the time he was twenty, she thought. "Where's your mother?" she wanted to ask, but what if his answer was, "She and my dad split up and my dad took me and now I'm an angry body-piercing freak with poor hygiene"?

She shifted uneasily, swallowing the thick taste in her mouth. Painkillers. The right kind—not the kind that included a sedative, like the ones she'd taken the day before. Her grandfather had pointed out the difference when he was finally able to rouse her. Too late to be of any help, of course. The minute Bruce realized Daria was sound asleep—for whatever reason—he'd hustled the girls into his rental car. "Screw this," he'd reportedly barked, "I'm taking you home where you belong."

"Don't blame yourself, Daria," her grandfather had said, trying to comfort her. "He was determined to leave. If you'd been standing between him and the door, he might have done something we all would have regretted."

She'd managed to book a seat on the earliest flight out of Rapid City, and Cal had supplied her with drugs that eased the pain without knocking her out. She felt miserable and nauseous, but at least her body managed to confirm that she wasn't pregnant. PMS and cramps were the least of her worries.

"Are you feeling okay, dear?" the elderly woman beside her asked. "You look pale."

"A bit of flu last week," she lied. "I'll be fine. Thanks for asking."

At least she knew the girls were okay. Bruce had called several times—probably to forestall her impulse to contact the police and put out an Amber Alert. He'd calmed her down by telling her that the girls regarded the impromptu road trip as an adventure. Miranda had backed up his claim, although the tremulous wobble in Hailey's voice had nearly killed her.

"My inhaler's almost empty, Mommy. What do I do if I need it? Will Daddy know what to do?"

Of course not. Bruce wasn't the one who slept on the floor beside Hailey's bed when she was having a rough night. He didn't fill the humidifier or know how to operate the nebulizer. "He can go to any pharmacy, sweetness," Daria had assured her. "They'll call your doctor and get it refilled. Don't worry. You'll be fine. I promise."

"When are you coming home, Mommy? I miss you."

"Soon, baby. I'll probably be there before you get back. Everything's okay."

No. That was a lie. Everything was not okay. She felt as though she was back to square one, but her lawyer had assured her they had options. She needed to return to Fresno, regroup and put any other plans she had on hold.

"You can't fight the devil with a water pistol," she'd told her grandfather that morning at the airport. "Thanks for trying to help, Grandpa. I'm sorry I turned your life upside down for nothing."

He'd insisted she'd done nothing of the sort and that she was welcome to return sooner rather than later.

"We are beginning our descent to Fresno," a voice said over the loudspeaker. "The flight attendant will be making one last sweep through the plane to collect any trash. Thank you for flying with us today. It's been a pleasure...."

Home again. Not really. It wasn't home without her daughters—nowhere was. Her pain returned on cue.

Once the plane had come to a complete stop, she pulled her backpack out from under the seat in front of her and edged sideways to escape the confines of her horrible seat. She slowly made her way to the front of the plane, the pain in her midsection radiating outward until it felt like someone was twisting a knife in her back. She gripped the handrail tightly as she descended the metal steps.

The sky was the dull color of lead, high fog totally obscuring the sun. The bite in the air felt every bit as cold as the Black Hills winter she'd left that morning, despite a forty-degree difference in temperature.

Another passenger held the door for her as she hurried inside. She smiled her thanks, scurrying to the main corridor where she knew she'd find a water fountain. She'd meant to ask the flight attendant for a water bottle but had forgotten.

She found the fountain, but a piece of yellow tape across it informed her it wasn't working. "Damn."

She considered buying a bottle but decided she needed to save her cash for the taxi ride home. The sooner she got there, the sooner she could call her lawyer and figure out a new plan.

She turned on her phone to check for messages.

"Please enter your password, then press pound."

"Daria?"

She stared at her phone a full second before realizing the voice wasn't coming from her in-box. She looked around. There, a few feet ahead, standing beside one of the artificial giant Sequoia trees that were part of the newly remodeled lobby, was William.

"Daria," another voice said, far more sharply and imperiously.

"Hester?" The pain in Daria's belly got worse. Bruce's mother stood a few feet to William's right. Two strangers meeting the same person? Didn't that kind of thing only happen in the movies?

Hester turned to look at William. Her eyes narrowed, identical to the way Bruce looked when he was preparing to rip someone to shreds, verbally.

Daria hurried forward to try to keep whatever was going to happen from happening, but her body suddenly froze as a punishing pain as great as childbirth ripped through her. "Oh," she cried. "Oh, no."

She staggered, one step, two. Strong arms caught her before she fell. "William," she gasped. He helped her to the closest bench. She leaned against him, afraid to move. "I think I need to go to the hospital," she hissed on a low groan of fear and pain.

Hester had pushed her way close enough to hear the last word. "Hospital? What's wrong with you? Are you pregnant? Oh, my God, you're having another miscarriage."

"No," Daria tried to say, but all she could do was groan.

"How far along are you? Does Bruce know? Of course not. He would have told me. In fact, we just spoke and he didn't say a thing about—" Her jaw dropped. "It isn't his baby, is it? That's why you ran away. What have you done?"

Daria's body started to shake, whether from shock or embarrassment or anger, she couldn't say. William cradled her tighter, obviously sensing her impending implosion. "You," he said, pointing at Hester. "Back the hell off." To the TSA guard who rushed to help, he ordered, "Call an ambulance."

"Already on its way, sir."

Other airport personnel appeared out of the woodwork, along with a few Good Samaritans. "I'm a nurse," a woman in a pink jogging suit said. "How can I help? Try to breathe slow and steady. Help will be here soon."

Daria tried to focus on the woman's voice, but her true lifeline was William, who only moved when the paramedics appeared. Even then, he remained close by, holding her hand.

Hester stayed on the perimeter. Daria caught a glimpse now and then of the woman's peacock-blue scarf. No doubt she was reporting a minute-to-minute play-by-play to her son, but she didn't attempt to talk to Daria again. Thanks to William.

"What are you doing here?" she managed to ask him through clenched teeth as the paramedic took her pulse.

"Making sure you're okay," William said softly. "Not doing a very good job of it, am I?"

She smiled. "How…?"

"Cal," he answered, cutting her off. "Shh. We'll talk later. I'm not going anywhere."

She liked the sound of that, but had to focus her attention on dealing with the emergency responders. She told them about her previous E.R. visit and gave them the name of her primary care physician.

"Okay. Let's get you to the hospital and see if they can do a better job of fixing the problem this time, whatever it is," the paramedic in charge said. To William, he said, "You can meet us there."

"I'll be right behind you." He squeezed Daria's hand and gave her one of his devastatingly handsome Cary Grant smiles. "Try not to get in too much trouble between here and there, okay?"

She might have been able to come up with a flip answer if not for the flash that suddenly exploded between them. "You're Congressman Bruce Fontina's wife, aren't you? Can I get a statement for the *Bee?*"

Daria turned her head and closed her eyes, wishing she had the power to disappear. *Just when you think things can't get any worse.*

"Who are you, sir? How do you know Mrs. Fontina? One of the bystanders said she might be having a miscarriage—is it the congressman's baby?"

William stepped in front of the man in time to block a second photograph of Daria on the gurney. He wanted to yank the camera out of the man's hand, crack open the back and pull out a yard or two of film, but unfortunately, that kind of satisfaction had died with the advent of the digital camera. Popping out the media disk and stomping on it didn't hold the same appeal.

So, he did what he was very good at—damage control. "Ms. Fontina is an old family friend. And if you know the Fontina family then you know they don't appreciate the press intruding on their private affairs. She was flying home after visiting her grandfather and was taken ill. Her mother-in-law was here to meet Daria's plane."

"And you are?" the reporter asked suspiciously.

"An old family friend," he repeated, dragging out each word as if the young man was a slow learner.

"Hey, man, I'm just doing my job."

"Seriously, *man?* Which job is that? The reporting of real news or the harassing of average citizens?" William asked, barely able to contain his disdain. "There's no story here. The lady is ill. It makes no difference that she's a politician's wife. Aren't they allowed to get sick?"

"But—"

William stopped him. "Do yourself a favor. Drop it. Have you ever met Bruce Fontina?" He let the implication hang in the air between them.

The reporter frowned. "A couple of times."

"Need I say more?"

The guy closed his notebook. "Whatever. But I'm going to follow up on this with a call to Mr. Fontina's office. If I find out…"

William didn't hear the rest of the threat because he was already on his way out the door. He had no idea where the hospital was, but his rental car had a mapping device so he wasn't worried. He paused at the curb to let a car pass.

"My question is the same as that reporter's. Who are you?"

He glanced to his right. The rotund woman with the ugly scarf. "You seemed pretty smoochy-woochy with Daria. Are you the reason she left my poor Bruce?"

"I assure you, madam, your poor Bruce is the sole

reason Daria chose to leave her marriage. I only met her three days ago."

She started to deny the charge but took a different route, instead. "Then why are you here? Do you live in town? You were obviously meeting her plane."

"As were you, madam. No doubt with the same intention—to check on her well-being. Her grandfather called me and told me Bruce had absconded with their daughters and Daria was ill. He thought she could use a friend."

He turned to leave.

"They're his kids, too, you know," the woman shouted. "He'll be here soon enough, and you'd better hope he doesn't find you hanging around his wife."

"Ex-wife," William would have liked to yell, but he didn't.

He shoved the unpleasant encounter out of his mind as he paid the parking fee and followed the verbal directions of the GPS device. He'd come to Fresno for a reason. A foolish one, but that hadn't stopped him from hopping in his plane the minute it was fueled and ready to go.

He couldn't stop thinking about her.

There was a chance he was falling in love with her. He wasn't an expert on love so he couldn't say for certain. All he knew was that he'd never felt this way before, and he wasn't ready to let go of this connection.

He found a parking spot in the visitor lot of the large, older-looking hospital and got out. He didn't know whether or not he'd be allowed entrance to the emergency room, but he'd wait, anyway.

At the E.R., he got in line at the information desk, but before he had a chance to talk to someone, an interior door opened and the paramedic who had helped

Daria poked his head out and looked around. He spotted William and said, "Come with me."

"How is she?"

"In pain. They're running some tests."

Was it a miscarriage? He wanted to ask, but didn't. He knew enough about the medical system to understand and appreciate patient confidentiality.

"Here you go," the paramedic said, pointing to a closed door. "I'm taking off now. Good luck."

William shook his hand. "Thank you."

"She's a nice lady. Tell her I hope things turn around for her, okay?"

William nodded. He hoped so, too. He also hoped he'd have the courage to say the right thing—even if that was goodbye.

CHAPTER TEN

"HELLO."

"William," she cried, reaching out to motion him in—until the tube attached to her arm stopped her. "I hate IVs."

He strolled in looking every bit as gorgeous as he had in her previous night's dream. She called it her guilty pleasure dream—emphasis on the guilty. Her life was such a mess—children missing, an undiagnosed pain in her gut and who knew what kind of nastiness Bruce might have in store for her. But as soon as she closed her eyes, there she was, making out with William. It had been the best part of her day, by far.

He came straight to her gurney and looked her over from head to toe. She was glad the gown they'd given her was one of the more modest varieties.

"You look better. Good color in your cheeks. Relaxed. And I love the gown. Very chic. Whatever's in that bag, I want some."

She grinned. "That's simple saline, I think. It was the lovely shot they gave me that did the trick. No pain. No problem."

"The pain. Same thing you mentioned before or did you—?"

She cut him off. "It wasn't a miscarriage. That would have been impossible because I was never pregnant.

My overactive conscience tag-teamed with my ongoing medical condition to make me think I was pregnant."

"Would it be too nosy to ask what your ongoing medical condition is?"

"Still waiting for the tests to confirm it, but this E.R. doctor—different one from last August—said he's certain it's my gallbladder. Now if I only knew what exactly a gallbladder was."

He pulled out his phone. "I have a vague idea, but I can check." He typed and tapped and a moment later said, "To paraphrase, 'a small sack beneath the liver that stores bile.'" He made a face. "Doesn't sound very attractive, does it?"

She agreed. "I might need surgery to remove mine."

"I can see why. Who wants a bile sack hanging around?"

She snorted but the pain medicine was catching up with her and she could feel herself starting to drift. But there was something she wanted to tell him first.

"I'm glad you came. And not just because you were there to catch me."

"Then why?"

"I wanted to tell you that it doesn't matter if Santa Claus is real or not."

He looked around, obviously puzzled by the non sequitur. "Okay. And what does that mean exactly?"

"The look on your face when I told you I'd slept with Bruce was exactly the same as Hailey's when her sister sprang the news about Santa. Disappointed doesn't quite cover it."

He shook his head as if to deny that he'd felt that way, but she knew better. "As part of our court-ordered marriage counseling, Bruce and I saw separate therapists.

Mine said Bruce put me on a pedestal and then waited for me to fall."

"Why?"

"So he could pick up the pieces. Smaller and more manageable than a whole, healthy, emotionally together person."

"That's very profound. Did Bruce agree?"

She laughed until she started to cough, which made her pain start to flare up. "He said his therapist called me a b-i-t-c-h, and he agreed." She made a face. "My point is I'm sorry to let you down, but I'm not standing on another pedestal for anybody. Santa might be perfect—if he existed—but I'm not. If that means you don't want to go out on a date with me, I understand."

"The divorce is still on, I take it?"

"Damn right. I'm petitioning for full custody as soon as I get rid of this gallbladder thing. Was that too blunt?"

He took her free hand and brought it to his lips. "No. Blunt is good, even if some of that attitude might belong to the narcotic in your system."

He had a point. She wasn't usually quite so direct. But she liked this newfound sense of freedom. She decided this might be her only chance to tell him a few other things, too. "You know, William, I like you. I think you're hot."

William did his best to hide his shock. He wondered if she was going to remember—and regret—this forthright honesty once the painkillers wore off. "Thank you. I find you very attractive, too."

She looked at him dryly. "Isn't hot easier to say?"

He nodded, biting down on his lip. "I think you're hot, too."

"Good. Because I'm going to be single and gallbladder-free one of these days."

"Shall we pick a date for our date?"

"No."

"Why not?"

"Because Bruce has my kids and I'm going to be busy jumping through legal hoops for a while. Dating a hot guy would probably make matters worse, don't you think?"

"Unless *he* was the one dating a hot guy." A thought struck him. "Would you like me to hire a P.I.? See if there's any dirty laundry we could air? Might take some heat off you."

"Heat is good. Don't you think so? Did I mention I think you're—"

"Hot. Yes, actually, you did. Now, about that P.I.—"

His question went unanswered because a brief knock on the door introduced a burly biker-type fellow in surgical scrubs. "Hi. Are you Mr....Fontina?"

William shook his head. "No. I'm a friend."

"Oh. Okay. Well, we're going to be moving her upstairs for the night. We need to run a couple more tests, but, Daria, it looks like we're going to take out your gallbladder sometime tomorrow. They're scheduling an O.R. Are you okay with that?"

She nodded. "The sooner, the better. I have a hot date."

The surgeon looked at William, who tossed up his hands. "Good drugs."

"Obviously they worked." The man made a notation on the chart then turned to leave. "Do you know anything about the large group of people in the waiting room? Rather loud and not very happy?"

"Her ex-in-laws, I'd guess."

"Should I let them in?"

"Could you give us a couple of minutes alone? Then I'll slip away and you can do whatever you think is in her best interest."

The doctor nodded and closed the door behind him.

William looked at Daria, who was sound asleep. Her mouth was open in the most adorable way and he wanted to scoop her into his arms and whisk her away from this place, those people, and all the problems coming her way. But what she said about him putting people he loved on a pedestal struck a familiar chord.

Bianca wasn't as educated and self-aware as Daria, but she knew people. She once told William, "You give people one chance and one chance only. They let you down, you drop them."

He'd argued that that wasn't true. He could point to several of his clients—JoE, for one—who were on their second or third trip to rehab, and William had stood by them.

"*Si.* But you don't *love* them," she'd maintained.

He'd loved her. Not as a girlfriend, but as a little sister, a daughter, a dear, dear friend. And when she disappointed him by going back to Ocho, he let her fall.

"Goodbye, Daria," he said, leaning down to kiss her lips. "Be well."

He didn't know whether or not they'd get their *hot date,* but there was something he could do to make her life a little easier, and he knew just who to ask for help.

Without bothering to calculate the time difference, he made the call from the rental car return lot as he waited for a shuttle to take him to his plane. If he woke his uncle, tough.

"Well, this is a surprise. Are you at the airport, needing a ride?"

"I'm at *an* airport, but not Heathrow. I need a favor."

Notty chuckled like a vaudeville villain. "It will cost you."

William sucked in a breath and answered, "I know."

"We have a deal."

"You haven't heard what I want you to do."

"William, whatever it is, trust me, I've either done it, watched it done or planned to have it done. You can't shock me."

William felt a small chill pass up his spine. His father joked at times about Notty being a spy, but Naughton always downplayed his civil servant job. "A boring paper pusher," he called himself.

Practically speaking, hiring a local P.I. made a lot more sense, but William was reluctant to do that for several reasons. First off, he didn't know who to trust. The last thing he wanted was for word of this investigation to get back to Bruce or his family. Daria had mentioned they were prominent business people.

"A friend of mine is getting a divorce and her husband is a problem."

"You want him killed."

"No," William sputtered. "I want to hire a P.I. to look into his past. I could call Cooper Lindstrom. He had—"

"Stop. Before you say anything else, let us be clear. If I do this, you will in turn return to England as soon as I give you the information I've collected. Agreed?"

"Yes."

"Done. E-mail me the man's name and any pertinent facts you're aware of. I'll call you if I have any questions."

"Done."

Notty chuckled. "Lovely doing business with you.

Now, if you don't mind, I'm in the middle of something."
He hung up before William could reply.

William didn't know if this was a good idea or not.
He pictured the envelope containing the voice mail tape
that Daria had given him for safekeeping. She hadn't
mentioned using it against her ex. Either her lawyer had
downplayed its usefulness or Daria had changed her mind
about using it. Another reason to keep this probe between
him and his uncle. Daria had a soft heart, a forgiving
heart. She might not have the fortitude to ruin the man,
but William could—and would—if Bruce became too
much for Daria to handle.

"DARIA?"

Bruce? How had he gotten here so quickly? Had he
abandoned the car and the girls, sprouted wings and
flown? On a broom, perhaps? She felt her lips respond
to the image with a smile.

She opened her eyes, looking for William. He'd been
there when she'd closed her eyes. Hadn't he? Or was that
a dream, too? She looked around. Not only was there no
William, she was in a different place. A private room by
the looks of it.

She took a breath to test her level of pain. A small
heated knot was still there and was starting to radiate
outward. She vaguely recalled a doctor telling her they
would do surgery.

"When?" she tried to say, but the word came out
garbled because her mouth and throat were so dry.

"Water," she managed to cry.

"You're awake. Finally. I've been waiting forever,"
Bruce said. He ran his hand through his hair in a gesture of frustration. "What a nightmare! The girls and I
grabbed the last three seats on a flight from Salt Lake

City. I actually had to bribe an old woman to give up her place. Cost me an arm and a leg, but when Mom called and said you were having a miscarriage…" His voice stumbled over the word.

Daria tried to tell him he was mistaken. There was no baby. No miscarriage. But when she looked into his eyes, she could tell he already knew.

"You're damn lucky it wasn't a miscarriage, Daria. If I thought for a minute that you'd run off to your grandfather's, pregnant with my child, to get an abortion, I would kill you." He leaned close enough for her to smell the alcohol on his breath. "Do you hear me? I mean it."

Her pain returned as swift and piercing as it had been at the airport. It made her groan and curl into a fetal position. Her nausea returned, too, and she started to retch.

Bruce ran to the doorway, shouting, "Nurse. Somebody. Can we get some help in here? My wife needs help." When no one came right away, he stormed into the hallway, his voice carrying.

Daria felt some improvement the moment Bruce left her side. She spotted a glass with a straw in arm's reach and took a sip. As she lay waiting for deliverance of some sort—medical, a lightning strike, something— she thought about William. She had a sketchy memory of them talking about going on a date. Was she crazy? What did it say about her that she raced headlong into a relationship with another man before she was completely rid of the last?

It says I'm just like my dad.

The thought unnerved her.

Her mom's ashes had barely been sprinkled at sea before Dad had started seeing the woman he would ultimately marry—six short months after Daria's mother's death.

Daria had been appalled. Until that moment she hadn't realized how needy and dependent her father was. He couldn't function alone.

Was Daria the same?

She hoped not. She wanted to think she'd asked the handsome…hot…Mr. Hughes out on a date because she liked him. Because her female radar had picked up on the fact that he liked her, too. She wanted to feel womanly, desirable, pretty and sexy. It wasn't that she was afraid to live on her own without a man in her life. She wasn't.

Was she?

The question flew from her mind the moment Bruce returned—with Miranda and Hailey. "Mommy. Oh, Mommy, I missed you so much. Are you okay? Please be okay. Please."

Her youngest daughter burst into tears as she pressed her face against Daria's leg.

"I'm going to be fine. The doctors finally know what's causing the problem. My gallbladder. Do you know what it is?"

Miranda shook her head.

"What is it?" Hailey cried.

Daria was about to repeat what William had told her, but she didn't have to because her surgeon joined them. He explained her condition in far more detail than either girl cared to hear, explaining how the procedure would take place and what she could expect to feel over the next few days.

To Daria's surprise, Miranda kept her distance from her father, choosing to stick close to Daria. She held her mother's hand and squeezed it hard when the doctor mentioned the size of the incision he would make.

Daria was anxious to talk to her girls, find out how Bruce had treated them and if they were okay, but Hester swept in a few minutes later. "Time to go, girls," she said, clucking like a mother hen. "You're staying with me tonight. Come on, come on. You'll see your mother after the procedure. Give her a kiss on the cheek. Don't want to spread any germs."

When everyone was gone, Daria let out a long sigh. Until someone coughed.

Her eyes flew open. Bruce again.

He walked to her side and bent low to whisper, "You had your diva moment, Daria, but that ends here. You're my wife and I'm never letting you go. If you try to leave again, I'll hire the best spin doctors in the country to destroy you. By the time I get done with you, everyone will know you're a conniving slut who used me, had an affair with some English errand boy and abused our children. Not only will your daughters hate you, so will everyone else. Including William."

He left before she could muster a reply.

"Bully," she whispered, closing her eyes to keep her tears at bay. She pushed his ugly threats out of sight. She knew Miranda and Hailey wouldn't stop loving her because of something he told them. She was their mommy and that bond was more resilient than Bruce could ever know. But her connection to William was new and untested. He might very well decide she and her baggage was simply too heavy to bother with.

She didn't know, but she would find out. Because no matter what Bruce threatened, she was never going to let him push her around again. But first, she needed to get healthy.

CHAPTER ELEVEN

"MOM, ARE YOU EVER going to talk about what happened between you and Dad after you got home from the hospital?"

Daria braked sharply to avoid hitting a pothole in the middle of the bike path. She'd invited Miranda on a bike ride specifically to sort through everything that had happened—the trip to South Dakota, Bruce's impromptu road trip and Daria's surgery. Four weeks had passed since Daria had been released from the hospital. She'd expected one or both girls to ask more questions. Neither had.

She put her foot down and hopped to a stop on the grassy shoulder that bordered the lane. "Let's sit, okay? I need to rest a second."

In truth, Daria felt healthier, more energetic and alive than she had in years, but she knew better than to overdo her recovery. She'd found out the hard way what happened when you pushed too hard.

The day she'd come home from the hospital—gallbladder-free—she'd discovered her ex had taken it upon himself to move back in. Without her permission, and in total disregard of their separation agreement *and* her lawyer's admonitions to the contrary.

Daria had been so furious, she'd piled everything of his on the front lawn, heedless of the weather forecast. She'd wanted everything done by the time Hailey and

Miranda got home from school so they wouldn't feel compelled to help. Unfortunately, the post-operative push had been too much.

Miranda had been the one to call Daria's friend Julie. They'd helped her to bed and waited on her hand and foot. Miranda also was the one to suggest they call a locksmith before Bruce returned from Sacramento.

The extra charge to get the man to come out at a moment's notice had been worth every penny when Bruce showed up and started cursing. The rain had started a few minutes later, prompting even more furious ranting. No one knew for certain who had called the police. Maybe the neighbors.

That was the last face-to-face contact she'd had with him in four blessedly quiet weeks. As per the court order her lawyer obtained, Bruce spent supervised time with his daughters at his mother's house every other weekend.

"I love spring in the valley, don't you?" she asked when Miranda joined her on the grass.

"Yeah, but I liked the snow at Great-Grandpa's, too. It was fresh and clean and we had fun throwing snowballs at William."

Daria cocked her head. "Are you saying you might not mind moving there?"

Daria was on the fence. Without Bruce breathing down her neck, she wasn't quite as motivated to leave Fresno. Even Hester had backed off to a degree.

"Maybe. I don't know. My friends are here. And the cousins, but…it's not much fun to hang out with them anymore because they say bad things about you."

Daria looped one arm around her shoulders. "I'm sorry you have to hear that. They've put your dad up on a pedestal. A pretty tall one, I guess, because they don't see his flaws. Not that—"

"It's okay, Mom. I love Dad, but you weren't with us on that road trip. He was different. More yelling and less fun. I know you tried to tell me there was another side to him, but I didn't want to hear it."

"Thank you. A mother likes to know her daughters are listening—some of the time."

Miranda got up. "Did Hailey tell you Dad's got a girlfriend?"

Daria put out a hand for a little help. "No. How'd you find out? Did he bring her to meet you?"

She shook her head. "Hailey overheard Dad describing her to Grandma. He called her a hottie." Miranda made a face. "Yech."

Hottie. The word brought to mind her last conversation with William. Daria felt her cheeks turn warm. Miranda noticed. "You don't care, do you? That he's found someone else? I know it seems pretty fast, but Hailey and I think you should start dating again, too."

A real date? William had asked. She'd been thinking about that. A lot. Too much.

"I'm going to. But you and Hailey deserve a mother who is there for you. This has been a turbulent time, emotionally challenging. And it's not over yet. We still have to go before the judge and iron out our final custody agreement."

Miranda rolled her eyes elaborately before picking up her bike. "I know. But that doesn't mean you can't call William. At this rate, I'll be dating before you."

"I think not," Daria cried, half seriously, half laughing.

"Uh-huh," her daughter singsonged, challengingly, as she hopped on her bike and took off pedaling.

Daria followed, but she didn't try to catch up. For one thing, she wanted to savor the moment. Her moody, teenage daddy's-girl was growing up. She'd seen signs over the past month—small kindnesses toward her sister, marked improvement in her grades and fewer arguments with Daria over trivial things that used to set off a tantrum.

While Miranda hadn't come right out and admitted that Bruce had scared the heck out of her on their rental car road trip, Hailey wasn't as reticent.

"Daddy was mean, Mommy. He yelled at Miranda for calling you when we stopped at the motel. And she had to take care of me when I couldn't breathe because he didn't know what to do. I don't want to go with him in the car anymore."

Daria wasn't happy that her daughters had been traumatized by Bruce's brutish behavior, but she was thankful they were more accepting about the divorce now. She was especially relieved that the details would be finalized very, very soon.

She hoped.

"ARE YOU PREPARED to ruin this man?"

William had been sitting at his desk for over an hour, staring blankly at the screen thinking about Daria when his uncle called.

"No," William answered.

"If you change your mind, the information you need is in the file I e-mailed a few moments ago. Regardless of whether or not you now have cold feet, our agreement still stands. Correct?"

William clicked on the attachment and quickly scanned the first couple of pages. "My God, where'd you get all this? Is it for real? Notty, I thought you were a paper-pushing bureaucrat. This stuff reads like a dossier from a spy novel."

Notty was silent on the other end of the line.

Finally, he said, "What you do with it is up to you, but, I repeat, our agreement still holds, correct?"

William already had his ticket, but he didn't tell his uncle that. "Yes. What I meant about not ruining Bruce is, I would gladly hand this to some eager investigative reporter and let them blow the man out of the water, but it's not my call. It's Daria's. She gets to decide what she wants to do with this information."

Notty let out a hearty laugh. "Well done, William," he said, the pride audible in his voice. "Your father would be proud of you. Now then, when are you arriving? I'll arrange to be in town so I can give you a lift."

"Soon. You have my word. First, I have to give this information to Daria. That's not something you do over the phone. And, as trite as it sounds, I do have a business to run. From the number of calls I've handled this morning, one might think the entertainment world was coming to an end."

"I leave it in your hands, William. I know you'll do the right thing. You know where to find us."

William let out a sigh as he hung up the phone then settled back to read the long list of damning evidence against Daria's husband. "Silver bullets," he murmured. "Very droll, Notty."

William couldn't imagine how Naughton came by the information, but it was glaringly obvious that one of the reasons Bruce picked Daria to marry was to add a little gloss to his less-than-illustrious past. If you wanted to rebrand yourself, it never hurt to align yourself with a photogenic young wife and two adorable kids.

William didn't give a damn about the man's greed and lack of integrity. The voters in his district could decide his political fate. The only part that mattered to William was how this information would impact Daria and her daughters.

And that was for Daria to decide.

"WHO'S THAT?" Miranda asked, slowing the bike.

Daria, who was following directly behind her, had to steer sharply to the right, narrowly missing a car parked in the street. They were half a block from home. "Where?"

"On our porch. I think that's William." Her voice went up an octave. "It is. Hurry, Mom. When's Grandma due back with Hailey?"

Hester had taken the younger girl to a birthday party for an old family friend at a senior center in Chowchilla. Miranda had flatly refused to go along. "No amount of cake in the world can make up for the smell of that place," she'd told her mother after Hester and Hailey had left.

"Not for another half hour," Daria answered, pedaling hard to catch up. Her heart was racing but she couldn't blame the physical exertion. William. William. He hadn't been far from her thoughts for even a moment these past few weeks.

"William," Miranda cried, letting her bike drop on the thick green grass of the recently groomed lawn. "What are you doing here?"

He stood up, his hands gripping a sleek leather brief-case. "Business, Miranda. I have something for your mum. How are you? And Hailey? Is the squirt okay?"

"She's with our grandma at an old people's party. Where's your car?"

He pointed down the street. "Your mum nearly ran into it. I was trying to be discreet. I called first but there was no answer. Is your cell phone turned off?" he asked, looking at Daria directly.

Her heart thudded so loudly she was afraid he might hear it. "I have a new number." She didn't want to admit that Bruce had thrown her phone against the wall of the house the night he'd come back to find all his belongings on the lawn, getting rained on. When he'd started breaking windows, she'd walked outside with her finger poised to dial 911. That was the last she'd seen of her phone. "Sorry. I meant to call you, but I felt uncomfortable asking Grandpa for your number. And I couldn't call Libby. I heard she's completely wrapped up with the baby."

"Oh, yes. Gannon. Ten pounds of perfection," he said, smiling. "Not to worry. I didn't want to intrude. We left things sort of loose given your health issues. You got the flowers I sent?"

"They were gorgeous. Thank you."

"You're welcome. How are you feeling? You look wonderful."

"Much better, thank you. Did you say you were here to talk business?"

He nodded. "I wanted to give this to you in person. It's a disk with some information that might be useful in your divorce proceedings."

Daria handed Miranda the house key and her cell phone. "Go inside and call your grandmother. Keep it casual but try to find out if she's on her way. Okay?"

"Sure, Mom." She smiled brightly at William, then hurried up the steps.

"You have a new ally," he observed.

"An old ally newly reinvigorated. Apparently, Bruce behaved poorly on their road trip."

"I'm not surprised. According to this report, it's what he's done most of his life."

"Really? What's in here? How'd you get it?"

"Police reports. Juvenile records. A few things that never went to trial thanks to some well-placed bribes. I have no idea how my uncle got this, and I'm not sure I want to."

"Oh. That's right. Now I remember you asked me about hiring a private eye. I was so out of it at the time, I completely forgot." She frowned. "I hope you didn't have to pay for this. My lawyer says Bruce's lawyer keeps giving her the green light. She thinks we'll have a fair settlement in place and ready to be signed within a few days."

"No, no charge whatsoever. Simply a little something to cover a worst-case scenario. What you do with it is entirely up to you."

Neither moved for a full ten seconds but she felt something shift in the air between them. She wanted him to kiss her, to confirm her memory of how amazingly wonderful it had been the first time he'd kissed her.

The moment he took a step forward, the door opened and Miranda poked her head out. "They're in Madera. Do you want me to tell Hailey to stall? She could say she needs to go to the bathroom. Or fake an asthma attack."

"She wouldn't do that, would she?" William grinned.

"Uh-huh. What should I do, Mom?"

"Ask them to pick up ice cream for tonight. And tell Grandma she's invited to stay for dinner."

William appeared surprised by the offer. "Hester apologized for what happened in the airport. I think she realized that her son doesn't give a darn whether his daughters spend time with their grandmother, but I do. She's been much nicer to me the past few weeks."

"Good." He didn't sound convinced. She wondered whether that was because of what was in the folder, or if it had something to do with his own family issues.

Before she could ask about his father's health, he told her, "I'm going to England in two weeks."

"Excellent. Is your father doing any better?"

"About the same, I'm told."

"Oh," Daria said.

She went on, "I'm going to Florida to see my dad. In June, after the girls are out of school. I had a sort of epiphany while I was in the hospital and I realized I was as much to blame as his new wife for creating a schism between us. I'd been holding in a lot of anger about him remarrying so quickly after my mother died."

He looked at her with that intense, questioning look of his. "And now you're not mad at him?"

"No. I realize he can't be alone. He needs someone in his life. I judged him for that, when, in a way, I did the same thing with Bruce. I stayed in an unhappy marriage for too long because I was afraid to be alone."

He touched her arm. The feel of his fingertips against her bare skin made something big and warm blossom inside her. "Maybe there's hope for me with my parents, eh?"

She hesitated a fraction of a second, then she kissed him. Too many long nights had separated them. Too many days filled with all the problems, issues, finances, job applications and planning that went into starting over. But always in the back of her mind was the spark of possibility that William had introduced in her heart.

It required all her willpower to pull back. Breathing shallowly, trying to regain her composure, she looked at him. "I love the way you kiss. Does that make me a wanton woman?"

"It makes me want to pick you up and take you back to L.A. with me."

Good answer. Suddenly feeling very brave, she tucked the folder under one arm and grabbed his hand to pull him with her. "What are you doing this coming weekend?"

He looked intrigued and slightly amused.

"Well, I planned to accompany one of my clients to a red carpet awards show, but that sounds far more grandiose than it is. I would gladly bow out if you have something else in mind."

She punched a code into the keypad beside the garage door then ducked under the door as it lifted and raced to her car. A few seconds later, she returned to hand him the three-fold flier she'd picked up on a lark. "I saw this at the grocery store yesterday. They sell these wines, but look at the B and B. Wouldn't it make a romantic first date?"

She worked her eyebrows suggestively, which made him laugh. He studied the photos and read the blurbs. "Paso Robles, huh? That's driving distance for me. How far is it from here?"

"Hop, skip and a jump," she said, visualizing the drive she'd made several times with Bruce. "It's not far from Hearst Castle. What do you think? Wanna go?"

The last time she'd asked a man out was at least fifteen years ago. She held her breath, waiting. Hoping.

"Absolutely. I'll have my secretary make reservations."

He started to put the flier in his pocket, but she snatched it back. "I beg your pardon. This is my date. I'll make the reservations."

Ever gracious, he bowed slightly. "Let me know the exact time, and I'll meet you there."

WILLIAM WAS STILL GRINNING when his phone rang ten minutes later. He hoped it was Daria calling to confirm their reservation. He honestly wasn't sure he could wait. A date with Daria. Lord, it was about time. He'd thought about it often enough.

He wriggled his Bluetooth into place and hit the receive button. "William Hughes here."

"This is Bruce Fontina. We need to talk."

William stepped on the brake without thinking. "No. I don't believe we do." The car behind him honked.

"I have a friend at the airport. He called to let me know you're in town. If you don't want to develop a little mid-air problem, you'll meet me at the Piccadilly Hotel across from the airport in ten minutes."

William's first impulse was turn around and warn Daria. They'd shared a kiss in the street—if Bruce had someone watching her, there was no way to pretend it didn't happen. "Very well. But it'll have to be quick. I have a meeting in L.A. this afternoon, and I will make note of this threat."

"What threat? I meant that the weather might give you a little problem. What a pussy."

He hung up.

"What an ass."

He quickly called his secretary. "I'll be a little late. Ran into a complication on this end. And FYI, if my plane goes down in a fiery crash, call my uncle and tell him the man he just investigated is to blame. He'll know what to do."

"What?" Moira cried. "A crash? William…"

He shook his head. "Sorry, I was venting. Don't worry.

The guy doesn't have the balls to commit murder. I'll call you as soon as I'm taxiing. Gotta go make nice with the biggest jerk on the planet."

He pulled into the parking lot of the older two-story hotel. He picked one of the many available spaces close to the building and hurried inside. The bar was easy to find—right across from registration. Bruce was equally easy to spot—he was the only person occupying a booth in the mostly empty bar.

William eased into the tufted leather seat, glad for the wide table between them. "Well?"

Bruce blew out a scornful huff. "So much for British class."

"As you'd know if you tried to follow through on your threat to get me deported, I'm only half English."

"Yeah. I found that out. And you're a hotshot agent. Isn't that a person who makes a living off other people's success?"

William shrugged. "Most of my clients would be the first to tell you that they wouldn't have attained their current level of success if not for my efforts on their behalf, but feel free to believe whatever you wish. Was there a reason you wanted to speak with me?"

Bruce motioned the waiter over. "Drink?"

"No, thank you."

"Hit me again," Bruce said, motioning toward his highball glass. "Jack and soda, easy on the soda."

He said the last with a jovial laugh that probably helped him fit right in with the bar crowd. William could see a hint of the *common man* charisma that had probably gotten him elected. On the surface, at least. Until you looked a little closer. Tiny red blood vessels spiderwebbed around his nose and eyes. He drank too much.

"Again. There was something you wanted to say to me."

"Leave my wife alone. I don't know how many times I gotta say it. She's the only reason you'd be in this lousy town, so don't try to tell me you were here on business. If I hadn't just gotten here myself I woulda caught you at my house, wouldn't I? Did you two do it in my bed?"

"I did meet with your ex-wife," he said, emphasizing the ex. "And Miranda. The girls left some things in my plane and I wanted to see for myself that Daria was okay." A partial truth was always better than a lame lie.

"You never heard of UPS?"

William sat forward and rested his hands on the table. "I don't owe you any explanation. I only came here to tell you to back off, or you'll be the one who is sorry."

Bruce's lips pulled back in a sneer. "I'm not afraid of you. Daria is having a moment, but she'll come to her senses. She can't make it without me. And I don't give a damn what her lawyer says about community property laws in California. That house she's living in was bought and paid for by *my* family's trust. The car is leased, and those children attend a private school that even you couldn't afford. Once she does the math, she'll come groveling back. Wait 'n' see."

William hated bullies. He'd heard the story a thousand times about how his father had beaten up the class bully who was picking on Notty, and suddenly, he felt a connection to his father he'd never felt before. He leaned across the table to look Bruce straight in the eyes.

"I'd think twice about trying to screw Daria out of her fair share of your property settlement, Bruce. I wonder what the media would do if they found about Kathy Scranton."

"Who?"

"You remember. The college coed who took out a restraining order against you. Some might call that stalking."

Bruce let out a scornful snort, but William read fear behind his eyes. "Ancient history. She said, he said. My lawyers would make mincemeat out of her."

"Maybe. But voters don't much like *rapists,* do they? You're up for reelection when?"

Bruce's shoulders bunched and he started to slide out of the booth, but William leaned closer, his voice dropping even lower. "This is no idle threat, Bruce, it's a promise. Daria is fully capable of making a fabulous life for herself and your daughters. I wouldn't dream of interfering in that—and neither should you. If I find out you threatened her or abused her in any way during this legal process, you will be sorry. And so will your brothers."

"My brothers? What do they have to do with anything?"

"A lot. How's the saying go? Oh, yes, follow the money. I believe that saying started with the IRS."

Bruce's eyes widened and he inched back slightly. "We're done here."

"I agree."

William left the bar feeling pretty cocky and proud of himself. The feeling lasted after takeoff and continued until the brownish-gray haze enveloping the L.A. skyline came into view. That was the moment he remembered what he'd told his uncle. "This is Daria's business. What she does with this information is her call."

He'd meant that at the time, but when it came right down to it, he wasn't able to stop himself from playing the hero. He knew without thinking too hard that she wasn't going to be happy about this if she ever found out.

Hopefully, Bruce was smart enough to take William's advice and never say a word about this to his ex-wife. Hopefully.

CHAPTER TWELVE

"DUNKE FROM Sonic Profile on line two, William. You might want to take this—JoE's contract is up in ninety days."

William heard the unspoken word *remember* in his secretary's voice. *I don't pay her enough.* Moira had worked her size-one butt off the past three days since William had returned from Fresno. Not only had he needed to clear his schedule for a trip to England, he'd also decided to bail on one of the most high-profile events of the year.

For a date with Daria. He got turned on just thinking about it.

"Put him through."

"Right away, but…"

Her hesitation made him ask, "What?"

"You do know that JoE is in rehab, right?"

William cursed softly. "When?"

"Friday. I texted you as soon as I found out. He'll be in virtual lockdown for six weeks."

William sighed. A complication, but not insurmountable, unless the record company decided the rapper was too much bother to keep on their label. William hated negotiating from a weak platform, but it was the nature of the business that some clients self-sabotaged to the point where he was lucky to even get them another chance. "Thanks for trying to keep me in the loop. Put him through. Here's when the buffalo crap really hits the fan."

Moira snickered softly. "Which is why you're worth the big bucks. Good luck." She was fifty, looked thirty and had a social life he usually envied from afar.

He pulled up his client list on the computer screen and opened the document he'd created regarding the young rapper's income projections and future album sales. The kid was gifted, with a real connection to the street, but how much of that gift was tainted by the drugs he procured on said street? The answer to that question would be the main point of negotiation, he guessed.

After a quick exchange of pleasantries, Dunke got to the point. "Can you guarantee your client isn't going to snort every penny of this up his nose?"

"Yes," William lied. Was it really a lie if that's what you believed? Because, deep down, that's what he wanted to believe.

"Well, bull-f'n good for you. I can't."

"Dunke, what my client does with the money you pay him to put his talent on your label really isn't any of your concern. The real question is how much do you love rap, and how much will JoE's next record earn."

"Don't give me that shit, Hughes. How many times does this asshole client of yours need to go to rehab? That's eight to ten weeks he isn't writing, recording, performing, promoting. You ever heard about Twitter? Fans love that shit, and where's JoE gonna tweet from—rehab?"

"I'm sure he would if he could. I'll look into it. In the meantime, do you want to open these negotiations or not?"

The question languished in the air for eight to ten seconds. Dunke let out a profanity-laced diatribe, b when he finished, the word William was waiting for emerged. "Yes."

They agreed to bargain over e-mail. William knew he'd be lucky to keep the same numbers from his client's previous contract, with no new perks. When JoE emerged from rehab, William would spell out very clearly that this was his last chance. Whether or not that made a difference would be anybody's guess.

"William," Moira said the moment he hung up the phone. "I've got Daria on hold...."

"Put her through." William's heart rate spiked. He jabbed the flashing light so hard the phone slid sideways.

"Daria. How are you?"

"I'm fine. Better than fine. Bruce signed the divorce papers this morning. No big fight or last-minute standoff. He agreed to all my terms. I'm finally a free woman." She laughed. "Well, not debt-free, but even that will be remedied when I sell this house. He agreed to split it fifty-fifty," she added in a hushed tone of awe, as if she couldn't quite believe her good fortune.

So much for his family's corporation owning it. "That's great. Congratulations. Did you have to use any of that information I gave you?"

Her tone went serious. "No. I gave my lawyer a copy but told her not to even read it unless Bruce started pulling some of his usual stunts. But he pretty much rubber-stamped every demand I put out there."

He wondered how much of that cooperation stemmed from the talk he'd had with Bruce. Very little, he hoped. "w are the girls handling the news?"

"ey seem fine. I've tried not to appear too joyful f them, but they know I'm happy. And they're about our date. They like you. A lot."

The feeling was mutual—especially where their mother was concerned. "So, you made the reservation?"

"Yep. I'm e-mailing you the link." His other line rang. Moira would pick that up, but Daria must have heard it because she told him, "I'm sure you're busy, especially getting ready for two trips. How's your father?"

"Surprisingly well. The chemo finally seems to be helping." Although Notty insisted it was William's planned arrival that boosted Father's spirits and made the treatment kick in. That, of course, added to William's guilt, which ticked him off and tempted him to cancel. *What do I have to feel guilty about?* he wanted to shout. But he didn't do either—shout or change his plans.

"That's great. I'm so glad."

Daria hesitated. She'd asked about his father as a stalling measure. She was glad to hear the man was doing better, but mostly she was unsure how to bring up the matter of sleeping arrangements. She felt foolishly out of date as far as dating went, but she wanted—needed—to know that she and William were on the same page, as they say.

"Um…in the interest of full disclosure and transparency—" She smacked the heel of her hand against her forehead. *Dumb.* "Sorry. Apparently I haven't completely purged the political lingo from my system. But I do want to make it perfectly clear that my intentions this weekend are…mostly dishonorable."

William made a choking sound, as if he'd been in the process of swallowing something. "You should warn a person before you say something that frank, Daria. I may need to buy a new monitor."

"Sorry," she said, reassured by his teasing. His tone gave her the courage to say what she wanted to say. "My girlfriend, Julie, and I had a long talk about whethe not I was ready—emotionally—for this sort of date. She thinks I need a great deal more *me* time before opening the door to another round of *we* time. But she is in favor of great sex."

He made that coughing sound again.

"And…and so am I," she rushed to add. "Does that work for you?"

William drew in a loud breath and let it out. "Of course. I'm a man. Great sex is never a bad idea."

Whew. "Good. Because I only booked one room."

She glanced at the calendar above her desk. Two red hearts—courtesy of Hailey—adorned the upcoming weekend. She wished she had a time machine to push the next two days out of the way. She couldn't wait to see him. *See* being the least of the things she'd dreamed about doing with him.

"Two rooms would have been a waste of money," he told her. "And your daughters aren't the only ones happy about this. Moira, my secretary, brought in a huge picnic basket this morning. Filled with everything necessary for a romantic getaway. She said it was about time I got a life."

"How sweet! Tell her I said thank you." Julie had given Daria a special gift, too. Sexy—some might say over-the-top—lingerie. Daria had blushed when she'd held up the black lace, but Julie had made Daria promise to wear it.

She waved her hand in front of her face to cool her cheeks. "I'd better go, William. It's almost time to pick up the girls, and I need to call my mother-in-law—I mean, my ster—I have to stop calling her that." She gave a squeal of glee. "I *get* to stop calling her that. She's keeping the girls for me this weekend."

"Does she know where you're going and who you will be with?"

Daria frowned. She'd almost forgotten that William and Hester had met. And that the circumstances had been anything but pleasant. "I'll admit that she's not crazy about me seeing you, but I blame Bruce for that. He hates you, William. But Hester is a realist. She's accepted the divorce and is doing her best to be nice to me so she can maintain a relationship with Miranda and Hailey."

"I can live with your ex's antipathy so long as it doesn't spill over on you and your daughters," he said.

"Time will help," she said. Everyone said so. Julie wasn't the only one urging Daria not to rush into another relationship. Even her father, who was certainly one to talk, had counseled her to take her time before jumping into the dating pool again. In fact, the only person in favor of her upcoming date—aside from her daughters— was Cal.

"Stop blaming yourself for marrying Bruce," he'd said. "So you fell for his line. You're no different from all those people who voted for him. The man is a con artist. He could sell God to the devil. You're a smart woman who deserves happiness. If William makes you happy, then I say, 'Go for it, girlfriend.'"

She'd giggled hearing the contemporary saying come from her grandfather's lips, but she'd taken his advice to heart. She wasn't looking for love—only a man who could make her feel loved. And she knew without a doubt that person was William.

AT 4:00 P.M. on Friday, William's grin—the one he'd been sporting since he'd left L.A.—widened as he pulled to a stop in the parking lot of the B and B Daria had selected for their weekend getaway. He parked beneath a gigantic oak tree—one of a dozen adding to the spectacular landscaping surrounding the winery. In every direction were rolling hills covered with grape vines proudly flaunting shiny new leaves. The main building had an antebellum look—white clapboard siding and black shutters. A large, graceful U-shape that welcomed its guests with warm, yet classy, appeal.

He got out, pausing to pop the trunk.

"William," a voice hailed from some distance.

"Daria." He waved to the figure on the second-floor balcony. Two white Adirondack chairs occupied part of the space, along with baskets of brilliant red geraniums. "You beat me. I thought you were coming later."

She held out a wineglass. "Change of plans. Chilled wine in every room. How cool is that?"

He yanked his suitcase out of the trunk, along with the picnic tote Moira had donated to the cause.

"Finally," she'd complained. "It's about time. You do know the only reason I took this job was because I thought a handsome, young Hollywood agent like you had to be living a dashing, romantic life. You have no idea how disappointed I've been."

Notty, too, was pleased and optimistic about William's chances for romance. "Ravage her to within a breath of her life," he'd advised with a gleeful cackle earlier that morning. He'd been promptly shushed by both of William's parents.

The memory made him smile. His father had sounded better. Stronger. And his mother had been less sharp with William when she'd given him the daily status report. He only hoped he'd actually be able to get there as planned. JoE was trying to get out of rehab ahead of schedule. Not because he was out of the woods rehab-wise, but because his record label had talked him into performing at a huge televised cable awards show.

William had not approved. He was afraid this could be a gigantic mistake—possibly even a lethal mistake. "You're not his babysitter," Moira had said, soberly. But she also knew about Bianca. It was a different kind of weakness, but JoE could wind up just as dead.

He pushed the thought aside as he hurried inside. He'd figure something out when he got back to L.A., but at the moment, he was here. Now. And life was looking very, very good. Daria—sans wine glass—danced down the wide, open staircase to his right and flew to his side. "William."

He catalogued a quick image of stone-washed jeans, classy flats and a white cotton sweater before she wrapped her arms around him. Her perfume was new, heady. "I'm so happy you're here. You have no idea."

He was still holding his bags and was afraid to let go for fear they'd land on her foot. "You look fabulous. You cut your hair. It's great."

She let go of him to ruffle her fingers through the much shorter bob. "I wanted something easy and different. I'd kept it long all those years because Bruce would have thrown a fit if I cut it. Julie said you'd be disappointed because men like long hair, but you're not, are you? Disappointed?"

He set down his bags and reached out to finger one feathery lock. "Of course not. It's your hair. Dye it pink if you want. Besides, the style suits you. It's fun."

She beamed and stepped back to do a little pirouette.

Something else was different about her. He studied the outward changes that had taken place since he last saw her. "You're glowing."

"I spent yesterday at a spa. And I joined a gym. I'm very strong now." She flexed her arm for him. "You should be afraid. Very afraid. I'm a force to be reckoned with."

He threw back his head and laughed. "You're even more beautiful than before. I like strong women—my mother claims she once fired a machine gun over the heads of a band of rebels who intended to steal drugs from the hospital. I'm not intimidated." But he was conscious of conducting this conversation in public. "Have you registered?"

She picked up the picnic bag. "All taken care of. Follow me. I'll show you our room."

William liked the large, airy room, which included a micro-kitchen and sitting area in addition to the deck. It was classy and beautifully decorated with antiques, including an armoire that doubled as an entertainment center.

He set his bag on the folding rack, deposited the picnic tote on a low table and did what he'd been dreaming about all week. He kissed her. Her arms went around his neck without hesitation. Her lips parted and she welcomed his tongue with a soft peep of pleasure. She tasted of wine and mint. The odd combination told him she'd gargled before racing downstairs to greet him.

His feelings for her sharpened to a fine point, so clear and defining he knew without a doubt that this was a life-changing moment that he would never forget. He was a heartbeat away from spilling his guts when she suddenly broke off the kiss and jumped back, excitedly.

"Perfect. That's exactly how I had our reunion scripted in my mind. I need to take a picture."

"What?"

"Not what—who. You. This room. Me. The new me. And the old you."

"I'm old?"

"The *same* you. That's a good thing, by the way. I really, really like the you you are."

"Are you by any chance channeling Dr. Seuss?"

Her laugh was pure joy, and William quickly forgot about spilling his guts. There would be time for heartfelt confessions later. Or not. Maybe the new Daria needed to enjoy herself without any encumbrances like the old William's declaration of love.

"You need wine," she said, apparently seeing something too serious in his face.

"Yes, I do."

She poured him a glass. The house chardonnay, she said, chilled to perfection in a special wine cooler.

"Now, about that photo," she said after his second sip. "Would you please stand by the door to the balcony? There. Ooh, yes, looking very dapper."

She clicked off several shots.

"Your turn."

He framed the shot. She looked gorgeous, exhilarated. But there was the faintest hint of worry in her eyes. He snapped the shot, then picked up his wineglass and walked to where she was standing.

"How are you? Really?"

She sighed. "I'm good. Excited and happy, but I feel a little guilty about being so excited and happy. Weird, isn't it?"

"No," he answered. "Some of us are taught from a young age to put other people's needs first. When we start making our own needs a priority, the conflict can get dicey."

She inhaled deeply and let the breath out slowly. "I'm

204 THE GOOD PROVIDER

also a little nervous. I've never asked a man on a romantic tryst before."

"Me, neither," he said with a wink. "So, let's agree to acknowledge any awkwardness by acknowledging that there will be awkwardness. Agreed?"

"That sounds very British. I like it. I like you."

"The *old* me? That stung, by the way," he teased.

She pouted playfully. "Poor you. Can I kiss that bruised ego and make it feel better?"

There was enough sexual sizzle in her tone for William to set down his glass and back her up against the wall. "Let me show you where to start."

CHAPTER THIRTEEN

THE LOOK in William's eyes told her her life was about to change. No more teasing. No more daydreams and what-ifs. He was here and very real.

She wet her lips and opened her arms to receive him. There was nothing tentative about his kiss. She tasted the tart wine on his tongue. She sensed his need, which matched hers completely. She loved that when he was kissing her, he made her feel as if she were the center of his world.

He pulled back enough to look into her eyes. "I want to be with you, Daria. Are you sure that's something you're ready for?"

"Yes."

He stepped back and offered her his hand. When she'd been alone, waiting for him to arrive, she'd entertained several fantasies about making love to him—in the fabulous four-poster bed, in the shower and on the balcony, where they were now standing. But not in broad daylight. She wasn't that bold. And she liked that William apparently felt the same.

He closed the French doors and released the drapery swags before he pulled her into his arms again. She pressed as close to him as possible, wanting to feel every bit of him against her body.

His hands roamed freely, touching her hair, her back, her butt. "I love the shape and texture and substance of you," he said between kisses, placing both hands beneath her buttocks to pull her closer.

His arousal took her breath away. She'd been thinking about this moment for far too long. She put her hand between them to touch him. Even through his pants he felt hard and thick. She gave a tentative squeeze. He cupped her breast, murmuring something low and encouraging.

She used both hands to undo his belt. Her fingertips slipped under his waistband to figure out the clasp. "Oh," she gasped. Her fingers touched something far too soft and silky to be jockey shorts. "You're not wearing underwear."

"I know."

He let her have as long as she needed to decide how she felt about that. "I am," she told him. "Victoria's Secret. Violet lace."

"I can't wait to see it. Shall we adjourn to the bed?"

She nodded, surprised and pleased by how easy he made what could have been an awkward moment.

Before she could move, he bent over and scooped her into his arms. "Oh, my," she exclaimed, wrapping her arms around his neck. "Are you sure about this? I'm not that light."

"Not to fear. I've been working out." After he set her down, he flexed one arm in a he-man way. "I'm strong. But you don't need to be afraid. I promise."

He couldn't have said anything that touched her more. He not only listened when she spoke, he understood the subtext of her words. She'd joined the gym to feel more empowered. After everything that she'd been through, why wouldn't she?

She did feel empowered. And she knew exactly how to prove it. She sat on the edge of the bed and motioned him closer. "You realize, don't you," she asked, getting rid of his belt, then carefully easing down his zipper, "that they call this 'going commando?' I don't think I'll ever be able to watch another action-adventure movie without picturing you like this."

His chuckle rumbled through his diaphragm, but it stopped the moment she touched him. Lightly at first, then less lightly, with her tongue.

"Oh. Uh…" His vocabulary continued to diminish in a way that fueled her courage. She liked knowing she had the power to rob him of thought. She liked the taste of him, too.

"Daria, stop. No, don't. Yes, do. Oh, bloody hell, wait." His voice had changed and he pressed on her shoulders in a way that told her she should stop. She didn't want to, but she rocked back and looked up at him.

"Stop?"

He let out a shaky breath. "Yes, thank you. That was quite delightful, but I can't be greedy."

He boxed his way out of his shirt and stepped out of his pants that were bunched around his ankles, kicking them aside. With a truly wicked grin, he dropped to his knees on the thick rug. "Your turn."

"LOVE AND OBLIGATION shouldn't be used together in the same sentence, but they so often are."

William hadn't intended for their dinner conversation to take such a deep and serious turn, but Daria was the one who'd brought up the subject of marriage.

"Does that mean you'd think twice before marrying again?" he asked.

She gave a small, bitter laugh. "I'd think five or six times and still probably say 'No, thank you.' Although, that could be the divorce talking. There's nothing fun about the dissolution of a partnership gone bad."

"One of my clients has been married five times, although she'll only admit publicly to three. She calls herself a serial monogamist."

Daria laughed. She was a changed woman, he realized. So beautiful and radiating a glow that had made men's heads turn when she entered the B and B's small, private dining room. Yet, she was so profoundly without conceit he couldn't quite believe his good fortune to be with her.

"Did she ever propose to you?"

He refilled their wineglasses with a cabernet that was so intense and flavorful they'd both groaned with satisfaction when they'd tasted it. "Of course. Twice. Between husbands three and four—no, two and four."

"But you declined."

"I told her I'd have to drop her as a client if I married her. And since we were in the middle of negotiating a movie role, she let me off the hook. The second time, I think she asked simply to be nice. She didn't want me to feel left out."

Daria shook her head. "You have a strange business."

"In all honesty, it's not the business that's the problem, it's me. Some agents handle things differently."

"What do you mean?"

He took a large swallow of wine before answering. "I was thinking about this on the drive up. Something you said to me about my relationship with Bianca made me ask myself whether or not I had let my clients fill some obvious holes in my life. Wife. Children. Family."

"At least your devotion to your clients isn't taking anything away from a wife and children and family."

He cocked his head, waiting for her to elaborate. "My father was a workaholic, too, but he had a wife and kids at home," she said. "Mom used to say Dad would give his customers the shirt off his back. She seemed proud of that. I don't ever remember her complaining, except once, a month or two before she died. She said wistfully that she wished we'd taken more family vacations."

She shook her head. "I think I told you that my dad remarried right away after Mom died. And less than a month after that, he sold his business and retired to Florida. Just like that." She snapped her fingers. "I was too upset and hurt to look very deeply at why he couldn't wait a respectable amount of time. Isn't a year the traditional mourning period?"

He gave a noncommittal shrug. "Everything moves at a faster pace where I live. Even the mourning."

She seemed to agree. "In all honesty, I don't think Mom would have wanted him to wait. But it took me a long time to figure that out. Funny, huh?"

William didn't think so. After all, he was still working through issues that most men his age would have cleared up or, at the very least, drunk under the table by now.

"The last time I talked to him he sounded…content. And I'm glad."

He lifted his glass. "To your father."

"And yours," she added, touching the rim of her glass to his.

He wasn't ready to talk about his family situation, although he had promised himself to completely come clean before the night was over. He stabbed one of the scallops on his plate and cut it in half. "The *coquilles St. Jacques* is fabulous. Would you like to try a piece?"

She'd been so caught up in their conversation she'd barely tasted her filet, but she leaned forward and opened her mouth. He swirled the scallop in the rich cream sauce then quickly lifted it to her lips. She moaned, chewing. "Yum. Oh, man, that could be the best thing I've ever tasted. Weren't you smart to order it?"

"Would you like it? Here." He picked up the plate as if to pass it to her.

She swallowed hard. "No. I couldn't."

"Why not?"

"Because it's yours." Bruce would have stabbed her with his fork if she'd tried to take something off his plate.

William frowned, his mellow gray eyes turning stormy. Without hesitation, he reached across the table to switch their plates. "I'm sure you're mistaken. I ordered the filet. I'm a steak man," he said firmly, sounding very American. "I hate seafood."

Daria had to laugh to keep from tearing up. She realized in that unlikely moment that she was very possibly in love with this man. *Too soon! Too soon!* the voices in her head cried.

William raised his glass, drank heartily, then attacked her steak with genuine gusto. He chewed and swallowed. "Perfect. Just the way I like it. Bloody but not raw."

The moment of panic passed—probably thanks to all the wine she'd had. After making love that afternoon, they'd polished off their free bottle of wine, then gotten dressed and taken a tour of the winery, sampling quite a few other varieties.

She reminded herself that she was here to have fun, to try new things—like *coquilles St. Jacques*—and she wasn't going to let her overactive imagination ruin the moment.

William held his breath, waiting to see if whatever the hell just happened had passed. Maybe he shouldn't have switched plates. Did his autocratic manner remind her of her ex? William hoped not. He wanted her to feel entitled, not guilty, about enjoying the bounty they were sharing.

Once she started eating again, he relaxed. Her steak was good. The scallops were better, but he'd never tell her that.

"I know this is a sensitive subject, William," she said between bites, "and you're probably tired of me asking, but how is your father?"

Now? Should I tell her everything? Now?

He pushed his plate aside and sat forward, resting his elbows on the table. "He's gay."

She coughed. Twice. And swallowed hard. She pressed her napkin to her lips a moment, then asked in a tight voice, "Is that a side effect of the chemo?"

His low chuckle helped defuse some of the tension he'd felt building. And her clever quip made him even more certain how he felt about her. "No. I've known for… ever, I guess. Although he didn't spell it out for me until I reached the age of majority."

The humor in her eyes faded. "Does your mother know?"

"Yes, of course. I think most of the world does, although he's such a good man and so well-loved by his constituents that his sexuality never became an issue. He advocates for equality for everyone, across the board. In her own way, so does Mum."

"Is this part of the reason you didn't want to go back?"

Her question took him by surprise. "No. At least, I don't think so. I've visited him and Notty—" Her small gasp told him he'd left out an important detail. "Yes. I told you he wasn't *really* my uncle."

"But you didn't say he and your father—" She didn't complete the thought.

"They're unbelievably discreet. London is not San Francisco, and although times have changed, they prefer to maintain a certain image. They share a majestic old house that Notty inherited. It sits on a corner lot and has two entrances that date back to the war, when the family needed some rental income. Technically, Father and Notty have separate addresses, but they've lived together pretty much all of my life."

"And your mother is okay with that?"

"Yes. Whether she knew about Notty before or after she agreed not to abort me, I really can't say."

"I beg your pardon?"

"Most of this I've gotten from Notty. Mum doesn't like to talk about the past. Father is far too softhearted to rehash anything sordid or sad. But he did tell me once that Mum changed the way he looked at the world. She was a force to be reckoned with—like a small sun. And when he was orbiting in the range of her gravitational pull, he felt like a different person.

"They were prepared to call what happened between them a college fling and be done with it, until she found out she was pregnant. To make a long story short, Father insisted they get married. The plan was to divorce after a year or two. He would raise me on his own, allowing her the opportunity to follow her lifelong dream of saving the world's poorest children."

"But they never divorced."

He shook his head. "Eventually Notty and Father reconciled. Apparently, Uncle was not thrilled by the whole marriage and child concept, at first. But he warmed to me after a few years." He polished off the last of his wine.

"It sounds like a British soap opera, doesn't it? That's why I don't talk about it."

She reached across the table to touch his hand. "I don't know, I've never watched one. But I think your parents were very brave. Especially your father. As you said, times have changed, but forty years ago, circumstances were very different. And being a single parent—gay or straight—is no cup of tea. No English pun intended." She smiled so sweetly, so kindly, he wanted to stand up and hug her, never letting go.

He flagged down their waiter. "We'd like to take this with us," he said, pointing to his steak. "And could we get our dessert to go, also?"

"We have a black forest cake that people have been known to travel thousands of miles for."

Daria shook her head modestly. Her lips said, "No, thank you," but her eyes said, "Two pieces, please."

"Two pieces," William said. "Is there flatware in the room?"

The waiter beamed. "Yes, sir. And we could send along a split of our very special port, if you'd care to give it a try. The combination is heavenly."

"Perfect. May we have the check?"

Daria sat up, adjusting the neckline of her midnight-blue silk dress. "I thought we'd put it on the room. My treat."

William forced his gaze away from the creamy skin and soft arc of her breasts to give her a that's-my-bill-don't-even-think-about-it look.

She blinked in mock terror. "Wow. I bet people quake in fear of that glare."

He snickered. "Not usually, but my pride simply can't take any more blows, Daria. You've insisted on paying for the room. I *will* get dinner. Are we clear on that?"

Her laugh was something beautiful and oddly healing. Sharing the truth about his family hadn't been as painful as he'd expected. Maybe because forgiveness was such an integral part of who she was. She didn't see someone's flaws; she saw how they acquired those flaws and empathized with their pain.

The waiter returned a moment later with their check and a small green bottle. William paid in cash, adding a hearty tip. He wasn't in the mood to wait for a credit card to be processed.

"Shall we?" he asked, extending a hand to Daria. "Dessert on the balcony, my dear?"

"Ah, William," she flirted coyly. "You do know the way to a woman's…heart."

Daria quickly slipped her feet into the too-tight-but-terribly-sexy shoes she'd borrowed from Julie and took William's hand. The night had been magical so far, even with the serious dinner conversation.

With their cleverly wrapped bag of goodies in Daria's hand and William carrying the mini-bottle of port, they made their way to their room. William opened the door using the key she'd given him earlier. That act alone had made her feel bold, powerful and a tiny bit brazen.

She lingered in the doorway, trailing her finger across the shoulder of his dinner jacket. "You're incredibly sexy. You know that, don't you?"

"I grew up watching old American movies with Clark Gable, Cary Grant, Tyrone Power and the like," he told her, shrugging the handsome white linen from his lean, beautifully contoured shoulders. Beneath it he wore a black, washed silk shirt that molded to his chest. No tie. He grinned. "Our cinema was very small and my nanny was very particular. She had her favorites, and those were the shows we saw. Over and over."

"You could do worse for role models," Daria said, kicking off her shoes as she crossed the room to open the patio door. The temperature was considerably cooler than it had been during the day, but she suddenly felt too warm.

William opened the port and poured them each a glass—a juice glass. "Have I told you honestly how glad I am to be here with you? Surprised, but pleased."

She swirled the glass, releasing a bountiful bouquet. "Why surprised? You knew I was attracted to you in Sentinel Pass. You kissed me."

He stood beside her, their shoulders touching, looking across the moonlit vineyard. Daria swore that if she looked hard enough she'd see the glow of fireflies, even though she knew that was impossible. But the area had such a magical feel to it.

Or was the magic what was happening between her and William?

He set both of their glasses on the flat, wooden arm of the closest chair and pulled her into an embrace. "You are so beautiful. Keats couldn't do justice to your beauty."

She hid her face beneath her splayed fingers. "Not true. You're embarrassing me."

"I shall forever regret not paying closer attention in literature class. I feel woefully inadequate to wax poetic about the perfection of this cleft, this hollow, this—"

"Quit," she cried, squirming as his tongue tickled a spot along her neck. "I'll concede that I clean up pretty good. Better than the person who shall remain nameless, though, or he might have taken me out more often, right?"

William studied her face a moment, then, apparently not satisfied with what he saw, took her hand and led her back indoors. He invited her to sit on the butter-yellow sofa, then returned for their port. He closed the door firmly and locked it, then looked at her. "Are there ghosts here that we need to exorcise? I'd like to know before I kiss you. Because we both know where that leads."

CHAPTER FOURTEEN

WILLIAM WATCHED HER as she thought about what he was asking. Even that oblique reference to her ex had worried him. He wanted some reassurance that she was here—with him—because she felt even a small degree of what he was feeling. "Tell me this isn't payback."

"No, William, this is not a threesome," she said, leaning forward. "It's you and me. Period."

The strap of her dress slipped over her shoulder, exposing a hint of black lace. The unintentional peek-a-boo turned him rock-hard. He wanted to believe her. Badly.

He sat beside her. "Good." He tugged on the bodice of her dress—one tantalizing fraction of an inch at a time until he could see the imprint of her highly aroused nipple straining against the fabric of her bra. "I'm a worldly kind of guy, but I don't share well with others."

"M-me, either," she stammered, threading her fingers through his hair to press him closer.

He rubbed his index finger in a slow, suggestive circle around her nipple. He watched her expression change; her eyes narrowed to passionate slits. She drew her bottom lip between her teeth.

"That feels good," she whispered, arching against his touch.

He slipped his hand into the cup of the stretchy material to free her breast and take the nipple into his mouth. He licked, nibbled and sucked, just as she'd done with his body the first time they made love. Her breathing turned ragged. Her hands dropped to his shoulders, urging him to move things along.

He angled their bodies so he could unzip the back of the dress and unhook her bra. William watched as she wriggled free of her clothing. His mouth started to water.

She looked down at herself critically. "Two babies. Nursing. My breasts aren't what they used to be."

He let out a low snarl. "Please. You dare defame these spectacular, womanly globes?"

He took her hands and placed them where her bra had been seconds earlier. "Feel their weight and substance, Daria. If they've changed, it's for the better. They couldn't be any more beautiful."

Her head cocked to one side and he could tell she was considering his words carefully. A second later, she looked at him and smiled. "Okay. They aren't bad."

He covered her hands with his then leaned in to bury his face in the fleshy V. He inhaled deeply before tackling her playfully. "You're far too modest. As an agent, I guarantee you I could book your breasts as a body double for several less well-endowed starlets," he said. "Not that I would. These beauties are far too classy."

Her laughter made her jiggle in a most provocative way. He repeated his earlier attention on the other breast until Daria was moaning again. Then he worked his way lower.

Her dress was bunched around her waist, so he pulled her to her feet and worked it downward. Her panties were miniscule but sexy as hell. "Those Victoria's Secret people know their lace, but if you don't mind…?"

She took them off, then gave him a pointed once-over. "I'd say one of us is terribly overdressed for this party."

Within a heartbeat, he was as naked as she.

They'd made love that afternoon, explored each other's bodies and created a new language, but this time was different. They knew each other better, and William, for one, had a great deal more invested. He loved her. He could admit it now. But could he show her how much he loved her without scaring her away? He knew his timing was problematic, ghostly ex-husband or not.

She seemed to sense his hesitation and took the initiative. She led him to the bed and pulled back the covers. "We have all night," she said. "Isn't that an amazing thing?"

Yes. All night. Her words took away some of his anxiety. This wasn't about performance, it was about love.

And he had all night to show her exactly what she meant to him.

She scooted to the center of the king-size mattress and patted the place beside her. "Are you coming?"

"Oh, yes, my dear. Again and again and again. Now, where to begin? Ah, but of course, the toes."

She giggled like a little girl when he picked up her foot and started kissing each digit. Her laughter faded as he started kissing his way upward, pausing to nibble the inside of her knee and run his tongue back and forth across her inner thigh.

"Ooh," she cried as he progressed farther upward.

That fabulous mix of perfume and pure woman beckoned. Her recent spa treatment showed a perfect, V-shaped arrow of pubic hair directing him to her warm, moist core. He tested the springy curls and parted them in search of that special spot. She bucked involuntarily, letting him know he was close.

"Tell me, Daria, what do you like?"

"Huh? Oh, um…well. Nobody's ever asked me that. But what you're doing now. That's nice." He flicked the tip of his tongue back and forth across the little jewel he'd uncovered. "V-very nice. I…like…that."

As his tongue toyed with her clitoris, he slipped his middle finger into her hot, juicy folds. She let out a welcoming cry that nearly unmanned him.

His body was resonating with her need, her readiness. He wanted to join her but she deserved more.

He spread her legs and sank lower, putting his tongue where his finger had been a moment earlier. She moved against his mouth, using him but giving back as much as he offered. He felt her climax build to a crest even before she cried out. And while her muscles still pulsed, he grabbed the condom from the bedside table where he'd stashed the package earlier.

His hands were clumsy in his haste and he couldn't get it open. The urgency of the moment made him fumble until he swore. "Bugger."

"Let me," Daria said, taking the package from him. She pushed him down so he was lying on his back. "When you've opened as many juice packs and bags of corn chips as I have, you get really good at certain things."

The ripping sound was most delightful. "Ta-da," she said with a sexy grin.

William sucked in a breath, which he held as she slowly, deliberately unrolled the prophylactic down the length of his penis. She surveyed her work, licking her lips like a starved woman. "You're beautiful, too. Did your English poets ever create an ode to a really great cock?"

He laughed, surprised and a little shocked to hear such

a word coming from her mouth. She looked at him several seconds. He felt her hesitate. "What? Is there a problem?" Was this the moment she changed her mind?

She inhaled deeply, drawing his attention back to her bare breasts. He was so distracted he only caught the last part of her question. "…on top?"

Me on top? You on top? He hedged his bet. "Obviously, I'm easy. Whatever you like."

Her smile was bold, her actions decisive. She quickly straddled him. After that, his brain went silent. No worries, no hesitation as his body eased slowly, deliciously into the hot, wet place that welcomed it.

"THANK GOD WE HAVE food and drink," Daria said a good while afterward.

They were snuggled under the twisted messy sheet, William's head resting on her chest. A position that allowed her to play with his hair. The man had great hair. Shiny, springy, healthy. And it smelled sexy. She loved his hair.

She loved more than his hair, she realized with a start. *I love him.*

He lifted his head, apparently sensitive to her slightest shift in mood. "Are you hungry?"

"Ravenous for something chocolate," she answered, more out of a need to move and digest her sudden revelation than to actually put food in her belly.

He rolled away, giving her room to slide off the bed. "And I want to show you the negligee my friend, Julie, gave me. Utterly scandalous. But I promised I'd wear it."

He got out of bed and walked to the table where he'd left their glasses. When he bent over to top them off with the remaining port, her mouth started watering and her lower body tingled with excitement. *Good lord,* she thought, *I've turned into a sex addict.* But she knew that wasn't true. She wanted him. Not any old Tom, Dick or Harry. She wanted William. Unfortunately.

"That's a serious frown," William observed, handing her a glass. "Was our lovemaking that terrible?"

She made a loud raspberry. "Fishing for compliments, are we?" She sighed. "I was just thinking how good it was, actually. Fabulous. You've completely ruined me for other men."

"Do there have to be other men?"

She wasn't ready for this discussion, but the one thing she knew for certain was that she could speak her mind with William without fear of creating a firestorm. "I have a lot of people—and every single woman's magazine—giving me relationship advice. And none of it is the same. Date, don't date. Wait, don't wait. Eat dessert first, too much of a good thing is bad for you. Who knows? Where's the cake?"

He returned to the bed, paper container in hand. "Do you want my advice?"

She tried a sip of wine to calm the sudden spike in her heart rate. "Yes."

"I say screw those know-it-alls. You're you. I'm me. And we get to decide what works and doesn't work."

"We do?"

"Why not? You can't change the past, but you can learn from it. How better to learn than through experience?"

She hesitated a moment, then pushed the pastry box aside. "The cake can wait. I'd like to *experience* a little more lovemaking, first."

His broad smile was all the answer she needed. They moved together without words. They'd learned shortcuts from their previous adventures. They threw themselves into the pure heat and sensation that had worked so magically earlier. There were moans of pleasure and groans of intense urgency. Some hers, some his. But for Daria, the only thing that mattered was the sensation that started between her legs and quickly swelled to encompass every cell of her body. Her mind lost track of everything but the need that built to a tantalizing precipice then radiated outward, leaving her shaking.

He was right. Every beginning had to start somewhere. Where this connection would take them, nobody could say. But she knew one thing. He was her dessert. And she planned to enjoy every morsel.

CHAPTER FIFTEEN

"WOULD YOU BE EMBARRASSED if I told you that last night I experienced the most fantastic orgasm any woman has ever experienced in recorded history?"

"Which one?" William asked, truly curious. "There were several, as I recall."

She held up three fingers that she wiggled, grinning. "The first was…well…orgasmic. And the third was beautiful. It nearly brought me to tears. But the middle one. The one that prompted our chocolate orgy? Yeah. That was classic."

He agreed, although he might have argued that number four—their early morning rhapsody—had moved them both to a climax as synchronized as humanly possible. Instead of arguing the point, he leaned back against the gaudy red-and-green plaid stadium blanket that he'd found in the picnic tote. They'd skipped the traditional breakfast part of their accommodations that morning in favor of sex, leftover steak and coffee. Moira's amazing picnic tote had provided lunch.

"In answer to your question, no, I am not embarrassed. I'm seriously considering taking out a full-page ad in *Rolling Stone* to share this accomplishment with the world."

She tossed a tiny piece of crust at him. Then she sat up straight, took a deep breath and hugged herself. "I am so happy, William. At this moment. In this place. With you. Thank you."

He stretched out, interlacing his fingers beneath his head as a cushion. He felt exactly the same. Satiated. Complete. Magnanimous to the point that the minute he returned home he planned to clear his calendar and invite Daria and her daughters to Disneyland.

What about your trip home?

As if reading his mind, she said, "Do you have any photos of your parents? In your wallet? Or on your laptop?"

My laptop? He cocked his head to look at her.

"I saw it in the trunk when we were loading all that wine you purchased yesterday."

"As a matter of fact, Notty's been scanning old photos recently and copying me by the dozens. Why do you ask?"

"I put together a short slide show set to music for Mary's funeral. I don't suppose you were there, were you?"

He shook his head.

"Me neither. That's one of the reasons I did it. Finding the right program was a challenge, but once I figured it out, I really liked being able to tell a person's story through pictures and music. I don't know if there's a call for that kind of thing in the marketplace, but I'd like to do it again."

He smiled, trying to visualize what she meant. The only videos he was familiar with involved rock music and all sorts of outrageous elements. It took him several seconds to realize she wasn't speaking in the abstract. She wanted to do this for him.

"What kind of video are we talking about?"

"Relax. It's not work. It'll be fun. And I'll get to know you better."

He didn't say anything right away. What could it hurt, he asked himself? So she saw a few old family photos. So she saw the big and important lives of his parents and felt sympathy—maybe a tiny bit of revulsion—for the surly, always frowning little boy they'd left behind.

No doubt she'd come to the same conclusion William had when he flicked through the shots. He was born a loner. He was an observer, not a participant. And he had not the slightest idea how to be part of a family.

Better she finds out now rather than later, right?

"Very well. Shall we get started?"

"These are spectacular photos, William. Your father is almost as handsome as you are."

He looked up from his phone, where he was checking some music apps for a certain song he claimed would fit perfectly with the slide show she was assembling. Claimed being the operative word—his obvious lack of enthusiasm for this project was a little disheartening, but she didn't let it stop her from going forward.

She loved working with this medium to tell the story of a person's life. Her sense of accomplishment once she exported the final version of "Mary's Life in Pictures" to Cal and Libby had assuaged some of the anguish she felt over missing the funeral. And the positive, glowing feedback she'd gotten for her efforts had been a nice thing at a particularly difficult time in her life.

"Look at this clip, William. It's of your parents' meeting in Boston. They look so young. And serious. Your mother has a sort of part-nerd, part-hippie look going. And there are some great shots of the three of you in England. You might well have been the cutest toddler on the planet." She grinned. "Of course, that was before my daughters were born."

He rolled over and shimmied closer.

She felt his warmth even though they weren't touching. She breathed deeply to smell him. She wanted to memorize that scent forever. She had no idea if it was cologne or soap or hair product or what. But on him, it was intoxicating.

"I was looking for a song that typified the early 1970s," he told her. "Something by the Beatles is the obvious choice, plus Mum once told me she had a terrible crush on Paul McCartney. But Father was a Stones fan. They had one of those Coke-Pepsi kinds of rivalries."

She hit the play arrow.

His eyes opened wider and he watched intently, a smile slowly coming into play on his lips. "'Ferry Cross the Mersey.' Nice pick. This is…very good, Daria. I'm impressed. Especially considering you've never met either of them."

"Anonymity provides objectivity," she told him. "Most of the homemade videos I've watched could have benefited from a little editing. It's much more difficult when you're emotionally attached to the person in the photos."

The clip ended and the song stopped. He looked at her. "What's next?"

She angled the laptop for him to see. She'd grouped another few shots together. He wasn't in any of them, but she'd realized how important these images were in telling the story of his parents. She also understood more clearly why he felt disconnected from these two, amazingly accomplished people.

"Good. Father's first election. I saw more of Notty than Father that year."

His tone was casual but she knew that blasé ruse was designed to mask his pain. She clicked on a shot of William and his mother standing before a mud hut of some kind. "The date on this one is the same year. You must have traveled with your mother more of the time because your father was so busy."

He stared at the image for several seconds before he shrugged. "If you say so. I can't remember that trip, specifically. All of these strange and exotic places began to blur after a time."

Her heart felt pinched by the image of a lonely little boy tossed back and forth between his busy parents like a sack of potatoes. She couldn't help but marvel at his resiliency and resourcefulness. She hoped her children would come away from this divorce with something good and lasting after all that she and Bruce had put them through.

Speaking of her children... She nudged the computer off her lap and stood up. "Break time. I need to call the girls and see how they're doing." She stretched, knowing William was looking at her. His gaze was never a burden or intrusive. He made her feel beautiful. Sexy. In fact, after she called home, she might suggest a communal dip in their room's oversize tub.

She grabbed her phone from the dresser and walked to the balcony. "Yesterday was Hailey's second dance lesson. I'm dying to know how it went. The first got mixed reviews. Hailey loved the dancing part, but hated learning the same steps over and over."

William smiled. "Does your ex-mother-in-law know how to e-mail photos? I'd love to see the little pigeon."

"I doubt it, but I'll ask. Bruce was supposed to be down from Sacramento for a visit. He might be able to handle it."

The question disappeared from thought the moment a male voice answered the phone. "Hello, Daria. Mom said you were going to call. The girls are outside. I wanted to talk to you before I give them the phone."

"Hello, Bruce. I thought you were happy communicating through my lawyer."

"That was before you went over to the dark side."

"What does that mean?"

"You're cavorting with the enemy. It's one thing to blink your pretty long lashes like a helpless, pathetic victim so he'd fly you around the country for free, but it's quite another to sleep with the guy to thank him for the blackmail booty."

Blackmail booty? "What are you talking about, Bruce? Wait. I don't want to know. William is a friend, and we're having a very nice time. I'm sure that irks you to no end, but I don't care. Please put the girls on."

"Fine. I will. But don't you want to know how he got his hands on that shit he threatened to use against me? Hell, he had some nerve talking about bribes when you know damn well that so-called proof came from a healthy under-the-table transaction. Is he really an agent, or is that his spy cover?"

"He's not a spy, Bruce. I don't know what you're talking about nor do I care. Could I please speak to Hailey or Miranda?"

He didn't answer. She thought he'd hung up but after a few seconds of dead air she heard the high-pitched squeal of her youngest daughter's voice. "Mommy. I danced. On my toes. Sorta. It was cool. Really cool. I wanna go again next Saturday. Can I?"

"Sure, honey. Tell me all about it," Daria said, but as she half listened, her mind was working feverishly in the background trying to pinpoint something that Bruce had

said that was bothering her. *Spy...bribes...blackmail.*
Pure craziness. Then it hit her. *That he threatened to use
against me.* When had William had any direct contact
with Bruce, other than those few minutes in Sentinel
Pass?

She damn well intended to find out.

CHAPTER SIXTEEN

WILLIAM LOOKED UP from the piece of art Daria had created. He was half-afraid he might humiliate himself by breaking down in tears. She'd captured certain elements of his parents' romance and first years together so eloquently, he could almost believe they had been in love. Not the comfortable mutually beneficial arrangement they presently shared, but the kind of blood-pumping passion and attraction he felt toward Daria. And hoped—was fairly convinced—she felt for him. Even though neither of them had said a word about love.

"Is everything okay?" He could tell something was wrong. He pushed aside the computer and leaped to his feet. "What's wrong? Did Bruce do something? Is it Hailey? Her breathing?"

She shook her head but didn't answer. In the space it took for her to get control of her emotions so she could speak, William experienced a precognition of doom. Something had happened to effectively kill the harmony and goodwill between them.

"When did you speak with Bruce?"

A dose of acid hit his stomach. He knew she didn't mean that morning in South Dakota. "He called me on my way to the airport. The same day I flew up to give you the file."

"The information you gave me to do with as I saw fit."

He didn't like the severity of her tone. "Yes."

She advanced a step and faced him, arms akimbo. "But then you took away my choice by threatening him behind my back."

"*He* called *me,* Daria."

"Did you threaten him?"

"He basically threatened me if I didn't show up." She waited for him to answer her question. "Yes. I'd read the file. I knew he was full of shit. I snapped. I told him if he didn't back off and do everything in his power to make your divorce go smoothly, I would ruin him."

She walked to the window and looked out. She didn't say anything for nearly a minute, then sighed. "Bruce was always making decisions *for* me. He never understood why I'd get upset about not being consulted over small, inconsequential things. Things like which phone company to use, what newspaper subscription to order. Dumb things. But every choice he took away made me feel smaller and less important. Feeling insignificant is a terrible way to live."

He hurried to her side. "I'm sorry. It was never my intention to make you feel badly. Just the opposite. I hoped that by playing the bad guy, you wouldn't have to make that choice."

She moved a step away to avoid his touch. "You're right. It's not a big deal. I'm probably overreacting. We both know I've been known to do that." Her words were conciliatory, but he could tell she was still upset. "Listen, I know we had plans for dinner tonight, but I'm feeling a little wiped out. Emotional. I've had a wonderful time this weekend—better than I could have dreamed for a first date. But I think I need to leave."

"You're leaving? Just like that?"

"I need some space to work things out in my head.

I'm sorry, William. I know you're not Bruce. You're not anything like Bruce, but going behind my back like that was so Bruce."

William had no excuse. He didn't know how to plead his defense when she was right. He'd felt superior, triumphant, self-righteous that afternoon at the bar when he'd verbally pinned Bruce to the wall. At that moment, he'd bested the bully as his father had so many years before.

But hadn't he always maintained he had nothing in common with his father? Nothing. Which of his other core beliefs were equally flawed, he wondered?

"Daria," he said, taking her shoulders between his hands. Her immediate flinch stabbed him in the heart and he dropped his arms. "Please, don't go. Let's talk about this. I'm sorry. I made a mistake."

She glanced at the bed where his computer sat open to a photo of his parents. "We all make mistakes, William. Like you said, it's how we learn. I'm simply trying to make sure I don't repeat the same one over and over."

She walked to the dresser and pulled open the top drawer.

"What about the slide show?" William asked, desperate to distract her from leaving. "It's only half done. Stay. We can work from opposite sides of the room. I'll sleep on the couch tonight."

She gave him a smile but shook her head. "I can't. I need to think. And plan. My grandfather invited me to move to Sentinel Pass after school lets out. He even had Libby's brother design an addition to the house so the girls could each have a bedroom."

She realized now that one of the reasons she'd put off answering Cal had been because of her feelings for William. She knew that his business was bicoastal.

Adding a stop in the middle of the country every now and then sounded like a pretty terrible way of conducting a relationship.

"Daria, please stay. I know you're angry with me, but we have something besides sex between us. It's real and good and filled with potential. Tell me you know that."

She didn't know anything anymore. "I know I need time to think. I can't do that while sharing a room with you. I feel too much when I'm with you. Remember when I told you you tend to put people on pedestals? Well, maybe I did the same thing to you. I told Julie you were my hero, but when you actually tried to save me—and I'm sure you had good intentions—I discovered I didn't want you to. I really do want to stand on my own two feet and feel as though I have control over my life."

"Does that mean you're never going to let yourself fall in love again? I've made a lot of mistakes in my life, Daria, but letting you go without telling you I love you would probably be the biggest."

"You don't mean that."

"I do."

"Well, I don't have any faith in the word. Bruce claimed to love me, too. Screw love. I'm sick of it. I'm going home. Regroup. Plan for the future. Period."

William looked hurt. Stunned. Why wouldn't he be? He was a terrific catch...if she were looking for love. But she wasn't.

"But you have a point...about your parents' video. That was my idea and I hate leaving things undone."

Plus, she felt good about the way the project was coming together. She'd be damned if she'd let either of the men in her life ruin her fledgling sense of accomplishment.

After she finished packing her few pieces of clothing

and sexy shoes, she zipped the suitcase and snapped the handle into its extended position. She still needed to get her cosmetics out of the bathroom, but first she walked to the bed and sat.

Drawing the computer onto her lap, she quickly typed away for a minute. "I'm copying the rest of the photos and my rough draft to an online storage site. When I get home, I'll finish the video and send you the link."

A few minutes later, she gave him a hug goodbye and left.

She couldn't say why she was leaving. Was she mad at William for doing something very Bruce-like, or was she afraid she might have fallen in love with the wrong man? Again.

She wasn't even sure she wanted to know the answer. All she knew for sure was that she had to go.

CHAPTER SEVENTEEN

NAUGHTON HAD WARNED HIM. "He's lost a lot of weight, William. And the drugs have left him a bit unsteady so he's using a walker."

Still, the moment William first spotted his father, his knees nearly gave out beneath him.

"William," his father called, his voice raspier than before, but filled with joy. "You're here. I'm so glad to see you. Come in, come in. I look like hell but I'm not contagious."

Whatever William thought he might say or do when he met his father again disappeared from mind. Here was the man who'd read to him every night that he was home, bought him his first bike, taken him to Paris when he was ten—because William asked what was so great about the Eiffel Tower.

"Father," he said, struggling to keep the sadness from his tone. Notty had demanded William "keep a stiff upper lip—as tired and cliché as that sounds. We must help him fight the good fight and never let him see us cry."

The two embraced, a process made even more awkward than usual because of the walker. "How was your flight, son? Did I hear you flew commercial?"

"From JFK. I hired a young pilot to be my copilot to the East coast then hopped a Virgin Air flight. Very nice, actually. I slept most of the way."

"I've heard they have seats that turn into beds. Lovely. Let's sit, shall we?" His father's breathlessness made William reach out to help, but Notty, who was standing a foot or so away, shook his head furiously.

"Where's Mum?" William asked, pacing his stride to baby steps as they slowly made their way into the study. William's eyes went wide as he took in the changes to the room that had been off-limits his entire childhood. Not until he'd returned from college had he been invited into this inner sanctum to share a brandy with his father and uncle.

"On her way. Should be here any time."

The leather tufted couch and matching armchair had been pushed aside to make room for a hospital bed. A moveable tray table was cluttered with medical supplies, a small vase of flowers and a plastic upchuck basin William remembered being given as a child when he was ill.

His father paused. "I know," he said, his tone resigned. "It looks pathetic, doesn't it? But the place is actually quite functional. Your mum can work on the computer while Naughton drinks my whiskey in front of the fire." He took a shaky breath. "And I suck down my oxygen."

"Would you like to lie down, James?"

Father gave Notty a dark look. "No. I'll be lying down for eternity soon enough. I'm going to have a conversation with my son. Leave us a bit, will you?"

The last he added less antagonistically than he'd started out. Notty gave a mock salute. "I'll make tea."

William took his father's elbow and helped him to the chair. "The ottoman, too, son. If you don't mind."

William's hands were trembling as he gently lifted his father's narrow, skinny feet to the overstuffed stool.

He tucked a woolen throw around him without being asked. "Is there anything else you need? A drink of water, perhaps?"

He shook his head. His near baldness wasn't as big a shock as his overall emaciation had been. James had started losing his hair in his thirties and had worn it closely trimmed for most of William's life. And while he'd never been fat, he had sported a bit of a spare tire around his middle for the past ten years or so. That small cushion of reserves was gone now.

As if guessing his son's thoughts, James said, "It's amazing how fast the body starts to fall to pieces once you place yourself in the hands of the medical experts. Specialists are the worst," he said, scowling. "They treat the one aspect of the disease they know best while entirely ignoring the host body. I told your mother recently how proud I was that she remained a general physician." He looked at William sadly. "Of course, now she's giving herself a hard time for bringing remedial health care to the children of the world instead of finding a cure for cancer. Imagine that? Lamenting all the good you've done simply because someone you loved was stricken by an incurable disease."

"I used to wish she were in research," William admitted. "A friend in school's parents were both doctors employed by some sort of pharmaceutical company. They were home every night. I was quite envious."

Father nodded, chuckling. "But did your chum ever sleep in a tent on the savannah? I bet not."

Or dispensed vaccines in Mumbai, breakfasted with monkeys in the Philippines, held the hand of a child dying of AIDS in some hellhole country that changed its name before William could memorize the previous one. "She helped a lot of people, didn't she?"

"More than we could possibly know."

"As did you," he admitted. "You were too modest to brag, but Notty's kept me abreast of the laws you helped bring about over the years. Civil rights. Human rights. Including the one about a patient's right to die with dignity."

Father laughed softly. "I can honestly say I didn't intend to be a test case of it. Life is a puzzle. Sometimes the pieces go together to form a picture completely different from what you'd envisioned."

"I agree," William said, thinking about Daria and the blissful future he'd imagined with her. For that brief moment in time, he'd seen it so clearly. And now his slate of dreams was blank.

"Are you happy, son? In California?" Father said the word as though it was the furthest, most exotic place on the planet. "I know you're a success in your field. You have famous friends. Naughton is most impressed, although he pretends not to be for my sake."

William sat forward, hands woven together. "What do you mean? Why for your sake?"

Father patted William's hand. His skin was dry and slick, like parchment paper. Old people's skin. *You're not that old,* he almost cried.

"Naughton has spent most his life protecting me from life's slings and arrows. His way of returning the favor from when we were young." He closed his eyes and smiled, no doubt recalling that earlier time. "You know the story."

"Tell it again. I've forgotten," William lied.

"Notty was small for his age—didn't get a growth spurt until seventeen or so. Youngest son. His sisters used to dress him in bonnets. Children can be cruel. I rather enjoyed standing up to bullies. Fancied myself a hero. Probably what pushed me into public service."

Father opened his eyes and sighed. "But once I was elected, I became a public figure and, in the minds of some, an open target. Notty created a public fiction to keep our private lives private. We told you, though, when you were older."

"Dad, you know I'm proud of you, don't you?" William asked. "My childhood was unconventional, but I've come to realize that different doesn't have to be a bad thing. Don't people always want what they can't have? I wanted the kind of family my chums had. The kind I saw in the movies. The kind I created in my mind."

"Hollywood's universal truth?"

"In part. I also saw my friends leading *normal* lives."

"With *normal* parents," Father put in, his tone rueful and a bit sad.

William turned his hands palm up in a gesture of acceptance. "A good friend told me recently that dysfunctional is the new normal."

They both laughed.

"Well, aren't we a happy bunch," a voice said from the doorway. "Hello, my son. Come give your old mum a hug."

William did as requested. Their embrace was the longest he could remember. She'd aged since their last visit. The lines around her mouth and eyes were more pronounced and her hair was considerably grayer, but the cut reminded him of Daria—spunky and unapologetic. "It's so good to see you, dear. Thank you for coming," she added softly, for his ears only.

Notty walked in a few moments later carrying a large tray. The four of them sat round the fire, talking and sipping tea, until someone noticed that James had fallen asleep. "The drugs," Notty said. "He's in and out all day."

"And night," Mum said, squeezing Notty's hand tenderly.

William understood then how amazing his family truly was. Unique in composition but strong and whole where it mattered. "I've fallen in love with a wonderful woman and managed to self-sabotage our relationship inside a fortnight," he announced to his profound surprise. "What should I do?"

Mum looked at Notty, who nodded. In unison, they said, "Grovel."

As his mother refilled his cup, she said, "Would this be Daria you're talking about?"

"Yes."

"Hmm...interesting. She's not talking to you, but I received an e-mail from her a few minutes ago."

"From Daria?"

She nodded. "She explained that she was a friend of my son's and the two of you had been collaborating on a video of some sort. She copied my e-mail address from a post that Notty had sent you. Clever girl."

William felt a jangle of nerves collaborate in his belly. "That was it?"

His mother smiled. "No, dear. She included an attachment." She glanced toward his father's desk. "I forwarded it to James's computer. His is newer and has a larger screen. Shall we?" She motioned them to follow her.

William hesitated. "But Father—"

"Is awake," James interjected. "Someone help me up. I want to see this. Whatever it is."

"A video of some sort, dear. From William's girl-friend."

"She's not— We broke up…and this can't be the video. She told me I could view it then pass it along if I thought you'd want to see it."

Notty leaned over James, who was seated in the desk chair, to hit the play button. "Change of plan, I believe."

The opening image was a black-and-white image of his father at age five. A handsome, clear-eyed, smiling lad holding an obese spaniel. "Brigit," Father cried. "Best dog I ever owned."

As "Somewhere Over The Rainbow" played softly in the background, the photos marched on through Father's life, introducing his parents, an older brother long dead, schoolmates, and, of course, Naughton.

"You really were a skinny kid," William said, giving the man a slight poke with his elbow.

"But look how lovely he was when your father and I met," Laurel said. "So handsome and dashing. I would have been hard-pressed to pick between them if I hadn't already fallen in love with your father."

The statement might have seemed odd given the fact both men were gay, had it not been the truth. And seeing a steady sequence of images placing the three friends together—along with a new baby—he understood. They truly loved each other—all of them.

And they loved him, too. The same way Daria loved Miranda and Hailey. But those two adorable children could no more hold their parents' marriage together than William had been able to make his family conform to some cinematic ideal. And yet, that's what William had tried to do. Every time he went to some far-off land to see his mother, he would beg her to come home. And every weekend that his father was in residence, William would try to make him act like other fathers.

As he watched the slide show move forward, he could almost hear Daria's voice in his head, saying, "There's that damn pedestal again." He shook his head in wonder. He had a family. An amazing family. He simply never appreciated it because he was too busy trying to make it perfect.

His love for Daria expanded exponentially. He would grovel, beg, do whatever penance she asked of him for however long it took to convince her that their story was bigger than its rocky beginning.

"Daria has an excellent eye for storytelling," Father said. "This is a life I would be proud to live. And I did." He looked at William, his eyes glistening. "How lucky is that?"

William had no words, but his heart had never felt as full. He watched the rest of the video in silence, holding his mother when she started to cry. Notty tried his best to keep the moment from becoming too maudlin by interjecting comments such as, "Look, James, you had hair then," and, "Didn't I warn you that those striped pants would come back to haunt you?"

The video ended with an image William couldn't remember posing for, at first. Then he recognized the oak tree behind this house. His graduation from college. William and his mother stood, arms linked, with the two men on either side of them.

"I remember this day so clearly. We were all so proud of you, William," his mother said, kissing his cheek.

"Top of your class, of course," Father added. "With your bright future opening up before you."

William swallowed the lump in his throat. "But I let you down. I'm not a doctor. Or a lawyer. Or a glorified paper pusher," he joked. They all knew Naughton was much, much more.

The three of them looked at each other and broke out laughing. "Is that truly what you think? That we're in any way disappointed in you, darling?" his mother asked.

Father looked at William. "Son, we've made our share of mistakes, singularly and as a collective, trying to raise a child we all loved. If we somehow made you believe that we harbored certain ambitions for you, I apologize. All we ever wanted for you was to be happy."

Notty and Mum nodded in agreement.

William didn't need to say anything—to them. But there was one person he couldn't wait to call.

"Can we watch it again?" Mum asked.

"Of course, but, if you'll excuse me, I'm going to call the movie's director and say thank you."

"Tell her we love it," Father said.

"Tell her we want to meet her," Mum said.

"Tell her you apologize for whatever you did and that she was right. Women love to be right," Notty put in.

"Because we usually are."

That, of course, set off a great debate which made William shake his head and chuckle. He was still smiling when he reached his room, but his expression turned serious when he pulled up Daria's number on his phone. She'd sent this video without running it past him for a reason. In contract talks, this sort of overture meant negotiations were still on the table. Or was this Daria's classy way of saying goodbye?

He held his breath as he waited for the call to go through.

She picked up right away, even though it was very, very early in California. "William. I was hoping you'd call."

"Your video is amazing. Not a dry eye in the house. Thank you."

"You're welcome."

There was a momentary pause, then they both spoke at once.

"I'm so sorry, William."

"I'm such an idiot, Daria."

William's heart filled with hope. "I love you, Daria. I truly, honestly, completely love you. And, some day, when all the dust from your divorce has settled and you're ready to try again—"

She interrupted him. "I'm up early this morning packing and cleaning and getting ready for a giant yard sale, William. I put my house on the market the Monday after I got back from our romantic getaway. I figure it will take months to sell given the current economic climate, so I'd better start right away."

"You're moving?"

"Yes."

"Where to?"

"I haven't figured that out yet. In fact, I was hoping you might help me. Is there a chance you could do me a huge favor and pick up my grandfather in South Dakota on your way home? Any time will work for him. We're totally flexible."

"Of course. I'd be glad to. Is Cal coming out to help you move?"

"Actually, we're talking about moving together. He wants to winter in California with me and the girls, and in the summer, we'll go to the Black Hills. I was inspired by your parents' story, William. I loved how they weren't limited by society's confines or simple geography. They made the family that worked for them. I want to do that, too."

"Is there a place in that family for me?"

"The answer is, bet on it."

He coughed. "What?"

She laughed. "I'll explain when I see you. And, William, I can't wait to see you. I was such a boob at the B and B. Talk about panic attack. I almost turned around halfway home, but then I decided maybe I was smart to give us some space. Dare I say I was under the influence of magazine therapists?"

Her tone was so Daria he couldn't help but feel hopeful. "And now you're not?"

"Exactly. I've put my faith in a much higher power." She laughed again. "I'll tell you all about it when I see you. I can't wait. But please, spend as much time as you can with your father. Is everything okay?"

"Amazing. And you'll see me sooner than you think. I've had to change my plans slightly because I have a client who needs me." He couldn't apologize for doing what he did best. After all, he was his parents' son. And he helped people. It's what he did. "But I've promised Father to return in a few weeks. When is Miranda and Hailey's spring break? Maybe we could bring the girls over at the same time."

Daria sniffled softly. "William, that's so sweet. I would love for them to meet your parents. We'll talk about it when I see you."

They pinpointed exactly when that would be so she could alert Cal and make her plans, then he hung up. But he called her right back.

"Did I remember to tell you I love you, Daria?"

"You did. And although I'd rather say this in person, face-to-face, I love you, too."

Face-to-face. He liked the sound of that.

FOUR DAYS LATER, William sat across from her in the passenger seating of his plane. He'd hired Lucas Hopper to be his copilot again so he and Daria could have some time alone on the last leg of their flight. He was jet-lagged and emotionally spent. Saying goodbye to his parents hadn't been easy, but Father promised to keep on fighting so he could meet Daria and her daughters in April, so he also felt energized and hopeful.

"Alone at last," he said, trying to get comfortable as the plane taxied to take off.

"You mean except for Lucas," she said, fussing with her seat belt.

"Don't mind him. He's blissfully content to listen to whatever comes across his noise-canceling headset," William told her. "But I picked the rear seats for a bit more privacy."

She let her head fall back against the plush upholstery. "It's about time, isn't it?"

The chaos surrounding their meeting a few hours earlier hadn't allowed either of them a chance to say what most needed to be said. William's attention had been swallowed up by Hailey, who explained that she was the one who'd fixed things between him and her mommy. "Asking the Magic 8 Ball was my idea," she'd bragged.

That had been William's first clue to Daria's strange comment about betting on them as a couple.

Miranda, not to be outdone, had described the scene in detail. "Mom was so sad after she came home from your date that Hailey and I decided you were to blame. But when we asked the Magic 8 Ball if you were to blame, it said no. So we asked Mom and she said the reason she came home early was because she was confused and thought it was too soon to fall in love again."

"So you consulted a higher power," William had guessed.

He approved of the end result, but his nerves went haywire when he thought about his fate hanging on a silly kid's game. But then he realized that wasn't the case. Daria, good mother that she was, simply let her daughters participate in a decision she'd already made.

"So your folks liked the video?" Daria asked over the revving of the engine. "They sent me the most gorgeous bouquet and a ridiculously over-the-top gift card to Macy's as a thank-you."

The latter had been Notty's idea. "New frocks for the girls when they come to visit," he'd said.

"My parents are madly in love with you. If you think Father's health improved knowing I was coming to visit, you should see what the possibility of meeting you three did for him. He even decided to try the clinical trial Mum was advocating."

Her jaw dropped. "Really?"

He nodded.

"But…" she hesitated. "Did you tell them about me? The real me, not that girl on the pedestal me? Divorced, single mom, nearly homeless—" She put up a finger to add, "And let's not forget that I invited my ninety-year-old grandfather to move in with me."

He glanced out the window as the plane began to level out and released the tension on his seat belt. "Daria, I promise, no more pedestals. If you catch me trying to put you on one, you can hit me over the head with it. And face it, when it comes to family craziness, you'll never win. Two gay fathers and a crusader mother trumps anything you can do. Did I mention Mum is opening a free clinic in our old carriage house?"

Daria shook her head, marveling at the changes she saw in William. He seemed lighter, freer. As if releasing whatever grudges or sense of failure had weighted him down had opened new windows, allowing him to see views of life he'd missed before. "How did it go with your client?"

He shook his head and sighed. "It didn't. JoE refused to listen to me. He decided his career was more important than his recovery. He checked out of rehab against my advice and doctor's orders and a court edict. Hopefully he'll get arrested before he ODs."

She made a small sound of horror.

"I know that sounds callous, but I realize now that, like Bianca, he's going to make his own mistakes. This time, though, I'm not turning off my phone. If he calls, I'll be there for him."

She reached out and took his hand. "You'll be there for him even if he doesn't call. That's one of the things I love most about you."

He leaned over to kiss her. "Thanks." He glanced toward the nose of the plane. "I'll try to thank you properly when we truly are alone. Now, tell me about your plans."

"I decided I can't stay in Fresno. Too many memories. The girls and I want to make a fresh start. I feel strongly about staying in California so Bruce can see Hailey and Miranda on a regular basis, but I also know Cal is at a point in his life where he needs family. Spending our summers in South Dakota seemed like a compromise we could all live with."

"I like the staying in California part of that plan."

"Then you'll like it even better when I tell you I'm meeting with a real estate agent to look at homes in Santa Barbara. Which, coincidentally, is quite a bit closer to Malibu," she added.

"Even better. Does that mean you're not quite as mad at me as you were?"

"It wasn't you," she said seriously, then rolled her eyes. "Okay, it was. For a minute. I thought you were another Bruce. But even when I was freaking out, I knew that wasn't true. I know why you did what you did. Bruce could make God's patience snap."

He wiped his forehead as if relieved to have dodged a bullet. But she wasn't completely letting him off the hook. "That doesn't mean I want you making decisions for me. If we're going to have a relationship, I need to know that you respect me and value my input—on the big things and the little things."

"I do. I will. How little?"

She gave him a look her daughters knew all too well. He merely grinned and changed the subject. "Did you just say we're going to have a relationship?"

"It's a given…when you love someone. Don't you know that?"

He reached over and unsnapped her seat belt then pulled her onto his lap. "I do now. Say it again."

She looped her arms around his neck and kissed him. "I love you. I tried to deny it, but I was flat-out miserable thinking I'd never see you again. That's when Miranda and Hailey decided to consult the Magic 8 Ball."

"So they told me. I've never tried one. Is there a chance it could have said, 'Run for the hills?'"

"I don't believe that's an option, but according to Miranda, four out of four tries came back with the same answer. *Bet on it.*"

"What was the question?"

"Does Mommy love William?"

The look in his eyes told her everything she needed to know. She might have forgotten how to trust in love, but her daughters hadn't.

"So Miranda and Hailey were the ones who did the

asking? You didn't actually participate in the séance or whatever it's called?"

She shook her head. "They were giving me permission to try again. That was the *higher power* I was talking about." She'd immediately tossed all her women's magazines and post-divorce advice books in the garage sale box. Her daughters were telling her it was okay to risk her heart one more time. On a man with a bit of a hero complex. But heroes had their place in the world so long as one had a strong heroine to keep him grounded.

William's kiss said more than words ever could, but all communication stopped when Lucas hollered, "We're at the Grapevine, William. Do you want to take her from here?"

"I certainly do," William said, his gaze never leaving Daria. He helped her up, then kissed her hard and fast before walking to the pilot's seat.

Before donning his headphones, he called out, "Buckle in tight, Daria. Things can get a little bumpy from this point on."

She did as directed, grinning the whole time. Things had already been a little bumpy. But without lows, how could you appreciate the highs? And the best part of the journey was having someone to travel with.

She was ready to fly—anywhere—with William.

* * * * *

COMING NEXT MONTH

Available November 9, 2010

#1668 THAT CHRISTMAS FEELING
Brenda Novak, Kathleen O'Brien, Karina Bliss

#1669 THE BEST LAID PLANS
Sarah Mayberry

#1670 A MARINE FOR CHRISTMAS
A Little Secret
Beth Andrews

#1671 A LOT LIKE CHRISTMAS
Going Back
Dawn Atkins

#1672 THE MOON THAT NIGHT
Single Father
Helen Brenna

#1673 LIFE REWRITTEN
Suddenly a Parent
Margaret Watson

LARGER-PRINT BOOKS!
GET 2 FREE LARGER-PRINT NOVELS PLUS
2 FREE GIFTS!

HARLEQUIN®
Super Romance

Exciting, emotional, unexpected!

YES! Please send me 2 FREE LARGER-PRINT Harlequin® Superromance® novels and my 2 FREE gifts (gifts are worth about $10). After receiving them, if I don't wish to receive any more books, I can return the shipping statement marked "cancel." If I don't cancel, I will receive 6 brand-new novels every month and be billed just $5.44 per book in the U.S. or $5.99 per book in Canada. That's a saving of at least 13% off the cover price! It's quite a bargain! Shipping and handling is just 50¢ per book.* I understand that accepting the 2 free books and gifts places me under no obligation to buy anything. I can always return a shipment and cancel at any time. Even if I never buy another book from Harlequin, the two free books and gifts are mine to keep forever.

139/339 HDN E5PS

Name _____ (PLEASE PRINT)

Address _____ Apt. #

City _____ State/Prov. _____ Zip/Postal Code

Signature (if under 18, a parent or guardian must sign)

Mail to the **Harlequin Reader Service:**
IN U.S.A.: P.O. Box 1867, Buffalo, NY 14240-1867
IN CANADA: P.O. Box 609, Fort Erie, Ontario L2A 5X3

Not valid for current subscribers to Harlequin Superromance Larger-Print books.

**Are you a current subscriber to Harlequin Superromance books
and want to receive the larger-print edition?
Call 1-800-873-8635 today!**

HSRLP10R

*See below for a sneak peek from
our inspirational line, Love Inspired® Suspense*

*Enjoy this heart-stopping excerpt from
RUNNING BLIND
by top author Shirlee McCoy,
available November 2010!*

**The mission trip to Mexico was supposed to be an
adventure. But the thrill turns sour when Jenna Dougherty
and her roommate Magdalena are kidnapped.**

"It's okay. I'm here to help." The voice was as deep as the
darkness, but Jenna Dougherty didn't believe the lie. She
could do nothing but lie still as hands slid down her arms,
felt the rope around her wrists.

"I'm going to use a knife to cut you free, Jenna. Hold
still."

The cold blade of a knife pressed close to her head before
her gag fell away.

"I—" she started, but her mouth was dry, and she could
do nothing but suck in air.

"Shhh. Whatever needs to be said can be said when
we're out of here." Nick spoke quietly, his hand gentle on
her cheek. There and gone as he sliced through the ropes on
her wrists and ankles.

He pulled her upright. "Come on. We may be on
borrowed time."

"I can't leave my friend," Jenna rasped out.

"There's no one here. Just us."

"She has to be here." Jenna took a step away.

"There's no one here. Let's go before that changes."

"It's dark. Maybe if we find a light…"

"What did you say?"

"We need to turn on the light. I can't leave until I know that—"

"What can you see, Jenna?"

"Nothing."

"No shadows? No light?"

"No."

"It's broad daylight. There's light spilling in from the window I climbed in through. You can't see it?"

She went cold at his words.

"I can't see anything."

"You've got a nasty bruise on your forehead. Maybe that has something to do with it." His fingers traced the tender flesh on her forehead.

"It doesn't matter *how* it happened. I'm blind!"

Can Nick help Jenna find her friend or will chasing this trail have Jenna running blindly again into danger?

Find out in RUNNING BLIND, available in November 2010 only from Love Inspired Suspense.

SHLISEXP1110